Avon Books are available at special quantity discounts for bulk purchases for sales promotions, premiums, fund raising or educational use. Special books, or book excerpts, can also be created to fit specific needs.

For details write or telephone the office of the Director of Special Markets, Avon Books, Dept. FP, 1350 Avenue of the Americas, New York, New York 10019, 1-800-238-0658.

MURDER by MAIL

M. D. LAKE

AVON BOOKS ◆ NEW YORK

MURDER BY MAIL is an original publication of Avon Books. This work has never before appeared in book form. This work is a novel. Any similarity to actual persons or events is purely coincidental.

AVON BOOKS
A division of
The Hearst Corporation
1350 Avenue of the Americas
New York, New York 10019

Copyright © 1993 by Allen Simpson
Published by arrangement with the author
Library of Congress Catalog Card Number: 93-90407
ISBN: 0-380-76856-9

First Avon Books Printing: December 1993

AVON TRADEMARK REG. U.S. PAT. OFF., AND IN OTHER COUNTRIES, MARCA REGISTRADA, HECHO EN U.S.A.

Printed in the U.S.A.

RA   10   9   8   7   6   5   4   3   2   1

This novel is for Pat, who writes mysteries under the name Ellen Hart, and her partner Kathy, who creates sculpture under the name Kathleen Kruger. Like all of Peggy's friends, they are generous in their support of others' creativity, and they behave inappropriately at the drop of a hat.

A lot of people helped: Officer Lee North of the University of Minnesota Police Department let me accompany him on patrol one summer night and gave me the setting for the scenes by the old river willow; Postal Inspector Robert Hausman answered my questions about hate mail and what the Postal Inspection Service can and can't do about it; Craig Kopperud shared his encyclopedic knowledge of money and how to get it, hide it, and lose it; Steve Benson helped clarify ideas I didn't know I had; and Lt. Regan Metcalf, without whom there would be no Peggy O'Neill, continues to share her knowledge of police work when asked.

A special thanks to my former editor and present agent, Nancy Yost, and my current editor, David Highfill, who refuse to let me settle for less than the best I can do.

One

It began like a painting by Norman Rockwell, with hot dogs and potato salad, beer, fireworks, and flags. Everything but a parade, in fact—but if you wanted to, you could imagine that. What you couldn't imagine was murder, which came later.

My landlady informed me one afternoon that our street was having a Fourth-of-July block party and she hoped I'd be able to attend. The emphasis she put on *hoped* was heavy. Mrs. Hammer thinks the fact that I'm a campus cop who works the dogwatch—from 11:00 P.M. to 7:00 A.M.—by choice is remarkable, and she likes to show me off.

Neighbors have never been my strong suit, so I told her I had other plans.

"And these other plans are what?" Mrs. Hammer is my height, five nine, but she's got better posture even though she's going on seventy. She was able to look down her nose at me.

I said I was going on a picnic with a couple of my friends, Paula Henderson and Lawrence Fitzpatrick, and afterward we were going to watch a fireworks display. That wasn't a complete lie because I'd been thinking of asking them if they'd like to do something like that on the Fourth, I just hadn't gotten around to it yet. Mrs. Hammer gave me a look that indicated she saw through my simple ruse and stalked back upstairs to her own apartment.

When I got to work that night, Paula and Lawrence had just finished writing up their reports and were about to leave. They had the third watch that month.

"What should we bring?" Paula asked me.

"Huh?"

"To the block party on the Fourth," she replied. "I suppose all your neighbors'll be bringing massive quantities of brats and burgers for the grills, and vats of coleslaw and baked beans, so how about if Lawrence and I bring a Szechuan chicken salad? You think anybody'd think that's un-American?"

"Hold on a minute!" I said. "Who said anything about a block party?"

"Am I invited, too?" asked Ginny Raines, eavesdropping. Ginny's a detective who likes food more than is good for her.

"Mrs. Hammer did," Lawrence said, "Your landlady. She said we could have the picnic you mentioned at the block party and watch fireworks afterward on Lake Eleanor."

"About this picnic," Paula said, trying not to laugh in my face. "Did inviting us just slip your mind, Peggy, or what?"

Score one for Mrs. Hammer.

Both ends of the block were barred to traffic, and picnic tables and volleyball nets had been set up in the street. Neighbors I'd never seen before, or seen but never talked to, milled around. Children tossed water balloons like swollen blisters at one another, trying, without much success, to catch them without breaking them. They were the only ones who looked cool on this hot and humid afternoon.

We all ate one another's offerings—hamburgers, hot dogs, chips, salads, and, of course, the ubiquitous bean casserole. People poked warily at Paula's Szechuan salad, full of chicken, sprouts, pea pods and Asian spices. Just about everybody who dared try some finished it, which is no surprise since Paula's a gourmet cook. I'd made guacamole—it's something I do—and surrounded it with corn chips. Nobody had any problems with that since I omitted the hot sauce in deference to the state's Scandinavian heritage. Kegs dispensed beer that was mostly foam into paper cups, and kids' plastic wading pools were full of ice and soda pop.

It wasn't getting any cooler as evening approached. There probably would be a storm later that night, but hopefully not before the end of the fireworks display.

My friends and I were sitting at one of the picnic tables with Mrs. Hammer and a man who lived across the street—a small, frail-looking, old man with shy eyes, dressed in a slightly threadbare gray suit and vest and a dark bow tie. He'd introduced himself as Harold Mullen.

"So you're Peggy O'Neill," he said, shaking my hand. "Mrs. Hammer's told me all about you. You're quite the feisty little woman, aren't you?" His hand was dry and hard.

"That's what we call her around police headquarters," Paula said. "We often say, 'What's that feisty little woman, Peggy O'Neill, up to now?' "

Mr. Mullen ignored her. "So your name is quite appropriate. *O'Neill* means 'descended from Njall', and *Njall* means 'champion', or 'military hero'."

"And *Peggy* probably means 'feisty little woman'," Ginny stuck in.

Mr. Mullen ignored her, too. "Did you know that the O'Neills have the oldest traceable genealogy in Europe, going back at least to the year A.D. 360?"

I asked him how he knew so much about my name.

He grinned. His teeth couldn't have cost much, for no expense had been wasted on trying to make them look real. "When Mrs. Hammer told me you were going to be here this afternoon, I took the trouble to look it up in one of my books. Names are one of my hobbies."

"According to Mr. Mullen, my last name means 'metalworker', or 'smith'," Mrs. Hammer said politely.

"Hammer's much better than Smith," Lawrence said.

"Or Metalworker," Ginny muttered. She'd eaten too many brats with all the fixings and wasn't looking well.

"Do you know what *Fitzpatrick* means?" Lawrence asked.

"No, but I could get one of my books and look it up," Mr. Mullen said eagerly. "I live just across the street, you know."

"Oh, it's not important," Lawrence said.

Somebody started a volleyball game then, and Paula, Lawrence, and I went over and played for a while. Ginny, who doesn't believe in exercise and wonders why she has a weight problem, stayed at the picnic table, nursing a paper cup of beer.

When we got back to the table, Mullen was waiting for us with a large old book open in front of him.

"*Fitz* means 'son of'," he told the sweating Lawrence. "It's from the Latin *filius,* which means 'son', and *Patrick* means 'noble', or 'patrician'. *Lawrence* means 'laurel-crowned'."

Lawrence tried not to let this news go to this head, but it was clearly a struggle.

Paula snorted. "How come nobody ever seems to have a name that means 'descended from nerd'."

"Maybe nerds don't survive long enough to pass on their names," Ginny suggested.

"They survive long enough to pass on their genes, don't they?" Paula replied, giving Lawrence a meaningful look.

"I think you'd make a nice match for Peggy," Mr. Mullen told Lawrence.

"Whoa there, Mr. Mullen!" Paula said, "I'm not ready to let Mr. Laurel-Crowned Patrician go just yet, thank you—and certainly not to Ms. Feisty Little Champion!"

Lawrence blushed and reached for her hand. He couldn't quite believe his good fortune in having won Paula's heart. "Look up Paula's last name in your book, why don't you?" he said to Mr. Mullen.

"Forget it," Paula said. "It's just the name of some slaveholder who owned my family 150 years ago."

"Maybe you should do a search, Paula, to see if you can find out what your name was in Africa," I suggested, "the way Arthur Haley did in *Roots.*"

"Why?" she asked.

"I don't know. Aren't you curious?"

"Were you curious about the O'Neills?"

"I wonder if your last name's in here, Ginny," Lawrence said, leafing through Mullen's book. "Here it is. *Raines:* 'dweller at a boundary line or at the sign of the frog'."

"Well, which is it?" Ginny demanded.

"I guess it could be either."

"Great." She belched, rather froglike. "Does anybody have a Tums?"

"You're all policemen?" Mr. Mullen asked. "Or should I say police men and women?"

"We're all campus cops, yeah," Ginny said.

"Mrs. Hammer tells me you work nights," he said to me. "I often see you riding home on your bike while I'm drinking my morning tea. The things women are permitted to do these days!"

"Permitted!" Ginny snorted.

"And do the rest of you work nights, too?"

Paula explained that they sometimes did, but not voluntarily, the way I did. Ginny told him she was a detective and worked mostly during the day and that I was the only night-blooming cop by nature among them.

"I don't suppose it's as dangerous being a policeman on a college campus as being a regular policeman," Mr. Mullen said. "I've met your boss, by the way," he added offhandedly.

"Which one?"

"Your president, Dr. Hightower."

He waited for one of us to ask how he happened to know the University president. When I did, he went on, "Oh, I don't mean to say I know him well, of course. But I did have dinner with him some time ago. It's nothing to brag about. I have a little money, you see, that I'm donating to the University."

"Too bad," Lawrence said. "You could've donated it to Paula and me. We're fixing up an old house, and Paula's starting law school in September, so we could use a big donation."

"In fact," Mr. Mullen went on, "I'm having dinner with a member of the University faculty tonight, which is why I'm so dressed up." He pulled a watch from his vest pocket and looked at it. "Dr. Hightower seems to be a very decent sort of fellow. A second-generation Englishman— his parents came over right after the war, he told me. He asked me to call him Bennett. And he has a very nice wife, too." A thought seemed to strike him. "Are any of you married?"

"I was once," Ginny said, "but it didn't take. How about you?"

"Me?" The question startled him. Ginny's direct approach has that effect on a lot of people.

"Yeah. What's your marital status, Mr. Mullen?"

"I never married, I'm sorry to say." He shook his head. "It wasn't God's will. It's not always easy, accepting what God wants for us, but we must all make the effort. Isn't that so?"

Smiling expectantly, he looked around at all of us.

Before anybody could come up with an answer, something across the street attracted Mullen's attention. He said, "Oh dear, there he is now—Mr. Oakes, I think he said his name is. I must have lost track of the time!" A man was standing at his front door.

He disentangled himself awkwardly from the picnic table, stumbled, but Paula caught his arm.

"It's been a lovely afternoon," he said, straightening up. As an afterthought, he turned back to me and added, "Some morning, why don't you stop in and have a cup of tea with me? I'm always up and about before you come biking down the street."

I told him I'd like that, and then he turned and crossed the street in an unsteady shuffle. The man who'd been at his door was coming down his walk, scanning the faces of my neighbors milling about in the street. When he saw Mullen coming toward him, he stopped and waved and gave him a pleasant smile. He was tall, thin, and blond. A little young to be a faculty member, I thought.

They went into Mullen's house together, and, a few minutes later, I saw them come out again, this time with Mullen wearing a raincoat over his suit. They walked to the end of the block, presumably to where the visitor had left his car.

I glanced back at Mullen's house. I guessed it was about eighty years old, the same age as most of the other houses on the block, but not as well kept. It didn't look like the kind of house a man of means would live in—one who'd been invited to eat dinner with the University president—but you never know.

"He forgot his book," Ginny said.

Mrs. Hammer picked it up, said she'd see that he got it back. "Funny old bird, isn't he? Before you all arrived, he told me the doctors didn't expect him to live until spring. Cancer, he said, but it went into remission. He bragged that he'd fooled the doctors. He's always been kind of a reclusive fellow—in fact, this is the first time I've ever seen him out among the neighbors. Maybe he figures it's time he got out and smelled the flowers, before he finds himself staring up at their roots."

Mrs. Hammer isn't a very sentimental person.

We stayed on until it began to get dark and then walked to Lake Eleanor, a couple of blocks down the hill from where I live, to watch the fireworks being set off from one of its islands. When the red glare of the last rocket had faded and the last bomb had burst in air, a brass band struck up "The Star-Spangled Banner." Unlike a lot of people I know, I've always kind of liked it: it's virtually unsingable, and the lyrics are a series of anxious questions about whether we're still here. Sometimes I wonder if anybody ever really listens to the words.

Afterward, Ginny, Mrs. Hammer, and I walked together behind Paula and Lawrence. They're both tall, and they were holding hands and strolling along as if they believed life only wished them well.

We call them Night 'n' Day because you can't have one without the other.

Two

A few weeks later, I was in the squad room nursing a cup of coffee and waiting for roll call. Lawrence came in from his watch. He got a Coke from the machine and came over and sat down at the other end of the table from me. I said "hi," and he said "hello" and started filling out his report. The expression on his face was grim, not a natural expression for Lawrence.

"Something wrong?"

He looked up at me again, tried to meet my eyes, and looked back down at his report. "No."

"I didn't think so. You always speak to me in dull monosyllables. That's what I like so much about you, Lawrence, and I wouldn't want it to change."

"Maybe Paula'll tell you about it, okay?"

"Okay."

Paula came in a few minutes later. She went over and sat down across the table from Lawrence. When he didn't look up at her, she said, under her breath, "You idiot!" and began filling out her report.

I wondered how serious this quarrel that was chilling the squad room in spite of the summer heat was. Thinking back, I realized that they'd been unusually quiet for several days. They'd been going together for almost a year, close friends for several years before that, and they'd just bought a house together that they were fixing up.

When it was time for roll call, I got up and said, "So long."

Lawrence didn't say anything. Paula looked up at me with sad eyes and gave me a little smile. I don't get involved in lovers' quarrels. I just worry about them, if they're people I love.

I was assigned the Old Campus that night, my favorite beat. Being a campus cop—or any kind of cop on patrol—is like being a fire fighter, except that cops spend their time between crises walking around, sometimes trying to look busier than they are; whereas fire fighters sit in front of the firehouse, making people shake their heads at the wasted tax dollars—until their homes start to burn. Campus cops stroll around the university, enter buildings at random, our only company being the soft metallic jangle of voices—the dispatcher's and the other cops'—coming from the portable radios on our belts or the little remotes clipped to our collars.

I'd been out about an hour when the dispatcher called my number. I responded and he told me Paula was looking for me. I told him I was over by one of the dorms on the bluffs above the river and that I'd wait for her in the quadrangle there.

She showed up ten minutes later, still in uniform.

"Want some company?"

"Sure."

We started walking. The dorms were dark—it was almost 1:00 A.M. and most of them were empty for the summer anyway. We walked down to the river road, crossed it, and went down the path through the trees and brush to the river. It's always cooler by the river in the summer than anywhere else on campus, and I usually take my breaks there if I'm in the area.

Neither of us said anything until we came to an opening in the brush that led to the shore. Soft voices drifted to us from upstream, where I could make out the shadowy figures of a couple sitting close to each other by the water. We turned and walked downstream until we came to an old, twisted willow that curves out over the river. It's survived a lot of years of ice and flooding.

We sat down with our backs against it. After a while Paula drew up her knees and put her head on them but still didn't say anything; she just stared out at the dark river.

"This consultation room is open from one to one-twenty," I said, when the silence had gone on long enough, "after which I have to return to my regular job, which is patrolling the campus, as you probably know."

"Lawrence and I have been getting hate mail," she blurted out suddenly. "Sometimes two, three pieces a day, each of us. Sick stuff—like this."

She pulled an envelope out of her shoulder bag and handed it to me. It was typed, addressed to Miss Paula Henderson, with no return address. I opened it, unfolded the sheet of paper and read: "In the long run, a white man won't be able to satisfy a black woman sexually. Then what happens? Either he leaves her because she's a threat to his manhood, or she goes looking for satisfaction elsewhere." That was photocopied. Typed in the margin was: "All flesh consorteth according to kind, and a man will cleave to his like."

"Here's one that was addressed to Lawrence," Paula said, handing me another piece of paper.

"A man's not a man until he's slept with a Negress. A man's not a man if he marries one." In the margin, somebody had typed: "Are you a man? Think about it, for God will not be mocked."

I stared up at Paula in horror. "How long have you been getting this stuff?"

"A week."

"A week! Why didn't you tell me?"

She shrugged. "I couldn't. I kept thinking it was going to stop. But it hasn't—if anything, it's increasing. And it's all the same, a sick mixture of racist pornography and racist piety. There's always a photocopied page or two from some cheaply printed book or pamphlet, and someone types messages that are mostly religious in the margins. Look at this."

She handed me another piece of paper. The text began: "Women of the lower races everywhere seek sex relations with men of the Nordic race." It ended: "The greatest injustice in the world is to produce a mixed-race baby. Race mixing is the only sin that God will not forgive, even though the child has no blame."

"This guy's got quite a god," I said.

"That's just a sample of what we've been getting," she said, her voice growing hoarse.

I put my arm around her. "Have you shown it to anybody at the post office?"

"The second day, I talked to a postal inspector on the phone. He asked me to describe it. When I did, he said it sounded like the kind of hate mail people have been getting for years, all over the city. They've never been able to find out who's mailing it. I gathered that it wasn't one of the post office's top priorities either."

"Why not?"

"Apparently it's not against the law to send this kind of filth through the mail. First Amendment rights. Can you believe the Bill of Rights was meant to protect this kind of slime, Peggy? Once law school starts, I'm going to talk to my professors about it."

A couple of months earlier, Paula had decided to become a lawyer. She'd been accepted by the University's law school in June and put in her resignation to the campus police department effective in September, just before school started.

"The postal inspector told me I could bring or send the stuff we've been getting down to him. He's got a huge file on this guy, he said, but he didn't hold out any hope that it would do any good."

"Kind of like when you report your purse stolen."

"Yeah, except that in this case it's just people like Lawrence and me walking down the street. All somebody needs is our address and he can try to steal our happiness and our peace of mind. Lawrence isn't taking it too well."

"How about you?"

"I'm not taking Lawrence very well, right now," she said with a shaky laugh. "He's a grave disappointment to me. I've had ugly experiences on account of my color before. Not as ugly as this, however—or as creepy. And I expected that Lawrence and I would encounter something like this sooner or later, although not on this scale and not this remorseless. I thought Lawrence knew what to expect, too—although I guess we never really sat down and talked about it."

Paula fell silent, her eyes following something unidentifiable that floated quietly past us in the slowly moving water.

"We've been going together how long now?" she asked after a while. "A year? I've seen the looks people give us sometimes and so has Lawrence. It isn't always because they think we shouldn't be together. I'm sure it's mostly that interracial couples are still a little unusual in this part of the country, and people do double takes when they see the unusual—I do, too. I don't mind it, even though you can't always be sure of the kind of look you're getting, the innocent second glance or the disgusted one."

"Lawrence must have experienced some unpleasant moments before now, too," I said.

"Of course he has, but he's big, you know, and in great shape and it's obvious to anybody that he can take care of himself. That helps. He told me last week—right after we first started getting this stuff—that a guy he knew slightly came up to him once and said he didn't think he should be dating a black woman. Lawrence beat him up. I got mad, told him I didn't want him to do that anymore. We're going to have to work out ways of dealing with these situations that don't involve violence. I don't want Lawrence getting hurt or becoming brutalized because he thinks fighting's the only way. There're lots of ways that are better than violence. There have to be."

She looked down at the hate mail she'd shown me. "But he can't handle this kind of violence. There's nobody to confront—nobody to beat up, walk away from, or try to talk to. It just keeps coming, a steady, wicked flood of malice and ignorance with no end in sight. Somebody out there wants to destroy us, somebody who doesn't know anything about us, only the color of our skin and where we live. And his only strength is that we don't know anything about him."

"Or her," I said, sticking up for my sex's right to include the warped.

She shrugged. "Yeah, I suppose. I was practically born knowing my color's a sniper's target. But I made a decision early on that it wasn't going to keep me from living my life just the way I want to, as much as anybody can. I've never ducked, I'm never going to. And I won't live with anybody who does."

"I think maybe you're being a little hard on Lawrence," I said. "Getting this kind of stuff, day in, day out, with no end in sight, would be a little overwhelming to anybody. As you said yourself, you've had experience with prejudice. This has to be new to a middle-class white male."

"I know that," she said. And then, quickly: "I'm wondering if maybe he's just using this as an excuse to break up with me."

"Why?"

"I don't know. Because I'm smarter than he is? Because I'm going to law school and he feels threatened by that?" She started to cry, then started to laugh, did both at once. "I just don't know!"

"I don't believe it. That would be making ugly uglier and Lawrence isn't like that."

"Isn't he?"

"No, he isn't," I said. I heard my voice rising, as if in panic, and realized that I really didn't want Lawrence and Paula to break up—at least not on account of the poison that some sick stranger was injecting into their systems.

She looked at me, surprised perhaps by the desperation in my voice. "Okay, Peggy," she said, as if humoring me, "okay." She pulled out a handkerchief and blew her nose.

"Do any of these letters contain threats?"

"Not really, not unless you count the promise of eternal hell as a threat. Sometimes I wish we were getting real threats. Lawrence could deal with those better than with what we've been getting." She thought for a moment. "But maybe it's better this way. I mean, what if I married him and then discovered he could only handle a situation like this with his fists—or a gun?"

The couple I'd seen upstream earlier lit a lantern and their faces were illuminated by the flame.

"You're talking like you're really thinking of breaking up," I said.

She didn't respond to that. "I didn't want to fall in love with Lawrence, you know," she said. "In my more rational moments, I used to think, thank God I'm not in love with this lout because that would make life a lot harder than it has to be, and who needs that? And then one day, there it was, as if it had been there all the time! What do you do in a case like that?"

I hadn't been there for that moment, but I'd been there when Lawrence fell in love with her. It was a memorable night, a night when somebody we'd been assigned to keep alive was murdered.

Paula and Lawrence had become friends almost immediately after he joined the campus cops. Nobody—not even Paula, she said later—knew that they gradually began coming to roll call earlier and earlier in order to be together longer, and they worked hard to get the same watches, month after month. They thought it was because of their love of word games, which they played in the office while waiting for roll call.

Things went on like that for over two years. Their banter, Paula's continued outrageous cheating at the word games, Lawrence's patient struggle to win honestly—he's not quick enough to cheat well—became constant background noise in the squad room whenever they were together, a noise that had suddenly ceased.

I asked her if they'd ever received any mail like that before.

"No, never."

"You bought the house what—a month ago?"

Paula nodded. "I've thought about that, too. When we moved in, maybe somebody thought there goes the neighborhood! and decided to try to slime us out. For that matter, Peggy, it could even be somebody in our writing groups. They see Lawrence and me coming and going together and some of them give us odd looks sometimes. Maybe they don't mean anything by it. After all," she added, and I thought I caught a glimpse of the old Paula's humor under the grimness, "Lawrence and I are worth a second glance, aren't we?"

Paula was writing a lot of poetry and she was occasionally published in magazines with names like *Florilegium* and *Whetstone Review*. Lawrence wrote true crime stories and he'd already garnered an impressive stack of rejection slips— campus crime apparently doesn't sell all that well. Paula had collected her share of rejection slips, too, for that matter. They were talking of making them into a collage to hang over the fireplace, if they ever finished stripping the old wallpaper from and replastering the living room walls.

"I suppose it could even be one of the campus cops," I said, reluctantly. Paula and Lawrence had thrown a party to celebrate buying the old house and they'd invited the entire University police force. About forty-five people showed up—cops, friends, neighbors. "Maybe actually seeing you two in your own home flipped somebody out."

"The reality is," Paula said, "it could be just about anybody. And another reality is that there'll always be ugly things happening to us, as long as Lawrence and I are together. Maybe not as hideous as this, but we'd have to be prepared for whatever comes, and not let it warp us. I thought Lawrence knew that, too. I thought we could deal with it together."

"He probably did know it," I said, "and thought he could deal with it. I'd like to be able to say I'd behave better than Lawrence if I were in his shoes, but I'm not sure I could."

She didn't say anything to that.

"Don't be disgusted with him, Paula," I said.

"I'm not disgusted with him. I'm disgusted with myself for getting into this with him in the first place."

"Don't be that either. You had every reason to think you deserved to be with whomever you loved."

"And I had every reason to know it wouldn't be permitted, too."

"Not without a fight. Did you take this hate mail to the postal inspector?"

"No. He sounded like it would be a waste of time for both him and us."

"Let's do it anyway. We'll at least be doing something."

"We? This isn't your business, Peggy."

"Really?" Then why are you keeping me down here by the river, leaving the campus defenseless?"

"I just needed to talk about it to a friend, that's all."

"I'll pick you up tomorrow at one," I told her. "That'll give you time to get back here for work." Paula and Lawrence were working the middle watch, 4:00 P.M. to 11:00 P.M.

She thought about it for a moment or two and then turned and gave me a wan smile. "Okay, Peggy," she said, without a great deal of enthusiasm. "You're right, of course. We have to try everything, don't we?" Her eyes are large and brown and they were still glittering with moonlight and tears.

We sat there a while, until it was time for me to get back to work. As we stood up and were about to leave, a string of barges floated quietly by in the warm July night. They seemed to emerge from nothing, on their way to New Orleans and the Gulf of Mexico. It was a lovely sight. Suddenly, one of the bargemen, invisible to us, began to swear, a long string of curses that shattered the peace and beauty of the night and the river.

But it was still a lovely sight.

Three

Paula called the post office and made an appointment to see the inspector she'd spoken to on the phone when they'd first started getting the hate mail. I drove to their house to get her and found her out in front, waiting for me.

"Isn't Lawrence coming?"

"No," she said flatly. "He doesn't want to take the time off from stripping wallpaper."

"At least he's working on the house," I said hopefully. "That's a good sign."

She shrugged. "Is it? He's doing it to keep from talking to me, touching me. And besides, we'd have to fix it up anyway, wouldn't we, if we're going to sell it?"

I didn't say anything to that.

The postal inspector's name was Ted Rossini, a man of about forty with an olive complexion and dark curly hair. Paula gave him a plastic garbage bag full of the mail she and Lawrence had received, and we sat and waited patiently while he looked through it.

Looking as though he'd eaten something that had gone bad, he carefully slid the last of the letters back into the bag and said, "Welcome to the club."

"You know who it is?"

"Not by name. By his method. He takes material from racist publications, types his own, usually pious, comments in the margins or on the back, photocopies it and sends it to the people on his list—mostly people in town, but his mailing list does include a few unfortunate people outside the city, too. All cases involve some kind of 'racial mixing', and most of the victims had appeared in the newspapers or on television shortly before they started hearing from him."

"Lawrence and I haven't hit the front pages yet," Paula said.

I asked him how long this had been going on.

"We've known about him for about eight years."

"But you don't have any idea who he is?"

"No. Only that he must have a lot of time on his hands. His work is time-consuming, and he must have some money in order to afford the photocopying and postage."

"You said there has to be some kind of 'racial mixing' to get his attention," Paula said. "You mean it's not just black-white relationships?"

"No. Caucasians who adopt Asian children also get on his mailing list—some of it is even addressed to these children. He's also opposed to Jews marrying Gentiles and Italians, Poles, or Russians marrying Scandinavians."

"In other words, he goes after people who are easily identifiable by their names or appearance."

"Right. As I say, he mostly get his 'leads' from the media. If your name is Larson, for example, or Nelson, and you announce in the newspaper that you're engaged to or going to marry someone named Goldstein or Cecchini, there's a very good chance that you'll begin hearing from our hate mailer. If one of you is black, and you're rash enough to include a photograph with your engagement or wedding announcement, you'll hear from him, too. I consulted a psychologist about this man. He said he almost certainly enjoys thinking about sex, perhaps especially sex with someone of a darker or more 'exotic' race than his own—his own shadow, he called it—but he has to justify it to himself by pretending that he's dwelling on it for some highly moral purpose." Rossini shrugged slightly, as if to say that didn't help much in locating the man. "Would you like me to keep this?" he asked Paula.

"What would you do if you found out who he was?" Paula asked him.

The expression on Rossini's face became even sadder. "As I told you over the phone, I'm afraid there's not much we could do. Nothing he's sent out yet has gone beyond his First Amendment rights, you see. He seems to know how to stay within the law. But we would like to know who he is, of course, because he's harmed a lot of people. Perhaps, if we could talk to him, we could try to convince him to stop. Not everybody who mails out this kind of stuff realizes that it hurts, you know."

"That's hard to believe," Paula said.

"He must realize it," I said. "Otherwise, he'd sign his name, wouldn't he?"

"Not necessarily. We had a similar case a few years back. When we caught the man, he explained that he didn't want people to know who he was because he didn't want to have to waste time arguing with them. He was on a crusade, you see, and he didn't have time for what he considered pointless debate or possible counterharassment."

"But you caught that guy," I said.

"Yes." Rossini permitted himself a small regulation smile. "A lot of the mail he sent out didn't have adequate postage. That's against the law if you do it on a regular basis. Unfortunately, this man"—he tapped the garbage bag—"is very careful. He always uses the correct postage. He may have learned from the mistake of his predecessor, which was reported in the newspapers."

"So as long as I can afford the postage, I can send you just about any kind of filth and hate through the mail, is that it?" Paula said.

Rossini had mild eyes. He looked at Paula with them and said, "I'm afraid so."

"Have you tried to find out who this creep is through fingerprints?" I asked him.

He looked uncomfortable. "We have to tread carefully here," he said. "It wouldn't look very good, would it, if it came out that the government was trying to trace a customer through his fingerprints, if what the customer was doing wasn't against the law? There's another thing about fingerprints," he went on, before Paula could say something she might, or might not, regret. "Everybody, as I'm sure you must know, seems to know about them now. This man does."

I laughed. "You've tried to identify this guy through his fingerprints?"

Rossini turned pink and grinned back, a real grin, not government issue. "I took over this case last year, when my predecessor retired. I spent part of a day reading through the file we have on this man—a file I'm not sure we're even supposed to have, by the way. We have hundreds of his letters—they're all much like yours. And, of course, I probably only saw the tip of the iceberg, because a lot of his victims may not even bother to get in touch with us.

"I decided I wanted to try to identify him, and I'd let the constitutional issue take care of itself, if and when the time came. So far, as I've told you, I've come up with nothing."

We sat in depressed silence in his cold office for a few moments. Then Rossini turned to Paula and said, "You're going to get more of this, I'm afraid, for a while. Then, as he exhausts his supply of old material, the volume will gradually decrease. In about two weeks, you'll only hear from him when he gets something new he wants to 'share' with you."

We listened in horror as he described what was going to happen.

"It sounds like Lawrence and I have a chronic disease and you're describing its progress," Paula said when he'd finished.

"I'm sorry," he replied.

We got up to go. I thanked him for his time and shook his hand. Paula hung back, angry and frustrated. Rossini walked over to her and stuck out his hand. After a moment, she took it, as if he'd written the article in the Bill of Rights that had caused her this pain.

"I don't like the way Italians are treated in a lot of novels and movies," he told her. "I feel strange sometimes, introducing myself to people—suspecting they couple my name with 'Mafia'. I wanted to name my first son Mario, after my dad, but after discussing it with my wife, we decided not to. We named him Mark instead. It's not as terrible as what's happening to you, but it's the same kind of thing."

Paula held his hand for a long time, looking into his face. "You should've named him Mario," she said.

Neither of us spoke for the first few miles, as I drove Paula to campus police headquarters. She was going to be a little late for roll call. Finally, I glanced over at her and asked if she wanted me to go over to their place and intercept their mail and weed out the filth for them.

"No. If Lawrence and I are going to survive this, we're going to have to deal with it ourselves."

We drove a little farther in silence, and then she said, "Lawrence should have come with us to meet Rossini. It was awful, some of the things he said, but I feel better now, realizing we're not alone with this. Even you so-called white people who adopt black or Asian children are getting garbage from him, whoever he is. And it's less personal, somehow, knowing he's got a kind of operation going, a mill that grinds it out."

"He must be a really lonely, angry person," I said, "collecting the names of people whose living arrangements he doesn't like, cutting and pasting hate literature together and then slinking out to mail it."

"I've always thought spiders were the loneliest of all God's creatures," Paula said. "You never see them with other spiders, you only see them alone, waiting for something to fly into their web. Well, I've decided that I'm not going to let a spider beat me. He might beat Lawrence, but he isn't beating me."

* * *

Lawrence continued to work on their house, either for their future together or to sell it, and he didn't want to talk about what was on both their minds. Paula decided she'd wait until the hate mail subsided, if it did, before demanding that he sit down with her and talk about what had happened and might happen again should they stay together. She bought herself a futon and moved into her study, leaving Lawrence the bedroom.

She usually got to the mail first, she told me, sorting it into "hers," "his," and "ours." She could recognize the hate mail, but made no attempt to keep his from him and, whenever he got to the mail first, he didn't withhold hers from her either.

"I could read only so many statements by animal breeders on the superiority of purebloods over mongrels and alleycats," she told me one night, "before realizing that if I ever get a pet, it's going to be from the Humane Society—pedigree highly suspect."

"Somebody once proposed," I said, "that there should be a law prohibiting marriages between people of the same race until all the races were completely mixed."

Paula thought about that for a minute and then shook her head. "No. The result would probably be what a human being would look like if the politically correct got together and designed one. Something bland, beige and always doing and saying the right thing, like a talking doll. Free will would have to go out the window, too, of course. No thanks! I think you have to learn to live with evil. If you abolish it, you abolish freedom, too."

That was a strange notion.

Paula and Lawrence had never held hands in front of the other cops, but I'd seen them brush against each other sometimes as if by accident and exchange the kind of glances only lovers use. That had stopped with the arrival of the hate mail. But now, in the squad room before roll call, they resumed playing their word games, a good sign, although Paula didn't cheat as much as she normally did, which was probably the most serious outward symptom of the trouble they were having.

As Rossini has promised, the hate mail began to taper off. A week after we'd gone to see him, it was down to just one or two pieces a day for each of them.

Four

It was the first day of August, and I was patrolling the Old Campus on foot. It had been drizzling most of the night, a warm, misty drizzle that glittered on the sidewalks under the streetlights and dripped from the ivy-covered walls of the old buildings. I didn't mind. I'd spent my student days on the Old Campus, and it was my favorite beat, for you could sometimes forget that it was part of a sprawling modern university and imagine that you were wandering the paths of an old-fashioned college in some more innocent—and probably fictitious—time.

That nostalgic mood lasted until a little after one in the morning, when I rounded a corner and found a figure huddled on a bench in front of the Botany Building, an open umbrella above its head. I circled around in front to see who was sitting there.

It was Professor Tate. His eyes lit up when he saw me and he said, "Oh, there you are, Officer! Thank you for coming so promptly. I seem to have misplaced my keys, and the janitor hasn't opened the building yet. I've complained about that before, you know."

I called the dispatcher and described the situation. All the campus cops knew Professor Tate. He'd been a botany teacher for forty years and now lived in a retirement home. He forgot occasionally that he no longer taught at the University and slipped away from the home, sometimes in the middle of the night. He walked all the way to campus,

25

convinced that a classroom of eager students was waiting for him. If it was late, he would try the doors and then, confused, would find a comfortable place to sit until somebody would find him.

A few minutes later, Jesse Porter, who had the squad car that night, pulled up to the curb, and I put Professor Tate, who was muttering about the caliber of today's students, in the cage. I crawled in after him.

"You don't need to come, Peggy," Jesse said. "I can handle it."

"I don't like him sitting back here all by himself," I said. "Besides, it's raining."

When we returned to the campus, Jesse dropped me off where he'd found me and I resumed my patrol. It was a little after two, and the drizzle had turned into a steady downpour by the time I reached the Psychology Building.

I used my key to open the front door and went inside. I don't like the place, which I call the Edifice Complex. It's a nearly new building, impersonal and without ivy—a violation of the Old Campus spirit—and it seems to have been designed as a maze so somebody could observe the ratlike workings of the faculty and students in order to write articles and books about them.

I usually avoid the place, pretending that it doesn't need patrolling since so many students and faculty members are there at night, but because it was raining, I decided to go in. I walked down the hall, past the administrative offices where a good friend of mine works, and continued on to the atrium in the back. Three of the atrium's walls are glass, with plants hanging from the galleries that surround the upper floors, and there are planters scattered about the ground floor as well, full of exotic flora.

I bought myself a cup of coffee from the machine in the faculty lounge and took it over to a leather sofa by one of the glass walls facing the river. I could see the road that passes behind the building, following the winding course of the river below it.

At the point where the road curves out of sight to the

north, a parking lot is jammed into the space between it and the low wall that runs along the cliff above the river, big enough to hold about a dozen cars. Only one car was parked there now, a small, white compact. Its lights were on, and I assumed its owner was preparing to drive home, but when I finished my coffee, the car was still there. Somebody, I thought, had forgotten to turn off his lights.

I took the stairs to the second floor. A lab halfway down one of the halls was lighted and the door was open. I glanced in and saw a young man sitting at a printer, reading the data it spewed forth. It must have been fascinating stuff, for he didn't seem to notice me.

I made a noise to attract his attention without scaring him and asked him if the car in the parking lot was his. He shook his head, his eyes still on some piece of data that would probably go into a luridly irrelevant and tedious article. His being there at that hour wasn't at all unusual. A lot of the psych grad students have to work far into the night, if they hope to have any chance to compete for the few jobs there are in academia these days.

I continued on to the third floor. A woman came out of a room as I started to pass and bumped into me before I could get out of her way.

She flinched back and then laughed a little breathlessly. "You startled me," she said. "You ought to wear bells."

"That would do a lot of good," I said, smiling. "Sorry."

"No problem."

I told her about the car.

"It sounds like Geoff Oates's," she said. She was tall and long-limbed. "If I see him, I'll tell him. You might check his office, if you're going that way. It's on four."

I glanced into the room she'd come out of—a plaque beside the door said it was The Grace Sterns Library—and then walked up to the fourth floor. At the end of one of the halls was an office with Geoffrey Oates on a nameplate beside it and next to that H. William Turner. I knew Bill Turner.

I knocked on the door and a sleepy voice hollered, "What?"

"It's Peggy O'Neill, Bill. I'm looking for Geoffrey Oates."

"Lucky man," he said. "How does he rate, after all the time and effort I've spent chasing you?"

He opened the door. He was wearing only an army blanket draped modestly around his waist. He needed a shave and his hair was uncombed, but that's how he always looked. "If I'd known you were coming," he said, "I would've ordered champagne and flowers."

Behind him was the cot he slept on and next to it was an open pizza box, the kind that's delivered, with a couple of slices still in it, and a few empty beer cans.

"Oates left his car lights on," I said. "It's parked out in the lot in back."

"Oh yeah?" Bill scratched his straw-colored hair. "I haven't seen him since around ten. I'll check his lab. If he's not there, he could be anywhere in the building."

I thanked him and turned away.

"You still dating somebody?"

"Somebody my own age," I said, and headed back downstairs.

I'd encountered Turner in the building so often, and at such odd hours, that one night about six months ago I used my passkey to look into his office. Leaning against a wall was the cot with the blanket neatly stacked on top of it. In a cabinet were several pairs of jeans, underwear, and shirts of various kinds, and a plastic toiletries kit.

I talked to him about it and learned he spent so much time in the lab that he'd finally seen no reason to keep an apartment. He'd got permission from his adviser to live there, he said. Every morning he took his shaving kit, clothes, and a towel over to the gym, where he showered and shaved.

I checked it out, and was told that we were to turn a blind eye to the unorthodox living arrangements of the psych grad students. The professors thought it made perfect sense for their students to live there. Bill Turner, as far as I knew, was the only one doing it, at least now. He'd asked me out once and I told him I was going with someone, and he shrugged and said if things didn't work out with Someone to drop by his mansion—I knew the address.

The someone I was going with was now in Central America, trying to live the simple life and writing long letters urging me to join him there, but I didn't mention that to Bill Turner. He seemed like a nice guy, but he must have been nearly ten years younger than I. Besides, I'd already had one Psych Department boyfriend, and one's enough.

As I started back down the stairs to the atrium, I saw that the car was still in the lot, its lights still on, only dimmer now. The woman I'd almost bumped into earlier was coming up the stairs, carrying a Styrofoam cup of coffee.

"You find him?"

I told her that I hadn't and she said what Bill had said, that Oates could be anywhere in the building. She had a nice smile, full of large, beautiful teeth.

"Maybe it's unlocked," I said. "I'll go see."

I went out through one of the back doors, crossed the road, and walked over to the parking lot. The rain had stopped. As I approached the car, I could see there was somebody in it, and when I got a few steps closer, I knew something was wrong. The head was thrown back at an unnatural angle and pressed against the driver's window. The eyes were open, staring wildly at the sky, as if making a last-ditch, agonized effort to find meaning there.

I didn't open the driver's door because I knew he'd fall out, so I went around to the passenger side. The car reeked of gunpowder, blood, and other smells of violent death. A thin stream of blood trailed from a wound in his forehead and disappeared into the collar of his white shirt. A pistol lay on the seat beside him, his fingers still curled around its handle.

I stepped away from the car, pressed the button on my portable, and reported what I'd found to the dispatcher.

Five

Buck Hansen was there, along with his assistant, Burke, who was taking notes in his eccentric shorthand. And Lt. Bixler, Melvin Bixler, my boss and the curse of my professional life, was there, too, trying to look as though he were in charge of the investigation.

It was about an hour after I'd found the body, and we were in the Psychology Building's faculty lounge off the atrium. Through the window, I could see shadowy figures moving around the little white car, the dead man still where I'd found him, the scene etched in the glare of harsh police floodlights, resembling a surreal funerary ceremony.

Buck was questioning the woman who'd told me the car belonged to Oates. Her name was Carly Bachman. She was twenty-eight, tall—close to six feet—with straight, dark, shoulder-length hair and large, blue eyes. Her mouth was wide and her smile, although I didn't see it that night, dazzling and full of self-confidence.

"What were you doing here so late?" Bixler asked her, looking as though he were homing in on the crucial clue. The fact that I'd spoken to her just before finding the body made her the prime suspect in his eyes.

I rolled my eyes to the ceiling because that sometimes helps me in the effort to understand Bixler. I do it so frequently that Bixler thinks that's the way real people consider questions, so he does it, too. It was my bad luck that he was the duty officer that night. He was mad that he'd been dragged out of his office and into the cold night, away from his *Guns & Gonads* magazine, and he needed a scapegoat. I've been his favorite scapegoat almost from the day I first reported for duty, and he lives for the day he can get me kicked off the university police force.

"There's nothing strange about that," she told him, looking at him as though she thought him simple, something else that happens to Bixler so often that he no longer thinks it's insulting—if he ever did. "I've spent a lot of the last five years working late in this building. I just finished my dissertation, I'm getting my Ph.D. at the end of second summer session, and I'm trying to finish up an article before I move to Berkeley. I don't have time to go home and sleep."

"Move to Berkeley?" Bixler repeated, as if he thought that meant flee the country.

"It's in California," she told him. "I have a job waiting for me there." Her eyes moved to mine and we exchanged several volumes of information.

"How well did you know Oates?" Buck put in, gently resuming the questioning.

"Not very well, I'm afraid," she said. "He was a year behind me and doing a different type of research. But he seemed like a nice guy, and I've heard that he was bright enough. He did kill himself, didn't he?"

"Do you know of any reason he might have had for wanting to end his life?" Buck asked her, without answering her question.

"No, I don't. As I said, I didn't know him well at all."

After a few more questions, Buck asked her to wait in the lounge with the other people the police had rounded up in the building, mostly graduate students, in case he thought of anything more he wanted to ask her.

A man came into the room and looked around. "Who's in charge here?" he asked.

"I am," Buck said.

"I'm Professor Gardner. Lyle Gardner, Geoff Oates's adviser. Where is he?"

Buck didn't tell him that the body had already been identified, he just got up and asked him to follow him outside. I watched them from the atrium window. When they returned, Gardner was looking green around the gills.

"He shot himself! Why? What a terrible, terrible waste!"

He was a broad-shouldered man of medium height who looked as though he'd once been athletic, but now he was putting on weight around the middle. Maybe fifty-five, I thought, with a full head of wavy white hair and fashionable glasses. He was wearing dark slacks, a short-sleeved white dress shirt, and loafers without socks.

Buck asked him if he knew of any reason Oates would want to kill himself. Gardner shook his head. "No, absolutely not. He was a good student. Not, perhaps, among the very top students," he added judiciously, as if formulating a letter of recommendation for Oates, "but good. Very good."

"What about his private life?"

"I know nothing about the private lives of my students," Gardner replied.

"How about enemies in the department?"

"You suspect foul play?" Gardner's eyes widened behind his designer glasses. "Surely not. But, of course, you have to look at all the possibilities, don't you, however remote? To my knowledge, Geoff had no problems with anybody on the faculty. Of course, students do have lives beyond the walls of academe."

Bonnie Winkler, an assistant medical examiner, came in then, to tell Buck she was through with the body and it could be taken away. "What happened to the man seems pretty obvious to me," she said. "Or it would, if Peggy O'Neill weren't the one who found the body."

We'd met before, Winkler and I, in similar situations, and it had colored our relationship. She gave me a smile to indicate she was only kidding, but it didn't quite come off.

I got tired of sitting there after a while, so I went back

out to the atrium, where other members of the homicide squad were interviewing the people they'd found in the building when they arrived. There were eight, all but one of them graduate students. The exception was a professor I'd seen in the building before, a plump, balding man with a blond ponytail and a lost air about him.

I looked for Bill Turner, Geoff Oates's office mate, and saw that he wasn't there.

I retraced my steps to the fourth floor, to Turner's and Oates's office, and knocked again.

"Yeah," Turner mumbled.

"It's Peggy O'Neill again."

"Jesus, Peggy," he said, when he'd opened the door. "What now?" He was sitting on the edge of his cot, the blanket covering him, too tired to make a joke about why I'd come back.

"You're wanted downstairs," I told him.

"Down . . .? Why? What's the joke?"

"You'll see. Get dressed. Let's go."

"Is it something about Geoff?"

I didn't say anything, just watched his face.

"It is, isn't it? What's wrong?"

I told him Oates was dead and saw a strange, thoughtful expression appear in his eyes.

"How'd he die? Was it an accident?"

I told him I didn't know.

We stared at each other for a few seconds and then he ducked his head and said, "All right. Just let me get dressed, okay?"

I followed him downstairs and turned him over to Buck's people in the atrium and then went out into the cool, wet night. I passed the squad cars with their flickering lights and ducked gratefully down a dimly lit path lined with oaks that had been planted a long time ago. I made my way across the deserted Old Campus back to headquarters to fill out my report.

Six

I biked home, working off the tension of the night by setting a new speed record. I live about four miles from the University, and unless the weather's really bad, I ride my bike to and from work year-round, avoiding the worst parts of town when I can, especially at night. When I get to Lake Eleanor I use the bike path that takes me to within a couple of blocks of where I live. Biking and a serious game of racquetball several times a week are my only forms of exercise. That's been enough, so far.

I was carrying my bike up my front steps onto the porch, sweating and panting, when somebody called my name, and I turned and looked over my shoulder. It was the old man, Harold Mullen, who'd been at our table at the Fourth-of-July block party. He was standing out on his front stoop and waving to me.

"How about coming over for a cup of tea?"

What I wanted was a shower and bed, but then I thought that tea with a neighbor might be relaxing. It would certainly be a change of pace from the night's activity. I enjoy the company of old people and plan to join their number someday myself, since the alternative is unacceptable. I finished putting my bike up on my front porch and crossed the street. Mr. Mullen held his door open for me.

Although it was early, he was dressed in dark suit trousers with suspenders and a bow tie, probably the same outfit he'd worn on the Fourth of July. He noticed my eyes

taking him in and he smiled and said, "When you're retired and you live alone, it's most important not to relax
your standards of personal hygiene. It's all too tempting
for the old to neglect their appearance. I often saw old
men in my store—and women, too, I'm sorry to say—who
had obviously stopped caring for themselves. I promised
myself that I would never become like that."

I suddenly realized how rumpled I was in my jeans and
sweaty T-shirt.

I said that I'd seen a lot of men his age—and women,
too, I added—who looked good in jeans.

"Perhaps I'm old-fashioned," he said, shaking his head,
"but I can't agree with you. Jeans are only appropriate to
the young, I think. You look like you rode your bike home
in a hurry."

"I did," I said. I thought of telling him about what I'd
been through that night but decided I didn't want to relive
it through his questions.

The interior of his house was dark and claustrophobic, like
a museum that was closed for the day, and smelled of old
varnish. As I followed him through his living and dining
rooms, I got a glimpse of heavy furniture, an upright piano
that grinned at me with yellowed teeth, and dull, nondescript
pictures on the walls that featured waxy fruit and dead birds.
I ran my fingers surreptitiously over the top of a picture
frame and checked my finger for dust. There wasn't any.
You could eat off my mother's picture frames too.

Mr. Mullen ushered me out onto his enclosed front
porch and sat me down at a little round table, making
fussy hostlike noises. He tucked the newspaper he'd been
reading under his arm, gathered up a plate containing an
eggcup with an empty shell in it and a few toast crumbs,
and took them away on a tray. He returned a few minutes
later with a teapot and a cup for me, a delicate china thing
that was chipped and matched his own.

We drank tea in silence for a few minutes and I was grateful for the chance to relax. I could feel him studying me with
shy glances. Finally he said, "A penny for your thoughts."

I said they weren't worth it, which was true. I asked him what kind of store he'd owned before he retired, and he told me he'd had a small electronics shop for many years—it had been just a mile away, over on Twenty-ninth.

"Small electronics," he added, "clocks and radios, electronic wares of all kinds." Mullen got a dreamy look in his eyes as he remembered all that he'd had in his store. "But it's gone now," he went on, his voice hardening. "I couldn't hope to compete with the chains, with their deep pockets. Electro-Mart put in a store across the street from mine and ran me out of business in three years! I hear they've sworn to put every independent store in the country out of business by the year 2000! It's Jap owned, of course." Mr. Mullen flashed his too-white, too-regular teeth in a grin. "I thought we fought World War II to keep those people away from our shores. But I guess our boys died in vain over there, didn't they?" When I didn't say anything, he went on. "It hurt to have to sell out like that. To have to sell my inventory and close my doors."

I wondered how much of his electronics inventory had been made in Japan, but decided I didn't want to get into that with him.

"It could have been worse," he said, brightening a bit. "Much worse. For you see, Miss O'Neill, I owned the property around my store, too—bought it a long time ago, long before property values began to climb, when people started to move into that part of the city. So when I sold it two years ago, I made a pretty penny off it, quite a pretty penny." The look of triumph faded quickly. "But I lost my store, driven out by the Japs, the way they drove us out of the Philippines."

It wasn't a perfect analogy, but it probably expressed how he felt about his loss. I said that it sounded to me as though progress had helped and hurt him in equal measure, since he'd made so much money from the increase in value of his property.

"Is that what you think?" he said, his eyes lighting up. "Not a year later, I got the cancer!"

"That's too bad." Mrs. Hammer had said something about that at the Fourth-of-July block party. I glanced through his front windows at my apartment across the street, wished I'd taken a rain check on tea.

"I blame it on heartbreak," he said, "the heartbreak of having to sell the business I'd put my life's blood into. My doctor doesn't agree, but it's the truth."

I told him he seemed healthy now.

"Oh, I am, I am!" He chuckled. "The doctor gave up on me—thought he had all the answers! I was supposed to die this winter, you see, but I fooled him. He tells me the cancer's gone into remission. It sometimes happens like that, he says, and I might live another five, ten years—or it might come back tomorrow, and I'll be dead in a month! But it won't come back—I've never felt better in my life. Either I've been very lucky, or it was God's will. Which do you think it was, Miss O'Neill?"

It wasn't a real question, so I just shrugged.

"It was God's will. God's will! There's no other explanation that makes any sense. God has always taken care of me. You see, I tried to sell my property ten, fifteen years ago but nobody would buy it at the price I was asking. So I hung onto it—had to. And then prices began to rise, and when I finally did sell, I got twice what I would have got earlier. I feel grateful, Miss O'Neill, and humble, too, and that's why I've decided to do something that would benefit humanity with my money."

"You said something on the Fourth of July about giving your money to the University."

"Yes, and that's just what I'm doing."

I asked him if he was going to leave the University his money for anything in particular.

"Anything in particular?" He chuckled. "Oh, yes, indeed I am!" He gave me a conspiratorial smile, waiting for me to ask for what.

When I did, he replied, "Research. Scientific research."

"Cancer research?"

"Cancer?" The word surprised him, as if he'd never

thought of that before. Then he laughed, a reedy noise without music. "Well, yes, you might say I'm giving it for cancer research—a very nasty form of cancer."

It had really been much too long a night for this kind of banter. "Are you going to tell me what kind of research?"

His whole face lit up because I'd asked that question. "Not now," he said, wagging a bony finger at me. "But soon, perhaps. Soon. We'll see. In the fullness of time. Until then, let me just ask you if you've ever heard of an 'endowed chair'?" When I told him I had, he nodded knowingly, winked, and repeated, "In the fullness of time."

Weirder and weirder. I made a movement to get up.

"You used to have a boyfriend, as I recall," he said. "I haven't seen him around lately."

"He's in Belize," I said, "in Central America." Mr. Mullen must have kept pretty good track of my comings and goings through these porch windows, I thought. And the comings and goings of my friends, too.

"For long?"

"I don't know."

"You couldn't feel very strongly about him if you didn't go with him, could you?" he asked.

"I don't know how to answer that one," I said with a weary laugh. I felt strongly about Gary once, but not strongly enough to give up my own life for his. I don't ever want to feel that strongly about anybody.

"Do you like being a university policewoman?"

"I think so, yes." Even after what I'd found last night— this morning, I mean—I added to myself.

"Why?"

"I can't think of another work environment I could put up with as well," I said, "or that could put up with me."

"What about marriage and children?"

"The world's full of married people and children, too. I'm not needed there." That was the answer I gave to people who had no business asking. I got up. "I really have to go now, Mr. Mullen. Thanks for the tea."

Mr. Mullen stayed where he was, watching me. "How's your friend—Lawrence Fitzpatrick, is it?"

"He's fine, I guess."

"He seemed like such a nice fellow. If you were married to another policeman, you'd have a lot in common, wouldn't you? You wouldn't have to give up your life for somebody else's."

I'd started for the door but turned back slowly and looked at him, a prickly sensation on my neck. Mr. Mullen's cheap false teeth were showing in a smile he may have thought was sly.

"That's true, I guess," I replied. "But one problem with it is, Lawrence is in love with Paula. You remember Paula, don't you?"

Then I recalled how, at the block party on the Fourth, Mullen had said Lawrence and I would make a good match, in spite of the fact that it was obvious Lawrence was there with Paula.

I came back to where he was now standing by the table. "Do you send out a lot of mail, Mr. Mullen?" I tried to keep my voice pleasant, but it wasn't easy.

"Mail?" He straightened up as if I'd hit him. "No, hardly any at all—I have no one to write to. Why do you ask such a strange question?"

He was lying, and he knew I knew it. He sat down and seemed to try to make himself smaller, frailer than he was—a harmless old man. "And why are you staring at me like that, Miss O'Neill?"

"Paula and Lawrence," I said, "have been getting hate mail, anonymously—really sick, disgusting stuff. You wouldn't know anything about that, would you?"

"Sick? Disgusting?" He was trembling, but then he pulled himself together, stood up and, with one gnarled, age-burnt hand supporting him on the table, said, "I don't know what you mean. I don't believe in white people being involved carnally with people of the darker races. It's a sin. God created the races, and it's blasphemy to mix them. Don't you think so, too?"

"No. I believe it's a sin to torment people who aren't bothering you just because you don't like them."

"I don't torment anybody! You're tormenting me, an old man who only asked you in for a cup of tea. I have a right to my beliefs."

I'd made a mistake by pushing it as far as I had. I wouldn't have, probably, if I hadn't been so tired and stressed from finding the body earlier, with its wildly staring eyes and one side of its face gone. I knew I was right about Mullen, but there wasn't anything I could do about it except call Rossini, the postal inspector, and let him deal with it if he could.

I turned and headed for the door.

"You should be ashamed of yourself," Mullen yelled, coming after me, his thin voice gaining strength. "I have friends at the University, young lady, important friends. If I wanted to, I could get you into trouble!"

I turned quickly, in time to catch the malicious glint in his eyes just before it winked out and left them as dull and watery as before.

Seven

It was too early to call Rossini, but not too early to call Paula and Lawrence. I started to pick up the phone—then hesitated. Paula's usually a lot more rational than I am. In the past, I'd been the one who'd behaved irresponsibly and got into trouble, and Paula had disapproved. Once, my behavior had almost wrecked our friendship.

But what would she do in this case, if I told her what I suspected? What would Lawrence do? One or the other of them might decide to confront Mullen. I had no real proof that he was the hate mailer, nothing that would stand up in court, at least. And even if I did, it wouldn't go to court anyway, according to Rossini, who had said the hate mailer wasn't breaking the law.

I was too tired and upset to think clearly. I decided to sleep on it.

I got up around two that afternoon, ground coffee and plugged in the pot and then padded back to the bathroom and brushed my teeth and showered. I went back into the bedroom and peered out through the venetian blinds to see what kind of afternoon I should dress for.

Across the street, a man was coming down the walk from Mullen's house. When he reached the sidewalk, he glanced left and right, then stared straight across the street, right into my eyes. Even though he couldn't see me, I flinched away. He was short and stocky, about forty, with dark hair slicked back that made his high forehead seem even higher. He was holding two grocery bags like fat babies to his chest.

Something about his furtiveness made me grab my bath-robe and run out of the bedroom as I wrapped it around me, not taking the time to put it on. I crossed to the front door and ran out onto the porch. A large green car, old and rusted, its paint almost gone, was pulling away from the curb. An American gas-guzzler from the 1960s or early 1970s, I guessed. I'm not good at identifying cars. There was no rear license plate. I thought I'd seen it before, parked on Mullen's side of the street, near his house.

I went back inside, got dressed, and drank a cup of cof-fee with a banana and a piece of toast. Then I called Rossini at the post office and told him I thought I'd found the hate mailer.

"That was quick," he said mildly.

I described my encounter with Mullen that morning. When I finished, he said: "I'm afraid I don't think we're much farther along than we were before. He denied to you that he was the hate mailer."

"But couldn't you just talk to him? Let him know that you're keeping an eye on him?"

Impatience crept into Rossini's precise voice. "You're not thinking clearly, Ms. O'Neill. This man has done and said nothing in your presence that could reasonably lead us to take any action against him at all. Surely you must see that."

"You weren't there," I said. "You didn't hear the slimy, insinuating way he talked about my friends. You didn't see his face when he saw that I knew."

"What would you think, if you were to read in the newspaper that a government agent had come to some-one's door and told them they were keeping an eye on them, on the basis of a neighbor's suspicions?"

"But . . ." That's as far as I got, because I knew exactly what I'd think.

"I do understand your concern, Ms. O'Neill," he went on, after giving me a few moments to let what he'd said sink in. "I'll discuss what you've told me with my superiors, to see if there's anything we can legally do to find out if this man is the man you think he is."

"I guess I hope there's nothing you can legally do," I replied with a sigh.

I was about to hang up when he said, "I assume you've told your friends about your encounter with this man."

I said I hadn't.

"You'll be doing both of them a favor by not telling them of your suspicions. They've been living with a great deal of stress on account of this person, whoever he is, and they might do something rash, something they would regret that would damage their lives more surely than this hate mail has."

I agreed with him that I didn't have to share my suspicions with them yet, and we hung up.

I didn't feel very good, withholding my suspicions about Mullen from Paula and Lawrence, but since there wasn't anything any of us could do without getting into trouble, I decided to keep them from temptation. My decision was made easier by the fact that they had the night off, so I wouldn't have to see them.

I biked over to Ginny Raines's apartment that evening for dinner and to watch a movie on her VCR. Ginny's my oldest friend among the campus cops, a detective who works days. We're both fans of old musicals and we get together about once a month to watch one. It was her turn to pick that night and she'd chosen *An American in Paris*. It's a great musical, but I'll never forgive Gene Kelly for dumping Nina Foch for Leslie Caron. Foch's the only woman in the flick with a brain.

Afterwards, I played Kelly's Jerry Mulligan and Ginny was Caron's Lise Bourvier, as we imagined they'd be a year after the movie ended.

"I'm going out to hoist a few with the guys, *ma cherie*," I announced, adjusting an imaginary cap over one eye and striking an apache dancer's pose. "Painting the kind of pictures that went out of style around 1915 really takes it out of a guy."

"Oh, no!" Ginny, a large woman, protested in her most gamine voice, trying to fade into the couch.

"*C'est la vie!*" I rasped boyishly. "Have a stick of this s'marvelous American chewing gum while I'm gone."

"Just tonight, Jerry, stay home and talk baby talk to me the way you used to in the rain, *s'il vous plaît,*" Ginny wheedled.

Her attempt at a moue cracked us both up.

I dragged my bike off her porch around ten and headed off to the University. "Next time, we're watching something with Fred Astaire and Cyd Charisse in it," I told her. I liked Cyd Charisse a lot.

I got to police headquarters a little early, bought myself a Coke, and sat in a corner of the squad room to wait for roll call. The silly mood I'd been in when I left Ginny gradually evaporated as I watched the other cops enter the room, coming either on or off duty. I wondered what they thought about the relationship between Paula and Lawrence. I've never heard any comments, but I probably wouldn't, since everybody knew I was their friend. I wondered if maybe I'd been wrong about Harold Mullen, and it was one of them who was behind the hate mail.

It couldn't be Jesse Porter, certainly, I thought as he came in, waved and smiled all around, then sat down and buried his little nose in a science-fiction comic book with a lurid cover. Jesse was too nice—nice to the point of tedium, in fact. Or so he appeared. But what did I really know about him? Harold Mullen had seemed nice enough, too, and I'd penetrated to something really ugly beneath his surface, even if he wasn't the hate mailer. All I knew about Jesse was that, as a rookie, he'd shot himself in the leg while practicing quick draws in front of a mirror in an empty campus building late one night. That had earned him the nickname Jesse James. He'd made up for that a few months later by taking a knife away from a man without even drawing his pistol and ended up in the hospital.

Still, being boring and a hero didn't exclude him from being a racist as well.

I didn't know any of the other cops well enough to make any judgment about them. Most of them did their jobs quietly and efficiently and then disappeared into their private lives when their watch was over.

I wondered about Floyd Hazard, a man with a perpetual chip on his shoulder, who was sitting over in the smoking corner of the squad room. He had no friends among the campus cops. I wondered if he had any friends at all and thought about what Paula had said about spiders being the loneliest of God's creatures.

Lt. Bixler stomped past the squad room just then, hollered "Let's go, shake a leg!" without looking in—his way of calling us to roll call. Bixler didn't like Paula much, but he didn't like any woman cop, regardless of color. With his mixture of arrogance and stupidity, it was possible he wasn't even aware that Paula and Lawrence were a couple.

I realized that Paula and Lawrence must have sat here and wondered about their fellow cops, too—maybe even wondered about me.

After roll call, I started out on foot for the Old Campus. I'd hardly begun when Ron, the dispatcher, asked me where I was and told me Lawrence Fitzpatrick wanted to meet me somewhere.

"What are you running, Peggy?" Ron asked. "A bookie agency?"

Grinning maliciously to myself, I told Ron to ask Lawrence if he knew where the old willow was on the river. He did, and half an hour later we were sitting where Paula and I'd sat when she told me about the hate mail.

"What's up, Lawrence? You've got your house all fixed up?" I didn't try very hard to keep the sarcasm out of my voice, but he looked so miserable that I felt bad about it immediately.

He didn't say anything for a few minutes, just peeled the bark from a twig and tied the twig in knots. After a while he asked me what had happened in the Psychology

Building the night before and I told him, making it brief because I didn't think that's what he was there for.

When I was finished, he said, as if he hadn't been listening to me at all, "Relationships are hard enough to make work, don't you think, without adding race?"

"You bet. Only an idiot would get involved in something like that."

"And there's the children to think about, too. Do we want to put them through this?"

I thought of Paula's and Lawrence's beauty and didn't see how kids could lose on the deal. "Why don't you wait and ask them?"

"C'mon, Peggy, be serious."

"I am serious. You should have thought of these things before you fell in love with her, damn you, and pestered her into falling in love with you. She's the idiot. You're just stupid. Or worse."

"It's easy for you, Peggy," he said.

I turned and looked at him. "You're not using this as an excuse to dump her, are you?"

"No! Paula asked me that, too, but it's not true."

"Good. So it's just that you're letting some hate-filled anonymous loser determine the direction of your life."

He started to say something in outrage, but checked himself.

"Paula said you haven't wanted to talk to her about it for almost two weeks. That's not a good sign, Lawrence, since you're not exactly the only one hurting here."

"Did she show you the kind of mail we've been getting?"

"Yes, right here where we're sitting now. It was incredibly ugly. The river was beautiful, though, and the night. Like now. And like Paula."

"I can't believe that Paula and I, just walking down the street together, can create such hatred in the mind of somebody who doesn't even know us."

"You didn't create it. You just activated what was there already."

"I know that, most of the time. I tried not to let it affect me when we first started getting the mail. But then I started to realize that it was never going to stop, and then I began waiting for the letter carrier, the way you wait for a blow you know you can't duck." Long pause. "And pretty soon, Peggy, I couldn't touch Paula anymore, and I didn't want her to touch me anymore either. I didn't know any longer why we'd ever wanted to touch each other—if I've ever known."

I suddenly had a vision of Harold Mullen as I'd seen him that morning in his house, spiffy in his dark suit trousers, white shirt, and bow tie, his faded eyes and soft, insinuating voice, his sly, false grin. Mullen was winning, and Lawrence didn't even know against whom he was playing. I wanted to tell him, but I didn't dare. If I wanted to see Mr. Mullen dead, what would Lawrence want?

"You're letting the sickos win," I told him. "I thought you were stronger than that, Lawrence, I'm disappointed in you. I figured you went into the relationship with Paula with your eyes open. How could you have lived this long and not know the kind of people who are out there? Don't you know that *anybody* who stands out in a crowd—for any reason at all—activates rage in a lot of people?" I heard my voice rising, tried to lower it. "Maybe it's just resentment—somebody who's lost a lot, or who's never won anything, who resents other people's happiness and uses race, or sexual preference, or religion as an excuse to try to stomp out that happiness. Or maybe it's a primitive thing, some kind of survival instinct that tells us to stay with the herd, and we get frightened when somebody breaks away. And when people get frightened, they get mad and want to hurt what's frightening them."

I'd once encountered a man who got enraged at the sight of handicapped people. He harassed them on the streets, usually only verbally, but at least once he went too far. I was there and arrested him and hauled him off to jail. He claimed it was a compulsion and the court ordered him to undergo therapy in lieu of jail time. I wondered if it worked.

"Christ, Lawrence," I said, remembering something else, "I didn't like *you* when I first met you!"

"You didn't?" He stared at me as if he'd never seen me before, his wide-set brown eyes glittering with tears. "Why?"

"You're too good-looking. Haven't you ever noticed?"

"Yes." He blushed. "I mean, I've been told that. But in most ways, I'm pretty average, I think."

I couldn't help but agree. "You are. But the fact is, Paula fell in love with you, Lawrence, and that was a miracle. Miracles don't happen so often that you can afford to walk away from one."

"But do you think we could ever get back to the way we were, Peggy?"

"So that's it!" I said, angry and disgusted. "You only want to be with Paula if you get to live your entire life in Cloud-Cuckoo-Land! Well, I'm sorry to have to tell you this but no, I don't think you and Paula will ever be able to get back to the way you were, and it's probably just as well. You can't go through life pretending evil doesn't exist. That's probably what the poor guy did whose body I found last night. Maybe he thought life was a bowl of fresh-picked raspberries and then one day he found a bug in the bowl and he couldn't handle it and—bang! he killed himself. Maybe Paula would be better off without you, if the minute a little reality enters your fool's paradise, you run away."

"You've run away from relationships, too, Peggy," he said.

That stopped me, but only for a moment. "Because the miracle hasn't happened for me yet, Lawrence!"

Eight

A little after seven the next morning, I biked home. As I turned up the hill from the path around Lake Eleanor I could already smell it: the acrid smell of wet ashes. And then, still half a block from my house, I saw where it was coming from.

The front wall of Harold Mullen's house was gone, leaving just the concrete steps that led up into nothing. The interior of the house was gutted, the first and second floors collapsed into the basement, full of charred timber. The front and side yards were littered with ugly piles of burned wood and broken glass and the sides of the houses on either side of Mullen's were scorched, with broken windows and missing roof tiles. The police had strung yellow tape around Mullen's entire yard to keep people out.

I just stood there straddling my bike, dazed.

"Too bad you left for work so early last night," Mrs. Hammer said, appearing suddenly in her door, which was next to mine, her voice jarring me back to reality. "You missed all the excitement." She'd obviously been watching for me to come home, so she could tell me about it.

"Where's Mr. Mullen?" I asked as I pulled my bike up onto the porch.

"They haven't found him, but he's in there somewhere—what's left of him is, anyway."

"When did it happen?"

"Around nine-thirty. Suddenly there was one hell of a

racket, with sirens blaring and people hollering and the street lit up like Judgment Day. It was the most excitement we've had around here since that night your apartment was full of people trying to murder you. Mullen's place went up like a torch. We're lucky we didn't lose the houses on either side, too.

"Do they know how it started?"

"The arson squad's coming this morning. But who'd want to torch old Mullen's place, unless it's some relative of his, greedy for his money and not willing to wait a few more months or years to get it? Most likely an accident, though. The wiring in some of these old houses is a hundred years old. Or else he left his stove on. Speaking of which, when was the last time you checked the batteries in your smoke alarm, young lady?"

I told her I couldn't remember. Wasn't it supposed to make a beeping noise or something when the batteries got weak?

We stood on the porch, staring across the street at the gaping wound in the neighborhood. I shuddered, remembering the last time I'd seen Mullen—just about this time yesterday. Then I remembered the furtive little man I'd seen coming down his walk that afternoon. That had been the last time I'd consciously noticed Mullen's house at all. And now it was gone, and Mullen, too.

I asked her how well she'd known him.

"I hardly knew him to speak to at all. Nobody around here did. We talked about him last night as we were watching his house burn up, some of the neighbors and I. He'd lived over there for thirty years, you know, and we didn't know a thing about him. Oh, he used to be friendlier than he is now—was, I mean. He'd stop to chat with the neighbors sometimes when he was out raking leaves or shoveling snow—not what you'd call effusive, you know, but pleasant enough. He kept up his yard," she added. In my neighborhood, that's the bottom line.

"All that changed about four, five years ago," she went on. "He let his lawn go, creeping charlie and clover took over, and he'd hardly speak to anybody. The kids learned not to go trick-or-treating over there. No point in it, he wouldn't answer the door.

"One of the neighbors thought it had to do with business—he had a little shop over on Twenty-ninth, where that new office building is now, and he was being squeezed by the chains. Maybe that was it. He sold his business a couple of years ago. I guess he owned the land it was on, and he sold that, too. He must have made a bundle off of it."

"Then he got cancer," I said, "and it went into remission."

"That's right. He wasn't expected to live, but he fooled the doctors, he said. After that he became friendlier again. He came to the block party on the Fourth, too, you remember. That was a surprise. You remember how he was explaining the meanings of all your names out of that big book of his—boring you to tears? Come to think of it, I've still got that book, I never did return it to him."

I asked her if he ever talked about any of his interests.

Mrs. Hammer looked at me suspiciously. "Like what?"

"I had tea with him yesterday," I said. "He made some racist comments."

"Oh. Well, so many people of his generation are like that, I'm afraid." Mrs. Hammer was of his generation, and she wasn't like that at all. "He never made racist comments around me, but then, I didn't talk to him much either. Why are you pumping me about Mr. Mullen, Peggy?"

"Just curious," I said.

"You think there might be something fishy about his house burning down?" Mrs. Hammer knows me.

I said I had no idea and after we'd talked a little while longer, I went inside and showered. Then I called Buck Hansen, a homicide lieutenant I know, figuring he'd probably be in his office, since it was a little after eight.

He answered on the first ring and I asked him if he'd like to meet me that afternoon for coffee.

"Why? To talk about Geoffrey Oates? You don't think

it was suicide and you feel responsible for the man, since you found him?"

"No, nothing like that," I replied. "I've got another death I'd like to talk to you about, a little closer to home."

"Who?"

"A man named Harold Mullen, a neighbor of mine. His house burned down last night."

"Arson?"

"I don't know. Maybe you could find out a little more about it before this afternoon."

Buck sighed audibly and said he'd see what he could do. We agreed to meet at a little espresso bar downtown at four-thirty.

"Sweet dreams," he said, as he hung up, but it didn't help—not, I think, because two violent deaths in two nights are enough to keep me awake anymore, but on account of the faint, sickly smell of wet ash that had penetrated my apartment.

Buck's in his late thirties, a little taller than I, lean, and has the silvery hair of somebody who'd once been very blond. I think he's beautiful. We see each other for lunch or dinner irregularly, sometimes as often as twice a month, sometimes not for several months. I like knowing he's out there and I think he likes knowing I'm around, too. Sometimes I wish we were more than friends, but I'm afraid to let my attraction threaten a friendship I value. I don't know what's prevented him from making a pass at me. Maybe the same thing.

When we had picked up our orders and found a place to sit, I asked him what he had found out about Mullen.

"It's Anne Meredith's case," he said. Meredith was another homicide lieutenant. "They found his body. There wasn't much left of it, but enough for a positive identification."

I shuddered, remembering his cheap false teeth. I wondered if they'd melted into a disgusting white mass.

"Was he a friend of yours?" Buck asked, noticing the shudder.

"No," I replied, "I only met him a few times. Do they think it was arson?"

Buck stirred cinnamon into his *latte*. "The fire seems to have started in one place, a room in the basement, a kind of study Mullen must have had there, full of books, papers, and some electrical stuff they think was plugged into inadequate wiring. All that points to its having started accidentally. You usually find more than one point of origin when it's arson."

"What sort of electrical stuff?"

"A number of things," he said, "but no smoke detector. A radio, television set—oh, and a copying machine, one of those expensive desktop models, the kind small businesses have."

"What would a retired old man want with a copying machine?" I asked.

Buck shrugged. "Maybe it was something from his electronics store, something he couldn't sell. It might not even have been in working order."

"Then why was he in the basement?" I imagined Mullen down there, alone, working on the hate mail he sent out, surrounded by the books from which he took his ideas. Did the fire start accidentally as he worked? Was he overcome by the smoke? Or did somebody come down there and kill him first?

"He had a washer and dryer down there, too," Buck said, injecting a note of reality. "Are you going to tell me what all these questions are about?"

I told him about Paula and Lawrence and the hate mailer. "According to the postal inspector, this guy's got a lot of time on his hands, and money—just like Mullen. He also photocopies passages from books and sends it out to people whose way of life he doesn't like."

Buck sipped coffee and listened, his blue eyes never leaving my face. That used to disconcert me, but now it only does when I'm hiding something from him, which I wasn't doing today. Buck has wrinkles at the corners of his blue eyes—laugh wrinkles, my grandmother would have called them—but Buck doesn't laugh all that much.

"I'm sorry about Paula and Lawrence," he said. "You think there's a connection between his alleged racist activities and his death?" He emphasized *alleged*.

"Why else would anybody want to torch his house and kill him?"

"You say he had a lot of money. That's a good enough reason for some people. When I spoke to Anne, she hadn't received a background report on Mullen yet. With all his records gone, she doesn't even know which bank he used."

I scraped the last of my whipped cream out of my cappuccino glass with a spoon. "He said he was leaving his money to the University—for research, but he wouldn't tell me what kind. He tried to make it a mystery."

"He was probably trying to make himself interesting to you, Peggy," Buck said.

I told him about the furtive little man I'd seen coming down Mullen's steps carrying grocery bags. "He could have been Mullen's helper, mailing out all the crud the old man created. Mullen was probably too weak to carry bags of hate mail down to the box on the corner. Besides, that much mail coming regularly from one mail box might attract attention, which is what he didn't seem to want. So the little guy mailed it for him from different places all over town."

Buck burst out laughing. "With your ability to see wickedness in the smallest thing, Peggy, you ought to be a tent revivalist or write mysteries. The poor guy might have been picking up Mullen's old clothes for the Goodwill for all you know."

"No. I think I've seen his car before, parked across the street. A big, old, rusted-out clunker."

"Maybe it belongs to a neighbor who was just dropping something off at Mullen's when you saw him."

"If the car's ever parked over there again, I'll buy that theory," I said.

Buck asked me what Paula and Lawrence thought of my theory about Mullen. I glanced up quickly, caught the look in his eye: the homicide cop look.

"I didn't tell them about my visit to Mullen," I said.

"Do you suppose it occurred to either of them that he might be behind the mail they were getting?"

"It's not likely, Buck. *I* didn't think of Mullen until I was actually in his house talking to him. And on the Fourth of July he seemed so innocent," I added.

"But you haven't been thinking about who the hate mailer might be as long or as hard as your friends have. And the mail did start coming right after the block party, you said."

"It was two weeks after, not *right* after," I retorted, trying not to talk too fast. "Lots of people could be suspect. Paula and Lawrence just bought a house, and somebody might not have liked having them in the neighborhood. Or it might even be a campus cop."

Buck leaned back in his chair and smirked. "Suddenly you're very concerned about giving Mr. Harold Mullen the benefit of the doubt, Peggy—very thoughtful of you! But you forgot to mention the most important thing: Neither Paula nor Lawrence would do anything rash, would they? Rashness is what you're noted for. Paula's chief characteristic is rationality."

"That's right," I agreed readily.

To get him off Paula and Lawrence, I asked him if he was satisfied that Geoffrey Oates had killed himself.

He grinned, seeing through my sudden change of subject. "Bonnie Winkler is," he said. "She couldn't find anything in the autopsy that said it was anything else. But I'm never happy when they don't leave a note. I'll wait to hear from the crime lab. It's only been a day and a half."

We talked about other things for a while and then he asked me if I'd heard anything from Gary Mallory.

"I get long letters from him," I told him. "He's in Central America now, working on a book on Belize, which he says is the last unspoiled country down there. Of course, if the book sells as well as his last one, Belize'll be the next hot tourist spot."

"Which will probably drive Gary back here to you," Buck said.

"He wants me to go there."

"Are you thinking of going?" I wondered if it was only my imagination, or if there really was a note of anxiety in Buck's voice when he asked me that.

"What would I do there?"

Buck wiped frothed milk off his upper lip with a napkin. "Stay out of trouble," he answered.

I laughed. "Come to think of it, I haven't heard from Gary for almost a month. Maybe he's met somebody down there and fallen in love with her."

"I wouldn't blame him," Buck said. "Nobody can live for long on hope alone."

"With Gary, anything's possible," I replied.

After we'd paid our bill and were walking out the door, Buck said, "I suppose you're going to tell Paula and Lawrence about your suspicions about Mullen, now that it's too late for either of them to do him any harm."

I said I couldn't think of a reason not to.

"You'll let Anne Meredith know, won't you, if they act strange—you know, the way Mullen acted in front of you?"

"You know I will, Buck," I told him, taking my time picking out the change for my share of the bill, to avoid meeting his unblinking blue eyes.

I waited until both Paula and Lawrence had come in from their watches, and then said I wanted to talk to them in private. We went into Ginny Raines's office, empty that time of night, and I told them about Mullen's house burning down last night and my conversation with him the morning before.

"But you didn't tell us about it," Paula said, giving me a half smile.

"I was afraid to. And I didn't have any proof."

She nodded. "I was starting to think of Mr. Mullen more and more often these past few weeks," she said. "We mentioned his name when I first told you about the mail, remember? But he was just one possibility among so many, and just because somebody's old-fashioned in his thinking—or even an outright racist—doesn't mean he's going to do anything about it. But I kept coming back to Mullen, since the mail started so soon after we'd met him, and he could easily have found out where we lived, since he knew our names. I kept remembering how he said you and Lawrence would make a nice match, even though anybody with eyes could see we were a couple." She turned and looked Lawrence up and down for a moment. "That grated, for some reason," she added, dryly.

"You never told me you suspected him, Paula," Lawrence said.

"No. Peggy was afraid to tell me of her suspicions and I was afraid to tell you of mine. That's one of the problems with this world—no trust no place no more."

Lawrence shook his head helplessly.

She turned to me and asked me if I wanted to know what she'd done about her suspicions. I gave an exaggerated sniff and told her I didn't smell kerosene.

She didn't smile. She said, "I went over to the old man's place last night."

"Paula!" That was Lawrence.

She ignored him, fixed her large eyes unblinkingly on me. "Lawrence was so busy painting the spare bedroom," she said, her voice flat, "the one we thought might make a nice kid's room someday, that he didn't even notice when I left the house."

Lawrence ducked his head.

"I drove over to your place, Peggy—I wanted to talk to you about it, since you'd known Mullen, too. I figured you wouldn't have left for the U yet, but you weren't home. So I thought, what the heck, I'm here, I'll just go across the street and discuss it with the man himself—nicely, in such a subtle way that he won't even suspect what I'm doing. And that's what I did."

"You actually talked to him?" I asked, horrified.

"There were lights on in the house. I rang his doorbell, waited, rang it again, and after a while I heard footsteps and then the door opened. Mullen was out of breath and angry. He said, 'Don't you have your key—?' Then he looked up and saw me. I thought he was going to have a heart attack. He backed away from the door, those false teeth of his bared in a hideous grin.

"As pleasantly as I could, I told him my name and reminded him of where we'd met before. He could hardly get the words out, but he managed to tell me he didn't want me in his house and to get out or he'd call the police. 'I'm not alone!' he said. He was shaking so badly, I thought he'd have a stroke. I tried to say something to calm him, but it just seemed to make him worse. He looked so old, helpless and pathetic. I realized that if I stayed there any longer, I'd just make things worse— probably for both of us. I'd never caused a reaction like that in anybody before—you'd have thought I was something from outer space. I was almost as shaken up as he was, Peggy. I didn't know what else to do so I just turned around and got out of there as fast as I could."

"Did anybody see you there besides Mullen?" I asked.

"I don't know. It was dark and I wasn't looking. Mullen said he wasn't alone, but I figured that was just something he said so I wouldn't try to force my way in."

"Poor Mullen," I said. "First me, that morning, and then you, that night. He must have thought he was under siege. What time were you there?"

"It must have been around nine," she answered.

I'd been munching popcorn and watching *An American in Paris* with Ginny. "And the fire department got there around nine-thirty," I said.

"Maybe it was my fault," she said. "Maybe I scared him so badly, he had a heart attack or a stroke while he was lighting a match or something."

"It wasn't your fault," Lawrence said. "It was his fault for reacting that way to you. He must've had a guilty conscience." He reached for her hand. She pulled it away.

"He did have a guilty conscience," I said. "Whether or not he was the hate mailer, he told me he was against whites and blacks marrying. If the fire was an accident brought on somehow by your suddenly appearing at his door—on top of me accusing him of sending out hate mail that morning—then he got what he deserved and I'm not going to lose any sleep over it. But it sounds like he was expecting somebody else when he opened the door for you."

I told them about the ferretlike little man I'd seen carrying the grocery bags away from Mullen's house. Paula said that didn't have to mean anything. He could have been anybody.

Buck had told me the same thing.

"I hope you don't think you have to tell Buck Paula was there last night," Lawrence said.

"Why should I? Paula's going to do it herself. She doesn't withhold evidence the way some people do."

I couldn't keep the snottiness out of my voice. Some time ago, I'd withheld evidence from Buck about a friend of mine, a humanities professor named Edith Silberman, who was a suspect in a murder investigation. It almost got Lawrence and me fired, and Paula had been angry with me because of it.

"No you're not," Lawrence said, turning to her. "Who cares who killed Mullen? And if it was somebody to whom he was sending hate mail, would you want him caught?"

"I don't play God," Paula said, getting up, "it's just too hard. And now I'm going home. You coming? We have some things to talk about."

She got up and walked out of Ginny's office without looking back. Lawrence went after her.

Nine

Geoffrey Oates's death was officially ruled a suicide and rated about one inch in a column on the paper's second page. His adviser, Professor Lyle Gardner, expressed the sorrow of all who had known him. "He'd been a young man of almost unlimited promise." That wasn't quite what he'd told Buck, but it was nice of him anyway.

I was more interested in what had happened across the street from my apartment than in a car outside the Psychology Building. The fire that destroyed Mullen and his house was given about the same amount of space as Oates's suicide. It was also on the second page, but included a good photograph of fire fighters putting it out. The cause of the blaze was unknown, probably unsound wiring in a cluttered old house. Mullen was described as a retired small businessman, survived only by a sister. Nothing was said about any bequest he might have made to the University.

I found a note on my door one morning when I got home from work. It was from Mrs. Hammer, announcing that she would be coming in to put new batteries in my smoke detectors unless I indicated that I'd already done the responsible thing. She'd let me know the price of the batteries and I could include it in my next rent check. She added a postscript that her labor would be free. There was a box for me to check, if I'd done the responsible thing. I left it blank.

I scanned the obituaries for several days, but none appeared for Mullen. I called Buck and asked about that, and he said Mullen's lawyer had called and explained that Mullen had left instructions that he was to be cremated and his ashes given to his sister, who lived somewhere in the area. The fire, Buck added, had taken care of just about half of Mullen's wishes along that line. He also told me that Paula had called him, and he'd passed her information on to Anne Meredith, who was handling the case. It wasn't a very high priority, since they hadn't established that the fire was arson and weren't looking for arsonists.

The next day, in the squad room, Paula took me into a corner. "I got an anonymous phone call last night," she said, "just after getting into bed. It was a man. He said he knew I'd killed Harold Mullen and burned down his house. He'd seen me do it, and I was going to pay for it because Harold was a nice man who wouldn't hurt a fly and didn't deserve to die. He said it was going to be easy to kill me because he knew who I was and where I lived and worked. He said I was going to find out what it was like to burn up. His grammar wasn't that good, and he threw in a lot of racial and sexual epithets, but I thought I'd spare you that. Oh, and he said he knew you were in on it, too—that redheaded bitch who lives across the street from Harold, was how he put it, but I figured he meant you."

"Who've you told about being at Mullen's place that night, beside Lawrence, me, and the police?"

"Nobody."

"That means somebody saw you, and either traced you through your license plates or followed you home."

"I didn't notice anybody following me, but then, I wasn't looking either."

"What did he sound like?"

"A sort of reedy voice, but I'd almost swear he was more frightened than he wanted me to be. Maybe it was stage fright."

"I'd be concerned if I were you," I said.

"I can assure you I'm not taking anybody who makes

anonymous threats and claims to be Harold Mullen's friend as a joke," she said. "Tell me again about that man you saw coming away from Mullen's house the day he died."

I did and described his car to her. "Maybe those grocery bags he was carrying contained Harold Mullen's last mailing."

"I'd like to meet him," she said grimly.

Paula's a serious student of *tae kwon do*—she's got a black belt, plus other stuff that makes even other black belts approach her warily. Anybody who attacked her from the front would regret it, but lately she hadn't been confronted by people who attack from the front.

"You haven't received any hate mail since two days after Mullen burned to death, right?"

"Right. But it's going to be a long time before I go out to get the mail without my heart in my throat, I can tell you that."

Paula and Lawrence didn't get any more hate mail or hear from the anonymous phone caller, either. It looked like things were returning to normal, at least as far as the outside world was concerned, but I knew things would probably never return to the way they had been for my two friends. I left them pretty much alone to pick up the pieces by themselves or leave them where they'd fallen, if that's how it was going to be. I just saw them occasionally in passing and gave them little squeezes now and then and quick, hopeful smiles.

Paula was to start law school the day after Labor Day. My feelings about that were mixed: I was happy for her but resentful, too, as if she were betraying me somehow. And, of course, her decision to go to law school made me wonder if I ever wanted to change jobs. But what could I do? I couldn't make the compromises necessary to work in any kind of corporate environment. Sure, the police force has rules and idiots like Lt. Bixler in positions of power. But rules and Bixlers are everywhere. At least by working nights, outside, I don't have to see Bixler very often, and I can sometimes bend the rules to fit the situation as I see it, not as some meathead does.

I couldn't leave my house without looking across the street and seeing the blackened remains of Mullen's home. It always made me think of my mother and how, when I was a child living in southern California, she would light a crumpled piece of newspaper and burn the black widow spiders she found in the garage. I always thought the smell was of the spider burning, not the paper.

The smell in my neighborhood was like that now.

I imagined Mullen, the frail old man with the cheap false teeth, sitting at the center of a web of psychological terror—until I realized that, if I had been right about him, I was giving spiders, even black widows, a bad name.

There was the possibility that Mullen wasn't the hate mailer, of course, regardless of his views on race. My reasons for thinking he was, after all, were pretty circumstantial. But the ugly ruins of Mullen's house, always waiting for me when I left or returned home, kept reminding me of the suspicions I had of him, the terrible things he might have done, and the questions that had survived his death.

What had he done with his money and why had he been so mysterious about it? And who was the man in the old green car? I never saw it again in the neighborhood.

Two weeks after the fire, I called Buck and asked him to get me the name of Mullen's lawyer.

"Why?"

"There's a pile of charred wood almost directly across the street from me," I said, "where a house and an old man used to be, and the smell of wet ash reminds me of poisonous spiders and questions I have. I want to know what Mullen did with his money. The nice thing about working nights is that I can spend my days indulging my curiosity about things."

"You said he told you he was going to leave it to the University."

"For 'cancer research' that wasn't cancer research. That's what he told me."

"He was just trying to make himself look interesting in your eyes, Peggy. Old people are like that, sometimes."

"There's more to it than that, Buck. I was there. I'm convinced he was behind the hate mail people have been getting for years. If I'm right, then I think I know what he meant by 'cancer'—the mixing of races through intermarriage."

"And you think he left his money to the University for some kind of racist research?"

"I don't know," I said. "That's what I'd like to find out. It's a harmless hobby—unless you'd rather I took up ceramics?"

Buck sighed. "No. Not that. Just a minute. I'll see if Anne's in. She has the lawyer's name."

He came back in a few minutes and gave me the lawyer's name and address.

As I was about to hang up, he said, "By the way, did you read the classified ads this morning?"

I said I never read them.

"There's one headed Hate Mail. It asks people who have received significant amounts of hate mail in recent years to contact a certain post office box number. Whoever wrote the ad is especially interested in hate mail directed against racial mixing."

"Have you found out who placed the ad?"

"Nope," Buck said. "I thought I'd let you ask your two friends about it first."

Mullen's lawyer's name was Dell Baker and his office was about a mile from where I lived, so I biked over. It was in a new building—square, six-storied, stucco and glass. I noticed that there was an Electro-Mart store across the street. If that was the store that had driven Mullen out of business, then the lawyer's office was probably in the building put up on the land Mullen had once owned.

I took the stairs to the third floor and walked into a reception room occupied by cheerful new furniture and dispirited-looking clients. I gave the receptionist my name and asked to see Dell Baker.

She asked me if I had an appointment and I told her I didn't, but I would appreciate it if I could talk to Mr. Baker for just a few minutes on a personal matter. She looked at me as though she couldn't imagine what else anybody would want to talk to Baker about and asked me what the personal matter concerned.

"A former client of Mr. Baker's," I told her, "who's dead now."

She pressed a button and communicated that information to her intercom and I heard a man's voice, resonant even through an intercom, ask her the name of the former client. I told her and she repeated Harold Mullen's name to him. There was a moment's hesitation, and then he told her to have me wait, he'd be free in about ten minutes.

I found an old hunting magazine, sank into a new leather chair, and looked at color pictures of a variety of animals who stared curiously back at me through the cross hairs of telescopic sights.

Twenty minutes later, a man with a pale face and thin, angry lips came slowly down the hall and slunk out the door. He was followed, a few minutes later, by another man—about five ten, heavy, ruddy, well-fed, with fluffy white hair and a bounce in his step. He spoke to the receptionist a moment and then turned and came over to me.

"Dell Baker," he said, running merry eyes like zippers up and down my body as he led me back down the hall and into his office. He was wearing an expensive but rumpled suit about ten years out of date and a loose tie, just what you'd want in a family lawyer.

His phone buzzed and he told me "Just a moment," then answered it. While he was doing that, I walked around the office, decorated in a hunting motif. A wooden paddle hung on one wall, with the Greek letters of some fraternity carved into it and a date. I was looking at it when he hung up.

"You know what that is?" he asked me.

"A paddle."

"Right. I had to make it myself, in order to get into that damned fraternity. And on initiation night, every member got to swat me with it on my bare butt!" He laughed loudly. "Hurt like hell."

"It must have been humiliating, too," I said.

"Humiliating?" Baker looked at me as though I were crazy. "No, it was just in fun. Besides, it's paid for itself over and over again—a lot of those guys are my clients now."

"Whatever it takes," I said, smiling. I wanted Dell Baker to be my friend, at least for a time.

"Exactly. Whatever it takes. Sit down, sit down, Miss . . . um . . . O'Neill," he said, glancing at his notepad. "So, you're interested in old Harold Mullen. Quite a tragic story, in its way. One day, his cancer goes into remission, the next he's a corn chip." He shuddered, leaned back in his swivel chair, clasped his hands behind his head, and studied me closely from under lazy lids. "You never know for whom those bells are tolling, do you? You're not a relative of his, by any chance, are you?"

"No, I—"

"Because Harold had just the one sister, you see. We're always a little leery of the long-lost niece or nephew popping out of the woodwork to challenge the will. Not that it works very often, but it costs time and money to fight it. The sister assured me that she's not going to fight Harold's will."

"She's not getting any of his money, then?"

He smiled at me. "May I ask what your interest is in Harold and the disposition of his estate?"

"Some friends of mine were receiving hate mail—racist stuff—and I think it was coming from Mullen. If I'm right, a lot of other people were receiving the same kind of mail, over a period of about eight years."

A look of concern darkened his face. "What makes you think Harold was behind that?"

I told him about my encounter with Mullen the last day

of his life. He listened patiently. Now he was holding his heavy face up with his hands, his elbows on his desk.

"That's it?" he said, when I was finished. "That's all you've got against the old boy?"

"The hate mail's stopped now," I said.

"Ah! The old *post hoc, ergo procter hoc* fallacy, eh? The hate mail stopped *after* Harold died, therefore the hate mail stopped *because* Harold died." Dell Baker smiled hugely into my awe at his erudition. I decided not to correct his Latin; he didn't look like he'd appreciate it.

"Mullen was a racist," I said.

Baker batted that away with a fat hand. "Aren't we all, when you get right down to it? But the point is, the hate mail's stopped now, you say. So everybody's happy, right? So why're you pursuing the matter?"

"Curiosity, I guess. I want to know if I'm right about him, and I want to know where his money went."

He shook his head. "My, my! The things some people will do to keep busy—but I suppose it's better than drugs, sex, and rock 'n' roll! I wish I had the time to pursue a hobby—although it certainly wouldn't be one like yours. Tell me, Miss O'Neill, are you retired—or perhaps you're practicing to be a private detective?"

"Neither," I said, struggling to keep my voice pleasant. "I told you, it's simple curiosity."

He stared at me a long time, trying to decide if I was telling the truth, then shrugged and relaxed back into his chair. "I was Harold's lawyer for the last fifteen years of his life, Miss O'Neill. He was a kindly old gentleman who lived frugally, even though he could have afforded to live much more lavishly. And shy, almost painfully shy. Although we didn't speak often on personal matters, I can't recall ever hearing a racist comment out of him. Oh," he added, flapping a hand, "he wasn't very happy with the Japanese outfit that put in the electronics store across the street, but you can't blame him for that, since they ran him out of business."

"He told me he sold his land for quite a lot," I said.

"I imagine he did."

"It was this property, wasn't it?"

"Yes." Baker chuckled. "We're probably sitting right over the spot where Harold sold his radios, clocks, and tape recorders for forty-odd years."

"So he must have had a lot of money," I said. "He told me he was leaving it to the University."

Baker's eyes narrowed. "He did?"

"Isn't it true?"

"Why, yes, it's true—I'm just surprised that he told you about it. You say you didn't know him well?"

"I only met him twice. I'd like to know for what purpose he left it to the University."

"Didn't he tell you that?"

"No. He hinted that it was for an endowed chair of some kind, for some kind of scientific research. I asked him what kind, and he said it wasn't advisable to tell me just yet but I'd find out in the fullness of time."

Baker smiled indulgently. "And, being young and impatient and having the day off, you can't wait until then."

"I'm not sure when it's going to be."

"What possible reason could you have for wanting to know where his money went?"

I'd given the question some thought before making up my mind to come clean with Baker. "If I'm correct in my suspicions about him," I answered, "Harold Mullen was an evil man. And yet, he gave his money to the University. Why? If he was the racist I think he was, why didn't he leave it to some racist organization? I'd like to know. If I discover that he left his money, say, to the children's wing of the University hospital, then maybe I'll try to find his grave and visit it and tell him I'm sorry—but I'd probably keep my fingers crossed, too, because I'd still be convinced he was the hate mailer who's caused pain to so many people."

Dell Baker shook his head and sighed noisily. "My God, I'll bet your pigheadedness has got you in trouble more times than you'd care to admit, Peggy O'Neill. I think you're all wet about poor old Harold. And I don't see any-thing sinister in his not telling you what he was going to do with his money, making a little mystery out of it. He was a very shy man. He wouldn't have wanted publicity."

"The impression he gave me was that he was looking forward to the day his gift would become known to the public. I was hoping you'd be able to tell me what it was, since he didn't get the chance."

"You know, Miss O'Neill, I'd like to help you, I really would. You've earned it, for the trouble you've gone to, coming here and wasting your time as well as mine—not that I begrudge it," he said, holding up a hand to stop the protest I didn't plan to make. "But I'm sorry to say I couldn't help you, even if I wanted to."

"Why not? You must have drawn up his will."

"No. All I did was advise him on the living trust he drew up with the University. Do you know what a living trust is, Miss O'Neill?"

I shook my head, looked willing to learn.

The phone on Baker's desk gave one discrete ring. He pressed a button and said, "I'll be down in a moment, Denise." Back to me, he said: "Put simply, a living trust permits you to keep absolute control over your money un-til you die, but then it passes to the people you've named as trustees. At that point, the trustees become, in effect, you, and they do with your money what you told them you wanted done with it. There's no will to probate, which means that the curious—like yourself—can't go to the Of-fice of Records and ask to see what's in it." Baker's face was aglow with the wonderfulness of it all.

"So I'll have to go to the University and ask them about it," I said.

Baker pulled himself up out of his chair and strode to the door, pulling me in his wake. "I'm afraid that's the case," he said with a chuckle. "And I wish you luck there, I surely do, because you'll need it."

"Would you happen to know whom I should ask at the

University?" He held the door, waiting for me to go through it before him.

"Somebody at the University Club, of course. That's who Harold named as trustee."

I told him I'd never heard of the University Club.

"I wish I had the time to tell you all about it. But they're in the phone book. You just take your busy little fanny over there and ask them to tell you all about themselves. But I can promise you this: you'll learn even less about Harold's money from them than you have from me."

"I can't imagine a quantity of information that small," I said to him.

He laughed heartily as he followed me down the hall. I was getting a sense of how the man who'd been in his office before me had felt.

"I could be wrong, of course," he said, "so if you do talk to somebody at the Club, and they tell you what Harold did with his money, I'd be most interested in hearing about it."

I thanked him and took my busy little fanny out of there.

Ten

Whenever I want to know something about the mysterious and often scurrilous workings of the University, I go to my friend Edith Silberman. Edith is a professor in the Humanities Department, and she was my adviser and favorite teacher when I was a student at the University. Buck Hansen once arrested her on suspicion of murder. She has never forgiven him and disapproves of our friendship.

I had to wait in the hall for her to finish with a student. It couldn't have been a pleasant encounter for either of them, judging by the expressions on their faces as the student stomped past me and she told me to come in.

"He thought reading ten novels and writing a paper was expecting too much of a summer student," she growled. "I thought he was going to threaten to file some kind of grievance against me for interfering with his sailboarding."

I flopped down on the old couch I'd spent so much time on as a student, and she pulled up her matching over-stuffed chair to the coffee table. Edith has dark hair that's going gray and a nose like that of a witch in the nightmare of a student looking for an easy grade. It would surprise her if you were to point out that she's short, barely five feet in her sandals.

"I read in the *Daily* about that graduate student in psychology being found dead in the middle of the night by a campus cop," she went on. "I wondered if you were the cop in question, but the article didn't say. Please don't tell me you're coming to me for help with that."

"No, that's not my problem. He's a suicide."

"Suicide," Edith said, nodding as if she'd thought so all along. "There've been a rash of those among graduate students lately. The competition's so damned stiff nowadays for the few jobs that're available, but suicide's not the answer. Some of these kids would be amazed at how many people live happy and fulfilling lives without having cushy positions in a college or university. You, for example, Peggy, with your wandering around the University and your poking your nose in where it doesn't belong. If this dead student's not your problem, what is?"

"I have a small fortune," I said, "and I want to leave it to the University."

"By the time you die, it'll be too late to do any good," she grouched. "This place is on its last legs—at least, as a place where kids can go for an education, assuming there are any kids left who want one," she added plaintively.

"That's not what I've heard," I said, teasing her. "I just read a big article in the newspaper about President Hightower's new Undergraduate Teaching Offensive."

Edith snorted noisily. "It's offensive, all right!" The University's not interested in undergraduate education—there's no money in it, no prestige, and it's hard work. The University's only interested in research. So, you have a small fortune and you want to leave it to the University, do you? What do you need me for?"

I told her Paula and Lawrence's story. When I'd finished, she said, "My son and his wife have received mail from that man." I'd forgotten that Edith's daughter-in-law is of Danish descent.

"They didn't want to show it to me at first," she went on. "They finally told me about it and let me read samples of what they were getting. It was unspeakably hideous and intellectually shabby to boot. They showed me a letter my daughter-in-law got that claimed that Jews regard the Nordic race as a good gene repository from which we can replenish our mongrel genes—just to give you an idea."

I told her I'd seen some of what Paula and Lawrence had received.

"They didn't know what to do at first," Edith went on. "They were afraid the letters might be a prelude to something worse, but nothing else happened, they just kept getting wave after wave of this terrible material. After a while, it tapered off and now it's down to about one a month—as if they were on some kind of reminder list.

"They have some friends who adopted two Korean kids who get mail like this, too. Even the kids, not yet a year old, starting getting hate mail addressed to them! That tapered off, too, and now they only get it on the anniversary of the day the adoptions appeared in the newspapers."

Edith got up and went over and fixed herself a cup of instant coffee. She knows better than to offer me any of that.

"If you're right about this Mullen," she said, talking over her shoulder as she stirred the chemicals, "he's the worst sort of creep—or was. You're not trying to find out who killed him, are you?"

I told her I wasn't even sure he'd been murdered. His death had been ruled an accident.

"Because it's quite possible," she said, when she came back with her coffee, "that if it was murder, whoever killed him was on his mailing list. He might have found out who Mullen was and killed him to stop him. I wouldn't blame him. I'd kill him, too, if I thought I could get away with it."

"I'm not trying to find out who killed him," I told her, "or even if it was murder. I just want to know what he did with his money."

"Why?"

"He made a mystery out of it to me. I talked to his lawyer, a bottom feeder named Dell Baker, about it, an hour ago. Baker sounded shocked when I told him Mullen was a racist—claimed he'd never heard a racist remark from Mullen. I think he was lying. And he said he didn't know what Mullen had done with his money, either. He claimed

Mullen left it in the care of something called the University Club. And that's why I'm here. What do you know about the University Club?"

"You've never heard of it?" Edith asked. "No, I don't suppose you would have. It's not a secret, but it does keep a low profile." She sank back into her chair and stared at me over the top of her cup of steaming chemicals. "Let me give you a challenge, Peggy. Suppose you're a state university. You know there's a lot of money out there, in the hands of corporations, foundations, and individuals. You know they're giving it to symphony orchestras, pet cemeteries, churches, public schools, hospitals—you name it—and you want some of it, too, since you're no longer getting all the money you want from the legislature now that the taxpayers are beginning to wise up to you. How do you go about finding out who's got it and then getting them to give some of it to you?"

"I don't know," I said, falling back into student mode.

"What you need are people working for you who already go where the rich people go, eat where they eat, and play where they play. And who would they be?"

"The rich people themselves, I guess," I said.

"Exactly. You have to have rich people working for you."

I asked her why they would want to. Edith ticked off some reasons on her strong, stubby fingers. "One, because they want to be members of something called the University Club—the wealthy like belonging to exclusive organizations with distinguished names, especially if they made their money selling rotten meat to old people's homes and they can't wash the stink off with soap. Two, because they believe in the University's goals—some rich people probably do. Three, the University gives them access to world-famous scientists, artists, musicians, etc., whom they can invite to their parties—people they'd never get within hollering distance of otherwise.

"The University Club's completely separate from the University," Edith went on. "It's got its own suite of offices downtown and all its operating costs are taken from the money it generates for the U. They have to do that so they can ensure the privacy of the donors. You see, if you give your money directly to the University, just about anybody can find out about it—through the state's 'open files laws' for public institutions. The University Club, being private, doesn't have to show its files to anybody."

"Why would anybody want to donate money to the University anonymously?"

"Lots of wealthy people don't want that kind of publicity," Edith replied. "You might want to make a big donation for tax purposes, but not have anybody find out how well-off you are, so you won't be hassled or put your family in danger of being kidnapped. Also, there are occasions when the University itself might prefer not to know where the money's coming from. With the University Club acting as a buffer between it and the donor, it never has to."

"Okay," I said, "so the members of the Club circulate among their friends, trying to talk them into donating money to the University. What happens when somebody bites?"

"When they hook a live one, the Club member calls the Club's director and tells him that Mr. Bottomfeeder, say, is interested in giving money to the U. Archie Bottomfeeder loves golf and his wife graduated from the U half a century ago with a degree in home economics. The director works with the U to see if they can arrange a dinner for the Bottomfeeders at which the golf coach and the chairperson of the Home Economics Department are present."

"In other words," I stuck in, "they tailor the pitch to the interests of the mark."

Edith downed some of her coffee. "Of course they do. It's a competitive market out there, a sea of hungry sharks. They wine and dine the Bottomfeeders, and if they think a punch bowl in the shape of a golf ball or holding a banquet in Irene Bottomfeeder's honor in the home ec kitchen will help, that's what they'll do. And they pretend to be wildly excited by what the Bottomfeeders want the University to do with their money.

"Sometimes donors make unacceptable demands. If, for

example, our Archie wants to pick the person for the golfing professorship himself or restrict the candidates for the job to white Christian males, that's a no-no—at least, it can't be guaranteed in writing," Edith added with an exaggerated wink. She does a white Christian male wink well.

"Big corporations," she continued, "are always trying to give money to the University for new professorships or programs with strings attached. They want to write into the contract the kind of research they want done—and sometimes even the results they want achieved—but that's a no-no, too, at least in writing. Professors can't be told what to do."

"Okay," I said, "so the donor's agreed to give the U a couple million bucks for a golfing professorship. Then what?"

"Then the University Club draws up a contract with the donor and presents it to the University. The University doesn't have to know who the donor is, if he wishes to remain anonymous. If the University finds the terms acceptable, the donor gives his money to the University Club and the University Club doles it out to the University as specified in the contract. Nobody has to know where Archie and Irene Bottomfeeder's money went except the directors of the University Club.

"More to the point, Peggy," Edith finished, "nobody has to know where in the University your Mr. Mullen's money is except the director of the Club, if that's what Mullen wanted."

I sat there and digested that. After a while, I said, "Mullen boasted to me that he'd had dinner with President Hightower and his wife. Is that possible?"

"Entirely possible. That's one reason for having a University president well-versed in all the social graces with a wife who's never spoken out of turn in her life. If, for some reason, the Club decided that the best way to get your friend Mr. Mullen's money was to have him meet the University president, they'd arrange it—assuming enough money was involved or the cause was worthy. I've heard that you can get lunch with Hightower for as little as $100,000, if you're willing to share your table with nine other guests. Dinner starts at a quarter of a million, but if you want to sit where you can talk to him, you'd better offer a little more."

I said, "You don't think Mullen could have left his money to the University for some kind of racist research?"

"No—at least, not with any written guarantee."

"So why," I said, "did Mullen make such a secret of what he was leaving his money for, if it wasn't for something nasty? He may have been a quiet, modest little man, but he couldn't have been so publicity-shy that he didn't want anybody to know even after he was dead. And if he was the man sending out hate mail for years to hundreds of people, I can't see him leaving his money to the University for something harmless."

"It could be, Peggy," Edith reminded me, mildly, "that you've got Mr. Mullen wrong."

"I know, I know," I said, annoyed. "I'm laboring under the tyranny of the original idea again." That was one of Edith's pet peeves. She'd accused me of laboring under the tyranny of the original idea on more than one occasion in our time together. "Since Mullen's dead now, do you think the University Club would tell where his money is?"

"Only if there wasn't anything in the contract with Mullen that would forbid it."

"I guess I'll have to go see, won't I?"

"Not dressed like that, Peggy. Go home and change into something a little more heiresslike."

And like Dell Baker before her, she wished me luck.

Eleven

It was too late to go there that day, so I went home and did a little light housework, the only kind I'm capable of. Then I poured myself a glass of iced tea and put a CD on my new stereo—Fats Waller, 1939. I sat in my easy chair and watched the sun set on bikers, skaters, and lovers on the shore of Lake Eleanor, a corner of which I can see in the distance from my living room window. By the time Waller slid into Ellington's "Solitude," with Rudy Powell on alto sax, I found myself wishing I had a lover, too.

I wondered if Gary was sitting in his window and looking out at a mangrove swamp or a pine savannah and thinking of me. Probably not, but he could have been, since Belize is in the same time zone we are—I looked it up once, in a moment of weakness.

I remembered something I'd said to Lawrence the last time we'd talked, "The miracle hasn't happened for me yet." I spent a few minutes wondering at myself for having said something so out of character. Luckily, it's not possible to get sentimental—or, at least, to stay sentimental very long—listening to Fats Waller, which is why I like him so much. Almost as much as I like solitude.

But I did dash off a letter to Gary before biking to work. The usual platitudes.

At police headquarters that night, I cornered Paula and Lawrence as soon as they came in from their patrols and asked them if they'd seen the ad in the paper Buck had told me about.

"Seen it? We were the ones who placed it," Lawrence said.

"It was Lawrence's idea," Paula said.

"We discussed it together and came up with it," Lawrence corrected her.

"What for?" I asked, my neck feeling the stress of swiveling between them.

"Because we thought it might be a good idea to get to know some of the other victims of this hate mailer," Paula said. "The mail's stopped now, but for all we know, the creep just figured he had too many other victims, he didn't need Lawrence and me, so he dropped us. Which means he might start up with us again someday."

"We want to try to get him, Peggy," Lawrence said, taking up the narrative. "We don't want to dread the letter carrier's arrival anymore."

I couldn't help it, I grabbed Paula and gave her a big hug and then grabbed Lawrence and hugged him, too. Because they'd come up with such a constructive idea and because they were saying *we* again.

I asked them if they'd heard from their anonymous phone caller again and they said they hadn't.

I went downtown the next afternoon, to the University Club, taking my car instead of biking on account of having to dress for the occasion: a skirt with a pseudo-ethnic print, cotton top—green to match my eyes—and a wooden necklace that Gary had sent me from Belize. I parked in a ramp and took a skyway to one of those reflective glass buildings without any personality except what they could absorb from the few older buildings around them that had survived the mindless venality of the 1980s.

The University Club had an entire suite on the fortieth floor. The elevator was as large as my bedroom and seemed designed to make me wish I'd either stayed away or spent a great deal more time and money on my appearance. I caught myself whistling tunelessly, stopped just as the elevator door opened onto a palatial waiting room.

A receptionist looked up, eyes professionally happy to see me under arched brows that looked like tattoos. What she was wearing probably cost her a week's salary.

"I'm Patty Mullen," I told her. "My grandfather, Harold—we called him Harry, my cousins and me—died recently and he left all his money to the University. That's just great, we don't have any problem with that at all! But we were wondering what he left it to this great university for, don't you know? He told us it was going to be a big surprise and that we were all going to be real proud of him when he sprang it on us—or is it sprung?"

Before she could say anything, I took a deep breath and rushed on. "Well, as you may know, Grandad Harry died tragically without telling us—I mean, without telling us what he was planning to do with his money, of course—and we haven't heard about any big surprises at the University yet. So I thought, hey, why not ask somebody at the University, maybe they'll know. I'm sort of in charge of keeping the family records—I'm kind of a Mormon that way, you see, but not really. We've got scrapbooks so fat you wouldn't believe it, going back almost a hundred years—and so I thought maybe I could find out what Grandaddy did with his money that he was so proud of he wanted to surprise us with it, and then I could put it in the scrapbook along with all the other things—the pictures of Gramps when he was in knickers and later, standing so darn proudly in front of his store with his new teeth, and all the rest."

The receptionist managed to keep an interested smile on her face throughout all of that, a tribute, perhaps, to her training and self-discipline.

"Harry Mullen?" she asked tentatively.

"Harold, I suppose it would be to you," I corrected her sternly.

"And he didn't tell you what he was giving his money to the University for?"

"He wasn't given the time," I said, and dashed a tear

from an eye with a finger. "My mother, his daughter, felt he was going to spring it on us at the reunion up at the lake cabin later this month, sort of a big surprise, you know. Unfortunately, Grandaddy passed away last week, if you can call being burned to a crisp in your own home passing away."

"I'm sorry about that," she said, although the accompanying expression of sympathy was diluted somewhat by the permanently startled eyebrows. "However, I'm afraid we aren't permitted to give out that kind of information."

"You're not? Really? You mean—we might never know what it was Grampa was so tickled pink about? That's terrible!"

"I'm sorry—"

"It's not like I'm asking for the details—the good Lord knows the scrapbook's full enough of those, we don't need the whereases and wheretofores. But just an idea, you know? Like, maybe he left it to the University for developing new and better electronics technology, so America can catch up with the Japs—Japanese. Grandad Harry was very concerned about what those clever, tiny people were doing along those lines, very concerned. Maybe it was something to do with—"

"I'm really sorry," she said, the melody having now departed her voice. "There's nothing I can do."

I stared at her sternly. "I find that hard to accept. Surely there is somebody here who can explain why a loving family can't find out something as simple and straightforward as what its patriarch left his money to the University for. May I see somebody with just a tad more authority than what you might possess?" I shook the beads on my necklace, making a noise like a rattlesnake having a fit.

A look of exasperation spread over her face beneath the startled brows. Jabbing a button on her desk with a long, tapered finger, she snarled, "It won't do you a damned bit of good."

Watching her lose her composure for a moment did me a world of good.

A minute later I was sitting in front of Stanford Driggs, and he was watching me through, over, or around a steeple he'd constructed of his long fingers and manicured nails. The desk between us was huge and empty, and the office as cold as his gaze.

I told him the same story I'd told the receptionist, this time trying to stick with one word for "grandfather" in my references to Harold Mullen. Driggs listened without interruption. He had a tanning room complexion and a health club body, but his good looks were fatally marred by a small, slightly bewhiskered mouth that I'd have thought would be more appropriate to some species of sucking insect.

When I'd finished, he sighed audibly and said, "Harold Mullen never married and he had no grandchildren."

"Oh," I said, feigning delight, "you knew him!"

"You told Brenda your name was Patty Mullen. What's your real name, please?"

I told him.

"Identification." He held out a languid hand. Against my better judgement, I showed him my driver's license.

"Are you a lawyer or a private detective?"

"Neither; I just want to know what Mullen left his money to the University for, and I've been told that it's not easy to get information like that from you."

"Why?"

"I wish I knew. You tell me."

"Why do you want to know how Mr. Mullen disposed of his money," he said, an edge creeping into his voice.

"Why is it such a secret?" I demanded, going on the offensive with the *why* questions.

"We did not ask Mr. Mullen why he wished to keep his gift anonymous," he said, as if speaking to an imbecile, "for it was none of our business. He was a very modest man, more concerned with the good to which his money could be put than with publicity. The fact is—and it is none of your business, Ms. O'Neill, but I will tell you anyway—that Mr. Mullen made a living trust and he named the University Club as trustee with the proviso that the purpose of his donation not be made public in connection with his name. Once he passed away, we became, in effect, Harold Mullen. Were we to violate his trust in us, it could be disastrous for the University Club. Surely you can appreciate that, Miss O'Neill. Now, what are you really after?"

"Answers," I said. "And the fewer I get, the more I crave them. You say Mullen was concerned with the good his money could do. Frankly, that scares me, since I have a pretty good idea of what Mullen thought 'good' was."

"And what was that?"

"He was a racist. And from the way he talked about his money and the University to me, I think he was using his money for something racist in nature."

"He talked to you about this?" Driggs leaned forward in his chair and moved his fingers away from his face, perhaps the better to stare into mine.

"Yes."

"You knew him well?"

Dell Baker had asked me the same question. "No, I just talked to him briefly on two occasions."

"And he didn't tell you what he wanted his money used for?"

"No."

I'd had this conversation before. Perhaps I was stuck in a time warp.

"Miss O'Neill." Driggs looked at his watch, a thin wafer of a thing that looked as though it would melt on your tongue. "I don't know what Mr. Mullen told you that has alarmed you so. But I assure you that he did not—and could not, even had he wanted to—give his money to the University for any illegal or immoral purpose. You may rest assured on that point. I personally spoke with Mr. Mullen on a number of occasions. I think I can say that we became friends for the very short time we knew each other. I found him to be a delightful man. A very shy man, ill at ease in company, and lonely. It may have been his awkwardness with people—especially people he did not know well—that led him to say something that you found disturbing. He never said anything of that nature to me."

He got up to indicate the interview was over. "We've wasted enough of each other's time, Miss O'Neill. I have other business to attend to today."

"A living trust, you say," I said as I got up. "That means Mullen could have revoked it at any time?"

"Of course. Just like any other kind of will." He began shepherding me to the door.

"But he wasn't given the time to revoke it," I said.

"There's no evidence, Miss O'Neill, that he ever had any intention of revoking it."

I stopped at the door and turned and looked at him. "The eerie thing is that there's almost no evidence that Harold Mullen ever existed. A lot of people seem to be trying to get me to think he's just a figment of my imagination. That gives me a very strange feeling."

"I'm sorry to hear that," he said, and shut the door in my face.

I stalked back to the waiting room. The receptionist watched me approach, amusement clashing with startled brows for dominance of her face.

"Did you get what you came for?" she asked me.

"Bovine fecal research," I said, pausing briefly at her desk.

"What?"

"Research into the fertilizing qualities of bovine fecal matter. That's what Grampa Harold left his money for. I just knew it was something we could all be proud of!"

Twelve

Disgusted that I'd got all dressed up and driven downtown for nothing, I retraced my steps into the skyway.

Now what? The only other lead I had was Harold Mullen's sister, who had received her brother's ashes and, according to Mullen's lawyer, nothing else. I wondered why Mullen hadn't left her anything. Maybe she had a lot of money, too, and didn't need his.

I found a pay phone, called Buck, and asked him if he could get me her name and address.

"Now what are you up to?"

"I'm following a trail so cold, my nose is getting frost-bitten, even though we're in the middle of a heat wave."

"I'm kind of busy, Peggy," he said. "Can't it wait?"

"I saw a great recipe for stuffed zucchini in the paper the other day, Buck. It's full of the kinds of things you like—bizarre mushrooms that you never used to be able to get in the grocery stores and herbs with names I would have thought were diseases. I'll fix it for you on Saturday if you'll do this one thing for me. Mrs. Hammer's zucchini is taking over the yard and my freezer's so full of her zucchini bread, I have no room for my frozen dinners."

"We'll have dinner at my place," he said. "You bring the zucchini, I'll cook it."

"If you insist," I said, hurt.

"Call me back in ten minutes."

I located an espresso bar, nursed an iced coffee, and

watched the people rushing this way and that through the skyway, earnest, self-important, and as similar as grease ants. Working nights and then having to be out and about during the day makes you realize how absurd the hustle and bustle of the overcrowded world is.

Ten minutes later, Buck told me Mullen's sister's name was Lillian Przynski and gave me her address. Since she didn't have a telephone, I drove over, glad I was wearing nice clothes.

She lived on a street of old wooden houses, the neighborhood was clearly on a downward slide, but not every home was going without a struggle. Some people still kept their lawns looking nice and had planted flowers, but many of the houses themselves looked like they needed work. Plastic toys in lurid colors littered a few of the yards, but most of the homes had the look of places where the last of many generations of children had grown up and moved away. Old cars sat at the curb, their rusted bodies glittering dully in the sunlight. Unless she lived frugally by choice, as her brother had done, Lillian Przynski could have used some of his money.

I went up onto the porch, twisted an old keylike handle that rang a loud bell somewhere inside the house, and waited. It took a long time, but the door was finally opened by a tiny old woman whom bone disease had almost doubled over. She shot me a glance from piercing blue eyes and asked me my business.

I explained that I'd known her brother, and I wanted to talk to her about him.

Her laugh, directed at the ground, sounded like the bell I'd had on my bike when I was a kid. "You've come to the wrong place, young lady. There's not much I could tell you, even if I was of a mind to. Before you interrupted me, I was sitting in the parlor staring at Bud's ashes, trying to decide if I should scatter him on the tomatoes or the lawn." Then she cocked her head and said, "What do you want to know about him?" A crafty note had crept into her voice. Her head trembled gently, from side to side, as if she were continually saying no to something, reluctantly but firmly.

"Your brother mentioned to me that he'd left his money to the University. I'm trying to find out what he left it for."

"You want some of it, is that it?"

"His money?"

"Of course. What else?" Her eyes darted quickly up and down my costume, fastened on my necklace with the exotic beads that may have told her of steamy pleasures under tropical skies. She poked a crooked finger up under my nose and said, "You're an adventuress and you thought you were going to marry him, didn't you?"

"Harold Mullen?" I blurted out.

She laughed at the appalled look on my face. "I should hope not, a nice-looking young thing like yourself! But stranger things than that have happened under the sun, let me tell you. Why are you interested in where Bud left his money?"

"Because he made it a secret," I told her.

"And you're making a secret out of why you're interested. Isn't this going to be fun?" She laughed again, a cackle of delight. "Come in, come in, no sense your standing in the door, toying with a helpless old lady, when you can be comfortable while you're about it. Care for some iced tea? It's rose hip, very good in this hot weather we're getting now. What did you say your name was again?"

She scurried on ahead of me as she talked. "Rufus, get down from there and let the lady have the couch. Come on, boy." She picked up the little poodle, who gave me a sleepy, incurious look, and deposited him on a pillow on the floor beside a rocking chair, then bustled out to the kitchen to get the tea.

I've never cared much for poodles, they have a tendency to yap and an equally unforgivable tendency to take nips out of strangers, but this one just rearranged himself on the pillow and went back to sleep.

Lillian Przynski's living and dining rooms contrasted sharply with her brother's. They were cluttered with small pictures on the walls and, in the dining room, two large black and white photographs in matching oval frames of a beautiful woman and a heavyset man with short hair and jug ears. They seemed to be staring at some common focal point in the middle of the dining room. A curio cabinet in the living room was full of ceramic animals of all sizes, and needlepoint pillows scattered around the room repeated a canine motif. The room smelled of the fresh-cut flowers in vases by the windows.

A square green box sat on a spindly legged table next to Lillian Przynski's rocking chair. I assumed it contained all that was left of Harold Mullen.

"Peggy O'Neill, what a nice name!" she said when she came back into the room carrying a tray that almost skimmed along the floor in front of her. "What are you, dear," she asked, "if you're not an adventuress? A reporter? Tell me a story I can believe about your interest in my poor brother and his money. These cookies are delicious, if I do say so myself."

There was no way I could lie to this woman or evade those bright eyes with their steady, curious gaze, so I told her the whole story—the hate mail and my conversation with her brother the day before he died.

She sipped iced tea and nibbled cookies as she listened. Her face expressed sympathy for Paula and Lawrence, interest in what the postal inspector had to say, disgust that somebody had been sending out hate mail for so many years, and anger at the way the University Club had stonewalled me. She was a wonderful audience.

When I'd finished, she leaned her crippled body back in the rocking chair and rocked gently for a few moments, her chin on her chest.

"I'm not surprised at what you've told me," she said finally, glancing up at me. "I'm afraid you're probably right about Bud. That was my name for Harold, you know—Bud." She turned and gazed at the green box next to her, as if addressing him, and said, "He always did have strange theories about everything under the sun, and above it, too: God, creation, politics, and who really runs the world—you name it, he had a conspiracy theory to explain it. Although I do think most such theories must have interesting conspiracies behind them, too, don't you?" she asked, shooting me a glance. "And Bud had strange ideas about race, too, part and parcel of all his other funny ideas. But I didn't know he'd become so bad as to spread his ideas through the mail to total strangers."

"I don't have any proof that he did," I reminded her, wanting to be fair to her brother's memory. "But you knew he was a racist?"

"Oh, yes," she sighed. "But I didn't realize how racist he was until I married Vince. Vince, bless his heart, was a Polack. That's him in the dining room," she said, turning and pointing, "and that's me next to him, although you'd never know it, would you? Bud was furious when I told him I was marrying Vince! Why, he didn't even come to the wedding. For years after that, I tried to bring the two of them together. I tried so hard to make Bud see that Vince was a fine human being, but Bud thought I'd betrayed my English heritage. He simply couldn't stand the idea of people getting married who weren't of the same race. He didn't like to hear about Chinese marrying Germans or Jews marrying Gentiles. Once I got so mad at him, I said, 'Bud, if you had a fulfilling life of your own, you wouldn't have to spend so much time worrying about other people's!' That made him mad. I think he would have hit me, if Vince hadn't got between us—and you know Vince wasn't a well man!

"Bud claimed he wasn't a racist. He called himself a 'racialist,' and said he was opposed to racial mixing—but I don't see that it makes much difference what you call yourself, if you go around hurting people on account of their race, do you? He said he believed that God made all the races and it was wrong to mix them—people of different races shouldn't even live in the same country. 'You mean, make everybody go back where their ancestors came from, before they were even born?' I asked. He said it would be painful, but in the long run it would be better for everybody."

"Harold was both ahead of and behind his times," I said. "Today it's called 'ethnic cleansing'. Where do you suppose he got his racism? You don't seem to be infected with it."

"No, I'm not. I just think people are people, some are good and some are bad. But I can tell you where he got it; he got it from a little girl who lived down the street. What was her name?" She nibbled on a cookie, thinking, her head trembling. "Bud fell in love with her when they were still just kids—eleven, twelve years old. He followed her around and wrote her name all over everything he owned—even scratched it on his own leg once with a nail. His leg became infected and Mother had to take him to the doctor."

Lillian Przynski shook her head at the memory. "She was a sweet little thing, too, with a round face and such a cute smile. Bud wouldn't even look at another girl. When he was fourteen or fifteen, he finally screwed up the courage to ask her for a date. She said yes and they went to the movies. He didn't have a car, of course, he was too young to drive and we were poor anyway, so they walked—and I followed them, sneaked along behind, hiding in bushes and running from tree to tree all the way to the theater. I sat behind them, too. Bud was so mad when he finally noticed me! I don't think they even held hands in the theater. Maybe it was on account of me, but I don't know—Bud was so shy, he might not have had the courage anyway."

Lillian picked up the green box, set it in her lap and stared at it, as if wondering how her brother had gone from the boy she was remembering to the ashes in the box. After a few minutes, she put the box back on the table, blew her nose with a Kleenex, and looked up at me with glittering eyes.

"That was the only time she went out with him," she went on. "Bud asked her again several times, but she always refused. Later, when he graduated from high school, he bought a car as soon as he got his first real job. He drove it down to her house, even though she only lived a block away. He went up to where she was sitting on her porch and asked her out again—as if she'd only refused him before because he didn't have a car! She told him no, she was going with another boy.

"He was so upset when he came home. I could see he'd even been crying. I asked him what was wrong and he told me the whole story. He kept coming back to the fact that the boy she'd 'jilted' Bud for was Jewish. I don't think he even knew what a Jew was until then."

Lillian picked another cookie from the quickly diminishing pile on the plate and took a bite, unmindful of the crumbs that dropped into her lap. "A year later," she continued, "she married her boyfriend in a Jewish ceremony. Poor thing, the next thing you know, she got polio and died. It wouldn't surprise me if Bud thought it was divine retribution, but he never said so. He never so much as mentioned her again. I think she was the only girl he was ever interested in."

"And that did it for Bud," I said.

"Well, that's all I can think of, but who really knows about things like that? I've never held much with psychology, myself. Bud was always a strange duck. Never had friends—at least, none he'd bring home—and, as I say, he was always full of strange ideas about everything. He lived in a world of his own."

She smiled down onto her bosom, added: "She didn't *jilt* Bud. I don't think she even knew he was alive."

Neither of us said anything for a minute or two. Then she said, "What I think is that Bud hated change—anything that smacked of change. God made the world such and such, and that's the way it was, is, and always will be! But I'd never in the world think he'd be the one to do anything about his ideas, the way you say you think he did. He was so quiet, he always kept to himself, and he just became more inward over the years. How many letters do you think this hate mailer sent out?"

I told her that he'd been doing it for about eight years and that there was no way of knowing how much he'd sent out and how many people he'd sent mail to, since probably not everybody reported it.

"But it's stopped now, you say? That sounds pretty suspicious, doesn't it, although maybe it's too soon to be sure. What does the University have to do with it?"

"I don't know. He made what he was leaving his money for sound very mysterious, and the more I try to find out about it, the more mysterious it gets."

"He was very mysterious about it to me, too," Lillian said.

"He talked to you about it?"

"A couple of times. You know, I didn't see hide nor hair of Bud for years, on account of Vince. He didn't even send a card when Vince passed away. But after he got the cancer and didn't think he was going to live much longer, all of a sudden he got interested in seeing his sister. He would have made a real pest of himself if I'd let him, but I had my life to live, too, you know, my volunteer work with the Humane Society and my clubs and such. But he told me how he'd been in touch with some people at the University about his money and he boasted that some very prominent men there had wined and dined him. I said, 'Why, of course they have, Bud! What did you expect them to do, pay some poor student to take you to McDonald's? They don't care anything about you and your crazy ideas at the University. All they care about is your money.'"

Lillian Przynski brought her head up and stared at me. "Now, you're probably thinking I wanted some of Bud's fortune myself, Peggy. Well, Vince left me enough for most of my needs, thank you very much, but you may have noticed that the porch is sagging a little, and it won't be long before the housing inspectors notice the roof and make me put on a new one, and I just don't know where on earth I'm going to get the money for that. So maybe I did have some selfish interest in Bud's money." She shook her head at the thought of her own depravity.

From where I was sitting, I could see water damage on the ceiling in a corner of the dining room.

"But mostly," she went on, "I was just afraid Bud was going to give his money to something useless when there are so many good causes that need help. Bud was so pleased that important people at the University pretended to be interested in him that he probably didn't care what they were going to do with his money. He told me he'd even had dinner with the University's president, if you can believe that!"

"Did he give you any idea about what it was he wanted the University to do with his money?" I asked. "Cancer research, for example?"

"Cancer? Bud never said anything about cancer research. As I recall, he just said it was for something dear to his heart and that I'd learn about it soon enough. I told him, 'I don't care to know what's dear to your heart, Buddy, but you'd be a fool to trust those people.' Then he got a sly look on his face and said he knew that, he wasn't anybody's fool. They'd find that out if they went back on their promises to him. 'Well,' I said, 'and what could you do about it once you're dead, if they did?' And he said he'd thought of that, too. He said he had somebody at the University who was looking out for his interests."

"But he didn't tell you who it was?"

"No, and I didn't ask."

"When was this?"

"Now when was it?" She scratched her face to help her remember. "It was right here, in this house, not more than a month ago. You think maybe the University hired somebody to bump him off, so they'd get his money sooner?"

"The University's pretty desperate," I said with a smile, "but I don't think they'd go that far—not yet, anyway. Do you have any idea how much money he had?"

"No, I don't. But he sold that property of his, where he had his store, for a lot of money, I do know that. At least he said he did, but you never know with Bud, he might have just been putting on airs. And I guess the land his house was on is worth something, too. That lawyer of his—what was his name?—told me I wasn't going to get

anything out of that either. I don't know what else he had.
You go talk to that lawyer, he'll know all about that. And
he'll know who Bud talked to at the University, too. He's
the one who put Bud in touch with some people there he
thought he'd be interested in."

I told her I'd already talked to Dell Baker and that he'd
told me almost nothing.

"That's it," she said. "Dell Baker. He came here, you
know, not two days after Bud died. There was something
about him I just didn't like. A smarmy man, if you don't
mind my saying so. He told me what a kind and gentle
man my brother was! Well, you can imagine how surprised
I was to hear that!"

"I suppose he came to break the news that you'd been
left out of the will," I said.

"Oh," she said, chuckling, "Bud didn't leave me out—I
got the contents of his house! I told Mr. Baker that I had
all of Bud's ashes I needed, thank you very much, right
here in this little box and I didn't need any more. I think
he was concerned that I might try to break Bud's will, or
whatever it's called. He asked me how close we'd been,
and how often we saw each other, and when was the last
time he'd been here. I told him Bud had spent more time
in my house since his death than in the past thirty years."

I stayed for another half hour or so. We talked about her
and her brother's childhood, her marriage, and what she
was doing, now that she was alone, to keep busy.

I got up to go and she came after me. "You know," she
said, "to this very day, I have to think how to spell my last
name." She spelled it slowly—"P-r-z-y-n-s-k-i"—like a
child delighting in letters of the alphabet, and then pro-
nounced it. "That's what I love about it, it's a name I can
never take for granted as long as I live—unlike Mullen,"
she added, her pretty head shaking, her eyes on my shoes.
"I'm only sorry Vince and I couldn't have children to
carry on the name.

"Why would anybody hate change, I wonder?" she went
on. "Sometimes I think change must be the only perma-

nent thing in the world. But not according to Bud. According to him, the world was created eight thousand years ago—no longer ago than that—and everything's supposed to stay the way it was then. That's a safe and comfortable thought to some people, I suppose, but I think it shows a shocking lack of imagination, don't you?"

At the door, as I went down the old wooden steps, she called after me, "Come back, sometime. Tell me how you're making out in finding out what my brother did with his money."

I said I would. I decided I very much wanted to make sure that the University was putting Harold Mullen's money to better use than fixing Lillian Przynski's rickety porch and leaking roof.

Thirteen

Harold Mullen had told his sister that he'd given his money to the University for research "dear to his heart." After talking to Lillian Przynski, I was sure there was only one thing that was dear to his heart—but where in the University would somebody be doing racist research? And who at the University was looking out for his interests? Would anybody there look out for the interests of a sick old man with money? Recalling Stanford Driggs, I doubted it.

His talk of knowing important people at the U and leaving his money for something secret might merely have been something he'd told his sister and me to make himself seem interesting. But it was true that he'd had a lot of money—he must have if he'd owned the property where Dell Baker's law firm was located. And his money had disappeared into the University without a trace.

I didn't even know how much money I was looking for. Most of it must have come from the sale of his land, and surely there must be some way to find out how much he'd sold it for. Since it was only about two-thirty, I headed for campus police headquarters to consult with Ginny Raines. After all, Ginny's a detective, and detectives know how to find out things like that.

She was in her stuffy little office, contemplating a bag of rice crackers without enthusiasm. A little fan on the wall swiveled back and forth, blowing dust and papers around. Ginny transferred her gaze from the crackers to me without feeling any need to change expression.

"You want something. Why else would you be here this early in the day, forcing your way into my office?"

"Good piece of reasoning, Sherlock. Now I know why they made you a detective. How do I find out what a certain piece of property sold for?"

"Why?"

"*Why* questions are to be encouraged in children," I said, "because it means they're starting to sit up and take notice. Adults' *why* questions are often an effort to kill curiosity."

"You know the address of this piece of property?"

"Sure."

"Then you go down to the county courthouse," she said, "to Public Records. Ninth floor, if I remember correctly. They can tell you."

"Can it be done over the phone?"

"Don't you wish."

I drove downtown for the second time that day. Public Records was where Ginny said it would be, on the ninth floor of the courthouse. I gave a pleasant young woman the address of Mullen's former property and she punched it into a computer, waited a moment, then scrawled something on a piece of paper. I asked her what that was and she told me it was the property's legal description.

"Take it up to Abstracts on twelve and they'll tell you everything you ever wanted to know about it."

On twelve I handed the slip of paper to a man who disappeared into a back room. He returned with a large metalbound book that he flipped open on a counter and turned so I could read what was in it.

Two years ago, Mullen had sold his property for almost a million and a half dollars. The buyer had been Dell Baker, his lawyer.

Baker and I had talked about the property in his office, but he hadn't mentioned that he owned it. Well, why would he, to a nosy stranger?

On the line above Mullen's property listing was the adjacent lot. A year earlier, it had sold for a half million more than Mullen's.

"I thought property values had gone up," I said.

The clerk shrugged. "Maybe there was something more valuable on that property," he said. "You can't tell from this."

"What do you think a person would end up with, after taxes, who sold a piece of property for a million and a half bucks?"

He punched buttons on a little calculator and said: "A little over a million. Nothing to brag about in some circles, but nothing to sneeze at, either."

I thanked him and took the elevator back downstairs, wondering how ethical it was for an old man's lawyer to buy property from him.

That night, around 1:00 A.M., I crossed the bridge over the river from the New Campus into the Old and used my key to enter the Psychology Building. I took my time walking its dimly lit, rat-maze halls. It seemed to be business as usual—I encountered the occasional grad student huddled over a computer, mindlessly feeding data into it to receive almost meaningless results. Geoffrey Oates had died; life goes on. When I got to the faculty lounge, I went in, bought myself a cup of coffee, took it over to a table, and sat down.

A glass case on one of the walls contained a display of snapshots that had obviously been taken at a summer picnic, probably one of the end-of-school picnics that various units of the Psych Department have in June. "Work hard, play hard," was the motto of the chairman back when I knew the department better than I do now.

As I sat there looking at the display, I recalled a picnic I'd attended once, when I was going with a graduate student in psychology. It was just after I'd graduated from the University and was in rookie school. The student's name was George. I've forgotten his last name and what I ever saw in him, but what I think he saw in me was a chance to try out the techniques he'd acquired in his field, learning disabilities in children. He wanted me to give up the idea of being a campus cop to marry him and be a faculty wife.

That picnic, in fact, had spelled the beginning of the end for George and me. I'd loaded up a plate of food and was looking for a place to sit when, suddenly, a hand closed over my forearm, and I felt myself being yanked into the lap of George's adviser, a professor who'd just gone through his third divorce and was in a celebratory mood.

"You can sit on my lap, Peggy," he said, "since there's nothing in it but me." He gave a fatuous laugh.

It's a peculiarity of mine that I don't like being yanked into the laps of men whose open mouths are full of potato salad. I twisted out of his grip and tipped my plate of food—coleslaw, baked beans, and a hot dog I'd slathered with ketchup, mustard, and chopped onion—onto the area he'd said was nothing but him.

"Oh, sorry." For all the feeling I put into those words, we might have been dancing and I'd stepped on his toes.

A pall fell on the proceedings. It was broken when George rushed over, his arms flapping, both hands filled with napkins like pom-poms, babbling apologies.

The professor laughed it off with thin, pale lips and eyes like a killing frost. He knew that what I'd done hadn't been an accident. I went over and got a new plate of food.

George's complete self-abasement apparently paid off, for when his professor got a better job somewhere else, he took George with him, and now George runs a research project of his own somewhere. Even after that picnic, he was still willing to marry me, for his professor had assured him that he held no grudges against clumsy women.

I shook my head at the memory, finished my coffee, got up, and went over to take a closer look at the snapshots in the display case, wondering if I'd know any of the faculty in them. I didn't—this wasn't George's area of specialization—but I did recognize some of the people I'd encountered the night I found Geoffrey Oates's body: Lyle Gardner, Oates's adviser; Carly Bachman; and Bill Turner, the graduate student who'd shared an office with Oates and lived in the building, too.

Most of the pictures were taken on a lake and on a patio with the lake in the background. Oates must be in here, too, I thought, somewhere among all these faces laughing for the camera, but I probably wouldn't recognize him. I'd only seen his face, horribly distorted in death, pressed against a blood-spattered car window, staring into the sky. With morbid curiosity, I looked at all the photographs, wondering which of the people in them was him.

A reflection in the glass moved and I spun around.

A man was standing in the middle of the room. He must have tiptoed in for me not to have heard him.

"I thought I heard voices," he said. "I see it's just your—what do you call that thing on your collar?"

"Portable radio."

I'd seen him the night of Oates's death, in the atrium, waiting to be interviewed by Buck's homicide team. He was about forty-five, plump, and pear-shaped, with blond hair thinning on top and pulled into a long ponytail. Because of the light reflected in them, I couldn't see his eyes behind his thick-lensed glasses.

"You're the policewoman who found Geoffrey Oates's body, aren't you?" he said. "I recognize your red hair. I'm Charles Bengtsson, associate chair of the Psychology Department. I'm also something of an insomniac, so I work here a lot at night, rather than go home to toss and turn in my bed. Perhaps I should have a job like yours." He chuckled, as though that were quite amusing. I resisted the impulse to tell him that he could do worse than have a job like mine. He had, in my opinion.

He came into the room and peered at the display. "Ah, yes, our June picnic." He studied the photographs a few moments, his nose almost pressed against the glass of the display case. "A summer afternoon on the lake! Who would've thought then that one of our happy little band would be dead so soon afterward? I see that poor Oates is in several of these pictures." He tapped the glass with a plump finger. "Here; and here he has one all to himself."

In the first picture, a young man was standing next to Bill Turner, both of them surprised by the camera. Geoff Oates had been tall and skinny, with short, blond hair and a serious expression on his face. In the second photograph, of Oates alone, he was pulling himself up onto a raft in the lake, grinning self-consciously and waving to the camera.

The picture stirred a memory in me—I'd seen that face before. I don't mean I'd seen it in the car, dead—I mean I'd seen Oates waving and grinning somewhere else.

"Rather ghoulish of us, isn't it?" Bengtsson was saying, his voice betraying his pleasure, "to be looking at Geoff like that, knowing that in only a few short weeks—what's wrong? You look as though you've seen a ghost."

I had seen Geoffrey Oates before. I'd seen him at the block party on the Fourth of July when he'd come to Harold Mullen's house to pick him up. Mullen had gone across the street to meet him, and Oates had smiled and waved, as he was smiling and waving in the photograph.

And then they both died, within a day of one another. One an alleged suicide, the other an alleged accident.

Fourteen

After I got rid of Bengtsson, I left the Psychology Building and continued on through the Old Campus, trying to make sense of it. I tried to remember what Mullen had said about Oates—something about him being a member of the University faculty who was taking him to dinner. He'd said it in connection with telling us that he was going to leave money to the University. At the time, I thought he was simply boasting.

The next afternoon, I called Susan Carlisle, the Psychology Department's principal secretary. We play racquetball once or twice a week, so I know her phone number by heart. I asked her if she'd be interested in a game that evening, provided I could reserve a court, and dinner afterwards, and she said fine. We agreed to meet at her office.

The nameplate on her desk says she's Pamela Reardon. That puzzled me the first time we met, since I'd known Pam Reardon, the principal secretary back when I was going with George. Susan explained that since the psych faculty never stopped calling Pam by her predecessor's name, which was Mary, she'd seen no reason to go to the trouble of requisitioning a new nameplate for herself. She's proud of the fact that, through a system of reward and punishment, she's trained all but a few of the faculty to call her Pam. Some of the nicer—or more alert—members of the department have even learned to call her by her real name. Susan is small and wiry, with a stubborn chin, blond hair and a wicked sense of humor. We have a mutual love of racquetball and we're about equal in ability. I've got longer arms, but she's got better reflexes and more bounce.

Because it was summer, I'd been able to reserve a racquetball court for an hour and a half, which was a good thing. After my discovery of the night before, I had a lot of energy to work off. I played like a fiend and didn't lose a game.

When we'd cooled down and showered, we walked across campus to an Italian restaurant on the New Campus side, the Via Appia, that I think serves the best pasta in town, although most of my friends think the noodles are overdone and the sauce mostly ketchup. For some of us, though, that's Italian.

"Either you've reached a new plateau," she said, "in which case we've played our last game together, or you played way above your head." She sprawled back in the red plastic booth and sniffed a glass of the house wine suspiciously.

"Harold Mullen," I said.

"Harold Mullen's the reason you played like that? Who is he, a new boyfriend?"

"You've never heard the name?"

She thought a minute. "I don't think so. But then, it's not exactly a name that clamors for attention, is it? It sounds almost like a common noun."

After the waiter brought us our salad, I told her who and what I thought Mullen was.

"He's dead now," I concluded. "His house burned down, with him inside, the night after Geoff Oates died. A few weeks before that—on the Fourth of July—I think I saw Oates at his place. Mullen said he was a member of the University faculty who'd come to take him to dinner."

"You *think* you saw Oates at Mullen's place. What's that supposed to mean?"

I told her about the photograph I'd seen of Oates and how it looked like the man I'd seen with Mullen.

"And they did die violently, both of them, and just a day apart," I added.

"Lots of people do," she said. "You don't think Geoff Oates was involved with this Mullen in sending out hate mail, do you?"

"I don't know. But don't look so skeptical. It's possible, believe me. I don't know what your idea of a hate mailer is, Susan, but Harold Mullen wasn't mine until he started talking to me about how terrible it is to mix the races. And his sister also thinks he's a racist. I don't have any idea what the connection is between Oates and Mullen—I'm just convinced there is one. How well did you know Oates?"

"Hardly at all. The Psych Department's crawling with graduate students and after a while they all start to look alike. I just remember he was sort of lanky and ordinary."

"Mullen left his money to the University," I said. "I haven't been able to find out for what, because it's being handled through the University Club, and they won't tell me anything. He said something about an endowed chair. Everywhere I've turned, I've been stonewalled, and you know how that affects me."

"You break out."

"I wonder if Mullen might have left his money to the Psych Department."

"I couldn't tell you offhand. But it's only been two weeks since he died. It would take longer than that for his will to go through probate. So we wouldn't necessarily know yet, if we didn't know before he died."

"His money didn't go through probate. It was in a living trust and when he died, the University Club took it over."

"Well, I don't think the University Club's notified us of any 'Mullen money' that's coming to us. I don't handle the budget directly, Andy Terry does that, but if we suddenly got a big windfall, I'd know about it. What did this Mullen look like?"

"Old, frail, with bright teeth that looked like he'd bought them off the rack next to the reading glasses at the dime store."

"Mullen," she said thoughtfully. "Mullen. Something's coming back to me. He used a walker, right?"

I hardly noticed our dinners arrive, huge steaming plates of spaghetti topped with hunks of Italian sausage. "Not when I saw him. But he'd had some kind of cancer before that, so maybe he did once. He told me it had gone into remission."

Susan nodded. "Well, if it's the man I'm thinking of, when he came into the Psych Building, he looked as if he were on his last legs."

"When?" In my excitement, I sprinkled too much cheese onto my dinner.

"Last fall, I think. Almost a year ago. The reason I remember is, he was bundled up in a heavy coat and had a black lambs-wool hat pulled down over his ears, even though it was Indian summer and hot. He could have turned around inside the coat, he looked so shrunken. He leaned heavily on a cane, too, and arrived in a taxi." Her eyes grew wide. "Geoff Oates went out to get him and brought him into the building!"

"Do you know what he was there for?"

"No idea. At the time, I thought he was a long-retired professor coming back to visit the scene of his crimes. But he could have been somebody the department was schmoozing to get his money." Susan twirled spaghetti onto her fork and poked it into her mouth. "The Psych Department likes to show off the facilities to prospective donors," she said when she'd swallowed. "The guy I saw doesn't have to be your Mullen, you know."

"But it was," I said.

She nodded, a little uneasily. "It's beginning to sound like it. Do you know what kind of research Geoff Oates was involved with?"

I shook my head.

"I don't either, exactly, but he was associated with the Human Genetics Research Project." She chewed spaghetti, waited for my reaction.

"That sounds right up Mullen's alley!"

"That's what I thought you'd think."

"What do they do there—create better human beings through genetic engineering?"

"I doubt it. I'm just a humble secretary, of course, and I don't keep up on all the things psychologists do to keep busy, but I think they conduct research on heredity and environment. Brice Ridgeway's the head of the project. It's one of the biggest—and richest—projects in the whole department. They bring people into their labs in droves—students, mostly—and run all kinds of tests on them, then run the results through their computers and write articles and books that have the shelf life of skim milk."

"And this is what Geoff Oates was working on, too?"

"He'd have to be. Oates was Lyle Gardner's student and Gardner's the associate director of the project under Ridgeway, so you know he'd have to be doing something Gardner was interested in."

"How do I go about finding out if Mullen left his money to this project?" I asked.

"Well, if his name's on an account, all we have to do is look at the books. I don't deal directly with the department's budgets—but I can ask Andy about it tomorrow. I can tell you right now, however, that we don't have any Harold Mullen Chair in anything."

I looked at my watch. It was early. Her car was still in the Psych Department parking lot and my bike was chained to a lamppost in front of the building. We had to go back there anyway.

"We could check the books tonight, couldn't we? It wouldn't take long, would it? We'll skip dessert here and I'll buy you a hot fudge sundae afterwards."

"He looked so weak and vulnerable," she said. "It's hard to believe. And you really don't have any solid evidence for any of this, Peggy."

"Some of the people he was harassing were weak and vulnerable, too," I said. "And you're right, I don't have any evidence that would stand up in court. But I do have the evidence of my own eyes and ears. I was in his house;

I saw his face and heard him speak when he realized I'd caught on to what he was doing. And the circumstantial evidence is getting stronger all the time."

She ripped off a piece of garlic bread, started to put it in her mouth, paused. "You think Geoff Oates killed himself because he was doing some kind of racist research for this guy Mullen—and he thought he was going to be found out?"

"It's possible, isn't it?"

"I don't think so," she said, chewing. "Nobody would be that stupid—to do that kind of research, I mean. They could never get it published. They'd be dead."

"Oates is dead," I reminded her. "And so is Harold Mullen."

Fifteen

We walked slowly back to the Psychology Building in the warm August evening. The office of Andy Terry, the budget secretary, was next to that of the assistant chairman of the department, Charles Bengtsson, the man with the ponytail who'd been standing with me at the photo display.

Susan used her master key to open Terry's door, let it close behind us, and flipped on the overhead lights.

She rummaged in Terry's middle drawer, and brought out a key that opened the files against one wall. She dug through them, brought out a large black ledger, and put it down on Terry's desk. We both pulled up chairs.

"This ledger lists all the money coming to the Human Genetics Research Project this quarter as well as where it comes from," she said. "The money we get from the University Club can be kind of tricky. The Club automatically deposits it—monthly, quarterly or yearly, according to the terms of the trust—in whichever of our accounts it's meant for and then sends us a statement, just like any bank statement you'd get. Then Andy enters it in here, and we spend it. Most of the statements indicate the name of the trust from which the money comes but not all. Some are just numbered accounts. If Harold Mullen was the publicity-shy fellow you say he was, he could have done it that way and we'd never find him."

"I'd feel like I'd struck gold if I even saw a number that I thought might be his," I said.

She laughed. "How would you know?"

"After all this time, I'll probably pick up his evil vibrations."

As I slid a ruler down the columns in the ledger, Susan explained each account. Most of the largest sums were from federal grants, with the next largest coming from foundations. There were several numbered accounts, and also accounts with the names of individuals on them—none of which was Mullen.

The ruler slid slowly down the columns, two page's worth. When I got to one account, she stopped me and said, "Andy's told me about this one. It's from an old man who'd read about Gardner's twins studies in the newspaper a few years ago—Gardner gets a lot of media attention, you know. Anyway, this guy was a twin himself, and somehow got the idea we were in the business of locating and reuniting twins who'd been separated at birth. So he left us the interest from $5,000 in his will—about $650 a year. It goes into our party fund. Professor Ridgeway's having a party for the HGRP's summer grads on Sunday. Six hundred and fifty bucks'll just about cover it, unless he brings in dancing girls."

"Are you going?"

"To the party? Are you kidding? I avoid those things like the plague."

The ruler moved down a little farther before she stopped it again, at the name Grace Sterns.

"The HGRP renamed its research library after her last year," Susan said.

"What does it take to name a library after somebody?" I asked.

"It takes me putting in a requisition for a brass nameplate that says Grace Sterns Research Library. Then a carpenter comes over and screws it onto the wall. Instant immortality, for as long as the wall lasts."

"You could have put in a requisition for a nameplate for Susan Carlisle while you were at it," I pointed out.

"Why bother?"

I continued running the ruler down the pages to the end. A glance had already told me that there wasn't any Mullen, but I was hoping to find some kind of significant change that might indicate that the human being behind the numbers had died and the amount of money given to the HGRP had risen. There were three numbered accounts that generated quite a lot of money for the HGRP each quarter, but none of them was new nor had any changed in the past few months. If Mullen's money was in here somewhere, I couldn't find it.

"Peggy O'Neill, stonewalled again," I said, staring bleakly at the ledger.

"Peggy, you're like a cat looking at a door that's slightly ajar. If it was completely open or closed, you'd ignore it completely. C'mon, give it up and let's go get that ice cream you promised me. You don't know that Mullen even left his money to the HGRP! You don't know he was a hate mailer. And you can't even be sure you saw Oates with him."

A noise made me turn and look over my shoulder. When we'd come in, the door had closed behind us but not all the way. Now it was open a crack. I got up and went over to it and pulled it all the way open.

Charles Bengtsson was standing just outside. He looked startled, and then turned red. He looked around me at Susan and said, "Working late, are you, Pam?"

A little too brightly, Susan replied, "Oh, hi, Professor Bengtsson. So are you."

He came into the room, his hands clasped behind his pear-shaped body. His eyes blinked myopically behind his glasses as he peered over Susan's shoulder to see what she had on the desk.

"An odd time to be going through the accounts, isn't it, so late in the evening? Besides, doesn't Andy Terry handle the budgets?"

I could see that Susan was undecided about whether to lie or tell the truth, so I stepped in. "An old friend of mine told me he'd left some money to the University. He never told me what for. When he died, I got curious. From something he said, I got the idea that he might have left his money to the HGRP."

"Indeed? And did he?"

"Apparently not. We can't find it here anywhere. The man's name was Mullen. Harold Mullen."

I thought I saw something flicker in his eyes that was more than the light on his lenses.

"Do you know the name?" I asked him.

"I'm afraid it rings no bells," Bengtsson said, trying to keep his eyes on mine without blinking. Turning quickly to Susan, he said, "It's nice of you to bring her over here so late, Pam, to satisfy her curiosity about an old friend's money." His lips curled up into a smile that knew better. "But isn't it something you could have easily handled over the phone?"

"We were passing the building anyway," Susan told him, "on our way to get ice cream. It would only have taken a moment," she added, "if you hadn't joined us."

He laughed. "Well, somebody has to patrol the building, when the campus police are out on the town." He turned and bowed to me. "So, you're Pam's new friend, are you, a campus cop?"

"Susan's friend," I said. "Not so new."

His little smile was knowing. "Well, I'll leave you to your dessert. I'm sorry my curiosity has delayed you."

As he backed out of the room, he said to me: "Perhaps I'll see you again on Sunday. Try to talk Pam into coming, won't you?" To Susan he said: "I noticed that you weren't signed up."

When he was out of earshot, I said, "I wonder how long he'd been standing out there before I heard him, and how much he overheard. He always seems to be in the building. He looks like he got into the 1960s late and failed to notice that they ended."

"Shh! Let's get out of here."

When we got out into the warm night air, heading back toward the New Campus and the ice cream shop, Susan said, "He's called Sparky, and not always behind his back, either, but he doesn't seem to mind. When he first started here, so I've been told, his research involved administering electric shocks to any living thing not covered by the Geneva resolution against torture. He'd write up the results of his experiments, which always seemed to be just that after a while, the animals would start drooling when they saw him coming with his tiny electrodes. Some people claim he even measured the drool and had a 'drool scale' for birds, fish, and mammals, but that's probably just a rumor."

"Maybe he wears the ponytail out of sympathy for his little furry subjects," I suggested.

"Probably. The University finally made the Psych Department unplug him, and he hasn't published anything since."

We got to the ice cream parlor and ordered hot fudge sundaes. "Bengtsson's only an associate professor," Susan went on, "the oldest in the department. They made him director of undergraduate advising for a while, just to try to get some use out of him, but he quit, he said, because undergraduate students made him nervous—he couldn't figure out what they wanted. Now he's associate chair of the department, which means he runs errands for the chairman."

I told her about my encounter with Bengtsson in the faculty lounge last night. "He knew who Geoff Oates was," I said.

"Every member of the psych faculty has to be officially associated with some research project, and currently Bengtsson's a part of the Human Genetics Research Project. He's been a member of just about every project the department's had in the last fifteen years, 'trying to find his niche,' he says. He sticks his nose into everybody's business, comes up quietly behind graduate students just the way he did us, peers over their shoulders. Scares the hell out of them sometimes."

"Maybe he's writing articles on scaring people," I suggested, "since he can't shock animals anymore."

Susan rolled her eyes. "Anything's possible in that godforsaken place."

Our ice cream arrived. "Tell me about the party on Sunday." I was scraping the whipped cream off my sundae and putting it on her saucer, along with the cherry. I hate cherries and there's always too much whipped cream.

"It's a party for the summer graduates, like the one at the end of spring semester for the June grads. It's always held out at Ridgeway's home on Forest Lake. The secretaries are always invited, to try to make up for our relentless exploitation the rest of the year."

"But you're not going."

"No. Kate's out of town on assignment and besides, she can't stand any of those people. So I probably wouldn't go even if I wanted to." Kate, Susan's partner, is a television reporter.

"Too bad," I said, staring out into space. "You could take me."

"But I'm not going to."

"No, I know that. I wouldn't either, if I were you. I'd almost certainly put my foot in it and get us both in big trouble."

She stared at me. "You want to go?"

"Yes!" I said fiercely. "I think Harold Mullen left his money to the Human Genetics Research Project and I think there's a connection between Mullen and Oates. I want to find out what it was. How am I going to find anything out, Susan, if I don't get a chance to talk to the faculty and students?"

"Jesus, Peggy—"

"I know, you could lose your job. I'm sorry I suggested it."

"It's not that. It's—"

"The embarrassment. I understand, Susan. I mean, if I get thrown off Ridgeway's property in front of all those people you have to work with day in and day out, it would be unbearably humiliating for you. You'd be afraid to go to work the next day."

"I know what you're trying to do to me, Peggy," she said.

"I'm so close!" I told her. "I started out with nothing, Susan, and now I've put Mullen together with Oates and the HGRP. But that's only a part of it—I want to know it all."

She scrunched up her face in thought. After a while, she said, "They'll think we're a couple. Bengtsson already does."

"Will that be a problem for you?"

She laughed. "For me? Hardly. But what about you? Won't some of them recognize you from the time you were with, what's his name, George?"

"He specialized in learning disabilities in children. None of those people'll be there."

"And anyway," Susan said thoughtfully, "you could have changed your sexual orientation. From what you've told me about George, any woman who went with him might. I've let you talk me into it, haven't I, Peggy?"

"You can change your mind if you want to," I said, having first convinced myself she wouldn't.

"Oh, right! Then you'd probably go alone, wouldn't you? And never be heard from again."

Sixteen

The light on my answering machine was blinking when I got home from work the next morning. I started my coffeemaker and then pressed Play.

"Oh, hello, Peggy. This is Lillian Przynski, Bud Mullen's sister. Excuse the noise, but I'm calling from a pay phone outside the gas station around the corner. I hate to pester you at this hour, but I've got some news that might interest you if you're still trying to track down what poor Bud did with his money. If it's no trouble, why don't you drop by sometime soon and I'll tell you about it? I'm sure it's not important." My answering machine indicated that she'd pestered it at a little after nine.

I was too tired to drive over to Lillian's that morning, so I showered, drank my coffee and went to bed. I went over to her place that afternoon.

"I met an old acquaintance of Bud's yesterday evening," she said, after she'd carried her poodle carefully to another chair and brought in coffee and cookies. "A man named Dewey. He worked for Bud at the store, a kind of handyman. Rufus and I were out for our evening stroll, when all of a sudden a big rusty old car pulls up to the curb, polluting the whole world, and lo and behold, out climbs Dewey! He comes over and says hello. Well, it took me a moment to remember who he was. Rufus growled and tried to nip him on the ankle—you can't fool an old dog, you know! When he told me how sorry he was that Harold had died, I remembered him."

"What does he look like?"

"Like something the cat dragged in, if you ask me. Short and thin, but with a large head. Bad complexion—he must have scratched his pimples when he was a boy. A high forehead that looks even higher because he combs his hair straight back. Dark, oily hair. Blackheads on his nose. Wears clothes he must have stolen from the morgue."

She'd described the man I'd seen coming away from Mullen's house on the afternoon he died.

"You're a cop's delight, Lillian. I'll bet you saw all that while giving him the impression you were staring at the sidewalk."

She cackled evilly, or as evilly as she was capable of cackling.

"Dewey what?" I asked.

"I don't know. Just Dewey, that's all I ever heard Bud call him. Oh, dammit," she exclaimed, "I should have asked him while I had the chance, shouldn't I?"

"He might not have told you," I said.

"I used to see him when I visited Bud in the store, since I could never get Bud to come visit me. I got the impression Bud exploited him something fierce—it was always 'Dewey, do this!' and 'Dewey, do that!'—maybe Dewey wasn't even his real name, but a nickname he'd earned!

"Anyway, I was surprised when he popped up on the sidewalk like that, bowing and scraping and telling me how tragic it was, 'poor Harold' dying in such a horrible manner. He said he was sorry he'd missed the funeral—which shows you what he knows, since there wasn't one. I could have told him that if he wanted to pay his last respects to Bud, he could just come over and mow my lawn, since that's where he is."

Lillian sipped coffee a moment and then said, "Dewey told me Bud had been murdered, and he knew who did it."

I had a feeling I knew who that was going to be.

"A black woman, probably in cahoots with a white woman with red hair," she said.

"So now you know."

"Pshaw, Peggy! He said this redheaded woman had come to my sick brother with false accusations on the last day of his life and then that night a black friend of hers burned down his house—except he didn't use the word *black*, you know, for this mythical friend of this mythical redhead."

"Did you let him know that you already knew about Paula and me?"

She smiled smugly. "I didn't think that would be a good idea, so I just let him do all the talking."

I told her about Paula's visit to Mullen.

"Well," Lillian said when I'd finished, "it served Bud right. He wouldn't have been scared, if he didn't have a guilty conscience, would he?"

"Did Dewey tell you how he knew about Paula?"

"He said he saw her coming away from Bud's house, the night of the fire. He'd been at Bud's that afternoon, helping him with something. That's when Bud told him about your visit. He was terribly upset, according to Dewey, because of the accusations you'd made against him. Then Dewey had to go off to his job—he has a part-time job around here somewhere. Well, after getting off work here, he drove back to Bud's, to take something to Bud that Bud said he needed, and as he was pulling up in front of the house, your friend Paula was coming down off the porch. She looked like she was in a hurry, Dewey said. So he followed her, all the way to her house where she lives with a white man—that's what he said, a white man. Then Dewey drove back to Bud's house, but the fire trucks were arriving, the police were closing off the street, and Dewey could see that Bud's house was just a mass of flames." Lillian paused to catch her breath. "I suppose Dewey must have been in on the hate mailing with Bud, don't you think?"

I said I thought so, too. I explained that I'd seen the man she'd described coming from Mullen's house the afternoon of the fire. "He was carrying two stuffed grocery bags. They probably contained your brother's last delivery of hate mail."

"I suppose so. Bud didn't have a lot of strength since his cancer, you know, so he probably paid Dewey to do the heavy work for him. I imagine mail with so much hate in it must be very heavy, don't you? Anyway, Peggy, I decided to do a little detective work on my own. So I asked Dewey if he knew what Bud had done with his money. I told him I hadn't been able to find out. And do you know what he told me? He told me Bud had left it to the University for a chair of some kind—a chair that was going to cost a million dollars. I laughed and said, 'Dewey, now don't be silly!' I shouldn't have laughed, because Dewey got furious and said Bud had known what he was doing."

Mullen had hinted to me that he was leaving his money for an endowed chair, too. I explained to Lillian what an endowed chair was: a position at the University that's funded from an endowment. Positions like that go to very distinguished, and often remarkably useless, people.

"How very interesting," she said politely, and went on with her story. "Dewey got a very suspicious look on his wretched face then, and he asked me why I was so interested in what Bud had done with his money. I told him I was just curious, but I could see he didn't believe me. I think he suspected that I was out to get it. He said that if Bud had wanted me to know what he'd done with his money, he would have told me. Then he said he had to get to work, and scurried back to his car and drove off."

"You didn't happen to get the license plate, did you?"

"Oh, darn it, I didn't think of that. What's happening to my mind? Some detective I'd make! But it was a big thing, old and green where the rust hadn't eaten it up."

We sat there a minute or two longer, the silence broken only by Rufus's quiet snoring and the rocking of Lillian's chair.

I tried to reconstruct the last hour of Harold Mullen's life. He'd been working in his basement, alone, expecting Dewey to return at any time. Dewey would use his own key to enter the house and come downstairs to help him with his work. There was a knock on the door, and then another, louder. Annoyed, he'd climbed the basement stairs, gone over and opened the door. He'd expected Dewey—but found himself face to face with one of his victims.

What happened then? Paula returned to her car and, tailed by Dewey, drove home. The fire must have started almost immediately after that, since the house was burning and the fire trucks were on the way when Dewey returned.

If it was an accident, that's the end of the story.

If it was murder, the killer was there at the same time Paula and Dewey were.

I'm not alone, Mullen had told Paula. But any old person, facing a potential intruder, might say that.

Saturday evening, I picked a sackful of Mrs. Hammer's zucchini and drove over to Buck's condo. He cooked it while I watched, the way a cat might watch Einstein working out something on a blackboard: a knowing look on my face, but without a clue as to what he was doing.

"That was great," I told him as I pushed my empty plate away and sat back. "I don't suppose dinners like that can be frozen in little individual servings and microwaved."

Sometimes I enjoy watching Buck squeeze his eyes shut in pain. Buck doesn't own a microwave oven.

We took our coffee into the living room and sat in front of his big picture window. From up there you can see the city spread out far below and, to the right, the University with the dark scar of the river cutting it in half. I enjoy visiting Buck's condo, but I wouldn't want to live in it. It's all rounded corners like a spaceship—but he seems to like being high above the violence of his working life.

I told him what I'd been doing since the last time we'd talked. He won't talk business over dinner.

"How certain are you that it was Oates you saw with Mullen on the Fourth?" Buck asked. "It was over a month ago, and you only caught a glimpse of the man."

"Pretty certain."

"Pretty certain. Would you stand up in front of a judge and swear to it, if somebody's life depended on it?"

"No."

"Good. Because a defense attorney would make you look like a fool if you did."

"How common is it that suicides don't leave a note?"

"Common enough. It would make it easier on everybody if they all did, but people who commit suicide usually aren't thinking of the consequences for those who have to clean up after them. Oates didn't have any really close friends here, and he doesn't seem to have been particularly close to any of his family, who live in California, so maybe he didn't think a note was necessary."

"Did you find a motive for suicide?"

Buck hesitated, sipped coffee. "Hard to say. According to members of the psychology faculty, he was a respectable student who wasn't having any problems with his work. The students who knew him said the same thing. But the student who seemed to know him best—Bill Turner, that fellow who lives in the building—he said he thought Oates had seemed depressed for the past several months."

"Did he say why?"

"No. Claimed Oates hadn't volunteered anything, and he hadn't asked. I had the feeling Turner wanted to say more, but changed his mind. I couldn't get anything else out of him."

"You think he's holding something back?"

Buck nodded. "I do, yes—but I wouldn't swear to that in court, either. Maybe I'm getting too suspicious in my later years. I'm starting to think everybody I talk to is holding something back." Buck stared morosely out his window.

Buck's feelings about people are usually very accurate.

"Did anybody hear the shot?"

He shook his head. "The car windows were up and the Psychology Building is sealed up as tight as a drum—air-conditioned. A couple of people in the building said they'd noticed Oates's car sitting in the lot with its lights on, but they'd just assumed it was somebody getting ready to drive out of there. They didn't wait to see."

"It's odd that he turned his headlights on before killing himself," I said. "You don't turn on your headlights until you've started the engine. Oates might've started his engine, turned on the lights, and then somebody killed him. The killer turned off the engine but, in his hurry to get away from there, forgot the lights."

Buck shrugged. "It's just as likely that Oates, about to kill himself, was a little distracted himself. He might have started the car and then decided to kill himself. He turned off the engine, but forgot the lights."

That was a plausible scenario, too.

"The University seems to be a pretty stressful place these days," Buck went on. "Two students have killed themselves there in the past year, before Oates. And whatever his mood was, I did get the feeling from talking to his adviser that Oates wasn't among the most promising students in the program."

I remembered how professor Gardner had assessed Oates: "Not perhaps among the very top students, but good, very good." I guess there were people who'd commit suicide over an evaluation like that.

I asked Buck if he could find out what Mullen had done with his money.

"By going to the University Club that stonewalled you and throwing my weight around? No, thanks, Peggy—not even for you. I do like my job, oddly enough. From what you tell me, it's a private foundation We'd need a court order to get into its files, and we couldn't hope to get one without reopening both the Oates and the Mullen case. And we don't have the evidence to justify doing that."

I told him about Dewey, Mullen's friend, and the threatening phone call Paula had gotten from him. Buck said that Anne Meredith had also received an anonymous tip that Paula had set the fire that killed Mullen.

"The man was very insistent about it," Buck said. "Almost hysterical. Anne invited him to give her his name, or come in, but he declined and hung up before she could trace the call. Since Paula had already told Anne about her visit to Mullen, and arson can't be proven, Anne hasn't followed up on it. We get lots of anonymous tips from people who hate their neighbors."

I got up, went over to the window, and looked down in the general direction of the Psychology Building. It wasn't hard to find, at a bend in the river, just where the bridge stretches over to the brightly lit New Campus.

"I think there's a clever—or damned lucky—killer loose out there somewhere, Buck," I said. "Somebody who killed two people in less than twenty-four hours. And he's getting away with it."

"Just because of a similarity between a snapshot and a man you saw a month and a half ago?"

"That, and the fact that the man in the snapshot was a student in the Human Genetics Research Project, and that sounds like something right up Mullen's alley."

"You think they're doing racist research, Peggy?"

I turned to him and said, "It's not a question of what they're doing. It's a question of what Harold Mullen thought they were doing."

Dessert was a chocolate soufflé that Buck served with espresso. We didn't talk any more about murder or possible murder until I was standing by the elevator, ready to go back down to earth. Then I asked him point-blank how happy he was with the suicide verdict on Geoffrey Oates.

"Don't do this to me, Peggy," he said, his eyes going suddenly to the wall behind me where he could watch the elevator's arrow moving toward his floor number, but not quickly enough.

"I think that's an answer," I said.

A look of frustration washed over his face, a look I'd seen before. "Okay, so I'm not happy with the suicide verdict," he admitted finally, "but I didn't have any evidence to bring to a grand jury to indicate it was anything else.

And I can't get the arson people to state unequivocally that the fire at Harold Mullen's house was arson, either."

I laughed, a little surprised. "But you tried!"

"Yes, Peggy, I tried, after what you told me about the possible connection between Oates and Mullen."

"I'm going to a party tomorrow afternoon," I told him. "At Brice Ridgeway's place on Forest Lake. Ridgeway's the head of the Human Genetics Research Project. A lot of faculty and students'll be there."

Buck shook his head. "Peggy, Peggy. Some of those professors have a lot of clout, you know. They don't like it when people like me come around, asking questions, acting as though I thought they were capable of committing criminal acts. If they find out what you're there for, you could lose your job."

I laughed. "Tell me something I don't know."

The elevator doors opened and I got in.

"If you're right about the double murderer," he said, "he could be there tomorrow."

"I've been to Psychology Department picnics before," I told him.

Seventeen

Sunday, as we zipped onto the freeway in her little red convertible, Susan said, "This is why I'm still working in the Psych Department. I'll be making payments on this sucker for another five years, so I can't afford to be fired, not the way the job market is these days."

"They can't fire you," I said. "You've passed probation."

"True. But they can make your life such hell that you quit."

"I'll try not to do anything that'll upset them. Now do me a favor. Slow down a little."

Forest Lake would be a forty-minute drive for me, but Susan's driving was probably going to make it ten minutes shorter. It was a warm day, and she had the top down. The wind played with the hair on top of my head like a nervous lover, a constant minor irritation. I've often wondered why you have to pay more for a car with a cloth top that rots than for one with a metal top that doesn't.

The party at Ridgeway's was to honor the doctoral candidates who were getting their degrees at the end of second summer session. "Brice Ridgeway takes these gatherings very seriously," Susan told me, "and he expects everyone who can to show up, so you're going to meet most of the faculty and students who aren't out of town. It's not exactly combat duty, because he's got a great place and the lake's wonderful. It's sort of like France, if you can stay away from the people, you can have a wonderful time."

"I'm not going to stay away from the people."

"I know. A working holiday; so I'd better fill you in on who's going to be there. Lyle Gardner, of course, you've met him. He's married to Shelley, who is his second wife. She's about twenty years younger than he is and they have two children. Gardner adores them. At least, he's forever showing pictures of them to anybody who'll stop to look."

"He can't be all bad if he loves his kids."

"Maybe not, but I can't imagine that he sees very much of them, since he's never home. He's either at the University or off in Europe or other parts of the country at conferences—Ridgeway doesn't like to fly, so he makes Gardner go in his place. I think he and Shelley were having problems for a while, but things seem to have improved in the last few months."

"What kind of a guy is Ridgeway?" I asked, watching cars fall away behind us in a blur and wondering where the highway patrol was when you needed it.

"A prima donna. They all are, of course, but Ridgeway's the worst because he has the most people working for him and access to the most grant money, which means he has the most power. Until he turned forty, I've been told, he was called 'The Prodigy'—the youngest person ever to get a Ph.D. in psychology at Harvard and the youngest to chair a major psychology department. He's about fifty now."

"But he's not the chairman anymore, is he?"

"No, he quit a couple of years ago. He couldn't stand the red tape—chairmen are supposed to be accountable, and accountability is a joke to men like Ridgeway. There's also not as much money or prestige in being chairman of a department as there is in heading a thriving research project. He's made the Human Genetics Research Project the biggest and best-funded in the department."

"He sounds formidable," I said.

"He is. He looks like the most agreeable man in the world, a lion at rest—until feeding time. And then watch out! As long as you do exactly what he wants when he wants it, he's pretty easy to get along with. He's much hated, but he's feared even more because he can break you."

I shook my head. "Things don't change around that place, do they?"

"It's probably gotten worse since your day. There's less money now and more of them to go after it. A moral upbringing and a moment's hesitation, and you find yourself lying in the dust with your colleagues' footprints on your back."

"Is that what happened to Professor Bengtsson?"

"Sparky?" She laughed. "Well, something's left him in the dust, all right, but I doubt you could blame it on a moral upbringing. Let's just say that Sparky's not enormously gifted, and leave it at that. He'll be coming alone. He once had a wife, they say, but, like Peter Peter, Pumpkin Eater, he couldn't keep her."

"What's that?" I said, pointing to a dial on the dashboard.

"The tachometer."

"What's it do?"

"I don't know."

She cut in front of a semi and sprinted onto an exit ramp, deftly downshifting as she went into the curve and up again as we headed onto a two-lane road that led into the woods surrounding Forest Lake.

"Five point two miles," she said, glancing at a piece of paper on which she'd written the directions.

Driveways with gates and No Trespassing signs began to appear on the right after a while, and occasionally I could see the windows of expensive homes through the trees and catch quick glimpses of Forest Lake glittering in the sun.

Susan screeched to a half-stop and then swung sharply into a driveway, its gate open. A sign nailed to a tree by the road read Ridgeway's Hideaway. A quarter of a mile farther, the driveway widened into a crowded parking area in front of a large house.

As I got out, I gave a low whistle of appreciation. The house was two-storied and Tudoresque, with lots of half-timbers and arched windows with small panes along with the inevitable ivy growing discretely here and there on its walls.

I asked Susan if Ridgeway was married.

"Sorry, Peggy. He's one of the few men in the department over forty who's been married to the same woman his entire adult life. My snotty opinion is, he decided life would be more convenient with a wife, found a suitable candidate, married her, and that was that. Then he could get on with the important things. Which reminds me—he has a son, Troy. He'll probably be here today, because he lives at home. Troy squandered his youth trying to make it as a professional baseball player, but couldn't hit curveballs, which is a big disadvantage for a ball player who wants to get out of the Bush Leagues. When he was pushing thirty, he came home, dragging his useless bat behind him."

We gathered our beach gear and headed to the house. "Does Troy have a job, or does he just live off his dad?"

"He invested whatever he'd managed to save during his minor league career in a sports bar. It's called A Whole New Ball Game. You might've seen it, it's out on the strip among all the other meat markets. Its only distinguishing feature is the roof, in the form of a baseball, and there're autographed photographs of famous ball players on the walls."

I told her I'd somehow missed it, I didn't get out that way much.

Behind Ridgeway's house was a patio, with a bar in one corner next to the house and several charcoal grills scattered around, waiting for dinnertime. Beyond the patio was a manicured lawn that swept down to a sandy beach and the lake, both littered with people in bathing suits. A raft bobbed in the water about fifteen yards offshore, with people on and around it.

It felt strange, stepping into a landscape I'd seen in photographs a few days before. I caught myself looking around for Geoff Oates.

"So we finally get you out here, do we, Susan?" A man in swimming trunks came striding from the house, changed directions when he saw us, came over, and gave Susan a big hug.

When Susan introduced us, he turned to me and nodded, gazing down into my face incuriously with dark eyes under heavy brows.

Brice Ridgeway was over six feet tall. He had a dark complexion, thick, dark hair and a nose that looked like it might have been broken once. His body was solid, muscular, and matted with dark, curly hair.

He pointed to a little cabin down by the lake and told us the changing rooms were in there. "Why don't you take care of the introductions, Susan, since you know most of the people here?" He nodded and strode purposefully off in the direction of the water.

"At least he knows your name," I said.

"Ridgeway doesn't neglect details. That's why he's got a place like this."

It was an August afternoon, the sky cloudless, the water a little cold, and there was a warm breeze. While splashing around and tossing Frisbees, I learned the names of a dozen faculty members and half that many students. Only a couple of the names rang bells, among them Shelley Gardner, Lyle Gardner's wife. She was somewhere around thirty and was wearing one of those thong swimsuits that are banned on many public beaches. Susan had told me she was the mother of two children, but she didn't look it. Then I realized that was my mother speaking. Most young mothers don't look it these days.

After a while, Susan and I swam out to the raft. As we pulled ourselves onto the deck and stood up, a man, lying at our feet, turned and dragged his sunglasses down out of his hair and over his eyes, the better to check us out.

"Hi," I said. "I'm Peggy and this is Susan."

"Troy," he said, and looked a moment longer at each of us to be sure he hadn't missed anything of interest the first time and then shoved his glasses back up into his hair and closed his eyes. He looked as though he'd gone back to sleep. He was long, lean, and was wearing a swimsuit very much like Shelley Gardner's.

"You're Professor Ridgeway's son," I said.

"You got it in one," he drawled.

Developing the art of conversation must be hard for a ball player, I thought, when your mouth's always full of chewing tobacco or sunflower seeds.

Troy Ridgeway was probably as tall as his dad, but a lot leaner and harder. He had the young-old face of somebody who'd spent too much time in the sun. His bleached hair was shoulder length and spread out around his head on the deck like a halo. His mouth was wide, but his lips thin.

Professor Bengtsson, who'd surprised Susan and me a few nights earlier in the Psychology Department office, was propped up on his elbows and looking our way, trying to see who we were. It was difficult because he wasn't wearing his glasses. His blond ponytail was wet and bedraggled.

As I was sitting down, a head popped out of the water beside the raft and its owner called up to me, "Peggy O'Neill, I thought that was you. What are you doing here?"

It was Bill Turner, Geoff Oates's office mate. "I came with Susan," I said.

"Oh." His glance went to Susan and then quickly back to me. His face fell momentarily and then understanding dawned and his expression brightened. "No wonder you wouldn't go out with me!" he blurted out.

"Huh?"

"I mean—you're with Susan!" He was a little flustered, but also pleased that he'd got everything figured out to his satisfaction.

"That's right," I agreed.

Out of the corner of my eye I saw Troy Ridgeway push

his sunglasses back down over his eyes and turn his head to check me out again.

"When I first saw you," Bill said, spitting water, "I thought you were here on duty."

Where are the man-eating sharks when you need them? I wondered.

Bill dragged himself onto the raft and stood dripping all over me like a big dog. "You know," he blabbed on, "on account of Geoff. Don't the police still think it was suicide?"

"Geoff Oates? What've you got to do with him?" That was Lyle Gardner, still in the water, holding onto the side of the raft and squinting up at me against the bright sky. His wife was pulling herself up onto the raft next to Troy.

"Nothing," Turner continued. "Peggy found Geoff's body. She's a campus cop. I asked her out once!" He launched a laugh out over the lake that might have attracted loons.

"I think—oh, yes," Gardner said, "I think I recall seeing you that sad night."

"A campus cop, huh?" Troy Ridgeway said, treating me to a lazy grin. "What do campus cops do? You find dead people all the time, or is it mostly just making sure nobody goes up the down staircase?"

"A little of both," I said.

Shelley Gardner was standing over him, straddling his body, dripping water on him. "Hey!" he said. "Knock it off, Shelley."

"You're going to get cancer and die, you know, lying in the sun like that." She stepped over him, sat down, and looked at me curiously.

Bengtsson was sitting up now and had crossed his fat legs, Indian fashion. His nearsighted eyes were thoughtful, something you don't relish seeing on occasions like this.

"Sounds like a nice, cushy life," Troy said, his reddish eyelids fluttering with the effort to stay open.

"Most of the time it is," I agreed. "But it's like everything else, just when you think things are going well, somebody throws you a curveball." I stared out over the water, pretending to be fascinated by a becalmed sailboat. Susan gave my back a shove with her foot.

Lyle Gardner was on the raft now, too, and sat down between Troy and his wife. "You're really a friend of Pam's?" he asked.

"Of Susan's. That's right."

"How long have you two known one another?"

"Since January," Susan said. "Why?"

"That's odd," he replied. "I saw you a couple weeks ago, walking across campus with a different woman."

Susan sat up, red spots on her cheeks. "I do have women friends who are just friends, Professor Gardner," she said, keeping her voice calm with an effort. "I've seen *you* strolling across campus with women who weren't your wife, and my first thought wasn't that you were fucking them."

Both Troy Ridgeway and Shelley Gardner laughed. Gardner's face turned crimson. "That was uncalled for, Miss ... Miss ... Pam. I really didn't mean.... that is...."

"My name's Susan," she told him evenly. She turned and stared out over the water, her mouth set in an angry line.

Shelley Gardner was still looking at me. Finally she said, "You never answered Bill's question—Peggy, is it? Don't the police think Oates's death was a suicide?"

I said that, as far as I knew, they still thought it was.

Her smile kept flickering on and off, as if she knew something amusing but wasn't sure she wanted to share it. It might not mean anything, I thought. People who don't know anything often affect that look to make you think they do. She had large eyes, of some deep color I couldn't identify.

"Of course it was suicide," her husband snapped. "What else could it have been? Come on, Shelley, I don't want to burn and I don't want you to burn, either. Let's go back to shore and get something to drink." He slid to the edge of the raft and into the water, treading water while waiting for his wife. She rolled over onto her back and stretched out on the deck, her hair mixing with Troy Ridgeway's.

I burn quickly, too, so I went in shortly after Gardner did, showered, and changed into a blouse and skirt. When I came out fifteen minutes later, Troy was approaching from the beach, looking like Tarzan in a loincloth that had shrunk in the wash. As he went past me to the men's side of the cabin, he said, in his mannered drawl, "We have a lot in common, you and I."

I raised an eyebrow.

He looked me up and down slowly. "We both like women," he said.

I looked him up and down slowly. "I do, anyway," I said.

Eighteen

Later, after we'd eaten, and the sun had gone down, Chinese lanterns swung in a light breeze on the patio, and Brice Ridgeway assembled the Ph.D. candidates. He gave a speech about all they'd accomplished in their student years and all they could expect to accomplish in the future, as they went off to begin their careers at the universities that had been astute enough to hire them. Then he called them up, one by one, and told us a little about them, as they stood next to him, his arm around each of them possessively.

I sat in the shadows watching and thinking about how polished and well-behaved they all were. There was something terrifying about it.

Brice Ridgeway's wife sat opposite me, also in shadow, a number of the Ph.D. candidates' wives and girlfriends around her, learning how to be faculty wives. I've been told that, in Japanese, there are three words for *you*: one for when you're referring to people above you in station, one for people below you, and one for people who are your equals. Faculty wives learn to make that distinction, too, except that, since English has only one word for *you* they have to do it with body language and tone of voice.

Ridgeway's wife was about the same age as her husband, I guessed, in her early fifties. She had a placid face, short, ash-blond hair, and a mouth that was still lovely but beginning to gather wrinkles. She knitted the entire evening and spoke only when asked a direct question.

I looked around for Shelley Gardner but couldn't see her. Troy Ridgeway was absent, too. I'd noticed him strolling up to and around the side of the house.

The only woman present who wasn't married or otherwise related to somebody who belonged there was the woman I'd met in the Psychology Building the night Geoff Oates had died. Carly Bachman. She'd changed from her swimsuit into slacks and a bright silk blouse that shimmered in the light from the lanterns.

I'd watched her throughout the afternoon and evening and admired the way she'd mingled with the men—faculty and students alike—totally unself-consciously. She had a wide mouth and strong, white teeth and I enjoyed the music of her laughter.

When it came her turn to stand up, Ridgeway told us that she'd accepted a position at Berkeley. I wondered how she'd made it through the Psych Department and even managed to get a good job out of it, with her sense of humor and vitality intact. Ridgeway had tried to put his arm around her, too, I'd noticed, and she'd gently picked it off and let it drop, smiling to show she had no hard feelings.

When it was over, I had to go to the bathroom and decided to try to find one in the house rather than walk down to the changing room where other guests were heading. I already knew what the changing room and its bathroom looked like. I hadn't been inside the house yet.

Ridgeway's living room was richly carpeted, with a large stone fireplace at one end and leather furniture that looked expensive. Off to one side was a paneled study. I went in and looked around. A leather reclining chair, suitable to Ridgeway's size, sat next to an oak desk littered with papers, books, and an ashtray with a pipe in it. A gun rack against one wall contained a collection of rifles, and photographs on the walls featured Ridgeway standing on the corpses of various things he'd killed. I recognized Troy Ridgeway next to his father, holding his own rifle.

Between two animals' heads on the wall above the desk

was a wooden paddle, and I remembered that I'd seen one like it in the office of Mullen's lawyer, Dell Baker. I wondered if all fraternities had the same dumb initiations or if Baker and Ridgeway had belonged to the same one.

I wondered if Mrs. Ridgeway had a room of her own in the house somewhere or if she had to live her life among all this male memorabilia.

There was a tiny bathroom in the study but, like Goldilocks, I was looking for something that was just right for me, so I left that room and found the stairs—carpeted, too—and took them up to the second floor.

There were two rooms on my left, a hallway on my right. The doors were closed and I didn't open them. I started down the hall. The first door on my right was open and I glanced inside. It was obviously Troy's room, with baseball artifacts scattered all over the place in no particular order. In the middle of the room, in the midst of the sports clutter, stood Shelley Gardner and Troy Ridgeway, but they were too involved in what they were doing to notice me. They were still in their thong swimsuits and kissing as if a stormy destiny had swept them together and could easily sweep them apart again.

I'd kissed that way, too, a few times, when I'd been much younger and still confused lust with a stormy destiny.

"You're nuts, Shelley," Troy Ridgeway said, laughing, when they came up for air. "Don't you ever learn?"

"No," she said, whispering. "Never."

She rested her head on his naked chest, opened her eyes, and saw me, reflected among photographs of baseball teams in a wall-to-wall mirror.

I admired her self-control. She stayed draped in his arms, made no sudden move that caused him to look around. But her eyes opened wide in surprise and then became as cold and as flat as the mirror I was watching them in, and her face turned to stone.

I went back downstairs, used the bathroom in the study, and then walked outside and over to where Ridgeway was sitting, surrounded by some of the other faculty and students. I pulled up a lawn chair and listened to their conversation for a while, waiting for an opening.

I noticed that Lyle Gardner seemed preoccupied and his eyes had followed me as I approached from the house. "You didn't happen to see my wife up there, did you?" he asked me, in a low whisper so as not to interrupt Ridgeway.

"She was waiting her turn to use the bathroom," I said. I don't know what made me lie for her.

When there was a pause in the conversation, I asked Ridgeway what exactly the Human Genetics Research Project was.

He held a kitchen match to his pipe and lit it, his eyes swiveling to me. "To put it simply," he said, blowing out the match with smoke, "we're trying to determine what's genetic and what's environmental in the human animal, and how much, if anything, can be done to change behavior."

I said it sounded interesting and asked him how they went about it. He talked about the various kinds of studies each of the faculty and students were working on, using terms like *psychometrics, information processing,* and *speech perception and production.* They drew most of their subjects from the students in the huge introductory psychology courses, he said.

I remembered having taken one of those courses. There were five hundred of us in the auditorium and the lectures were all filmed. I later found out that two of the professors teaching the course had been dead two years or more even as I'd sat there taking down their words of wisdom and smiling faintly at their desiccated academic jokes.

"And what kind of results are you getting?" I asked Ridgeway, when he stopped talking.

He puffed a moment or two on his pipe, then replied: "Quite dramatic results, I believe. We're coming increasingly to believe that personality—your personality, my personality—is determined far more by genetics than by environment. Many people, of course, believe—or *choose* to believe—the opposite, since obviously it's considerably easier to change environmental factors than genetic ones."

"You're saying we're prisoners of biology," I said. "We can't do anything about it, and maybe we shouldn't even try."

"Well, of course, environment plays a role," he said, waving his pipe to indicate that it was only a nuisance role. "But it's a role 'scripted'—if I may continue the theatrical imagery—by your genes."

"Some people are just born to play the bad guys," I said.

"I wouldn't use a value-weighted word like *bad*," he said. "But some people are born less capable of dealing with stressful situations, say, than other people."

" 'Stressful situations', like poverty and prejudice, with no relief in sight?" I asked. "Some people have a harder time dealing with those conditions than others, you think, because of their genes?"

Carly Bachman laughed.

A look of mild annoyance flitted across Ridgeway's face. "You sound like you've been talking to Carly," he said to me.

Professor Bengtsson broke in with an eager smile. "You've read something about us, haven't you, Miss O'Neill?" he asked. "You've read some of the things that got in the papers after the flap about the Scripter Fund money."

Out of the corner of my eye, I could see Shelley Gardner stroll down from the house. She'd changed into brightly colored slacks and a matching jacket.

"It sounds vaguely familiar," I said.

"The Scripter Fund is a large, private foundation that the media, in their wisdom, decided has a racist agenda," Ridgeway grated. "None of us in the Human Genetic Research Project knew anything about that—or, to be honest, cared—none of us who actually are engaged in any meaningful research, that is," he added, glaring at Bengtsson.

"Money is money, after all. Value neutral, like good research."

"Ha!" Carly Bachman said.

Ridgeway made a face. "But then somebody leaked word to a newspaper reporter that the Scripter people were racist right-wingers and that some of our funding came from them. We found ourselves in the glare of publicity."

"Some psychologists at other institutions," Carly said, "have been accused of using Scripter money to do research with the intention of showing that race is a factor in such things as intelligence, job performance—even morality."

"But we don't do that here," Ridgeway said.

"You don't do anything that's consciously racist," Carly said with a smile, with emphasis on *consciously*. I wondered how she had not only managed to survive in the Psychology Department but to have landed a good position at Berkeley.

"I know, Carly, I know," Ridgeway said roughly. "I agree with you that there's some cultural bias—how could there not be? But we can compensate for our biases, and, over time, our tests are getting better."

"But they're still flawed—yet being published and disseminated just as if they were objective science—whatever that is," she replied.

There was a pause while Ridgeway and Carly Bachman stared at each other. Then Ridgeway laughed without much humor and said, "I don't want to get into a pissing contest with a skunk tonight, Carly. Anybody interested in your ideas can read your dissertation."

Troy Ridgeway had joined the group, strolling up from the lake. He must have left the house by the front entrance and taken a roundabout course. He was still in his thong, as though he suspected that a body was all he had to offer. As he approached, I watched him to see whether he knew I'd seen him with Shelley. I couldn't tell. His eyes met mine incuriously and then passed on.

Ridgeway suddenly remembered me, turned, and said,

"We dropped the Scripter money. I personally saw to that. God knows we didn't need it—although Lyle apparently thought we did."

"That's not fair, Brice!" Gardner protested. "I said I didn't think we should bow to public pressure. By giving back the Scripter money, we were as good as admitting that they're a racist outfit."

"They are, Lyle," his wife said, softly and sweetly. He turned and glared at her.

"The only reason I asked about your project," I said, "was because a neighbor of mine told me he was giving some of his money to it."

"Oh, who?" Lyle Gardner asked.

"His name's Harold Mullen."

There was a silence that was broken finally by Brice Ridgeway. "I hope he does," he said, relighting his pipe and squinting at me through the smoke.

"Mullen . . . Mullen," Lyle Gardner said, as if trying to place the name. He was watching Ridgeway, as if waiting for a signal of some kind.

Bengtsson turned to Ridgeway and told him how he'd found Susan and me looking for Mullen's name in the project's budget book late one night.

Ridgeway gave Susan a long look and then turned to me. "And did you find it?"

"No."

"That's too bad."

One of the graduate students burst out, "Mullen! Harold Mullen. I knew that name rang a bell! Feeble old man with wispy hair who used a walker, right? All bundled up, even though it was Indian summer." When I nodded, he continued, "This old fellow came to the department one afternoon and we showed him around—don't you remember, Professor Gardner, you were there, you chatted with him for a bit. He asked all kinds of strange questions about what we were up to. He'd obviously read some of the bad publicity about us and the Scripter Fund, and he wanted to know if it was true."

The student's eyes kept going to Gardner, as if checking his facts. He didn't seem to notice that Gardner wasn't enjoying his story. I glanced at Ridgeway. He looked as though he wished he'd flunked the kid out years ago. The student seemed to realize he'd put his foot in it and shut up as he was about to say something else.

Gardner stepped into the silence. "I didn't recall the name," he said, "but now that you remind me . . . it does ring a bell."

Bengtsson turned to Ridgeway, his face alight with malice. "You took this Mullen person to dinner at the president's house one night, Brice, didn't you?" He laughed, his ponytail bobbing on his plump rounded shoulders. "You thought he was rolling in money, I seem to recall. How much did he leave us, anyway? Enough so we don't need to write another grant proposal for the rest of our lives?"

Ridgeway chuckled dryly. "Oh, yes," he said, "I do remember this Mr. Mullen. He was sent to us by the University Club. Somebody there—Stanford Driggs, I believe— assured me he was quite well off, although I'm not sure what grounds Stanford had for thinking so. He suggested some of us in the HGRP might want to talk to him. Mullen had read something somewhere about what we're doing, and he was interested in knowing more."

I turned to the graduate student and asked him what he'd meant when he said that Mullen had obviously read some of the bad publicity about the HGRP.

"Well," he said, glancing nervously at Ridgeway and then Gardner, "he seemed to know about the Scripter money and he wanted to know if having to give it back would hurt us. That's all." He clamped his mouth shut.

"I don't think he mentioned Scripter to me," Ridgeway said.

"Do you take any prospective donor who happens by to dinner at the president's?" I asked him incredulously.

"Of course not. But I happened to be having dinner with Hightower that week, so I thought, Why not kill two birds with one stone? The old fellow looked to me to be on his last legs, and I figured it might do him some good to meet the University president and his wife. And who knows how much money he might have? Driggs said he thought he had quite a bit. God knows, the University needs it—more than we do, I can assure you." He smiled grimly. "Besides, dinner with the president and his wife is always a waste of an evening. How's the old fellow getting along?" he asked me.

"He's dead."

"I'm sorry to hear that," he said, not missing a beat. "I think he did say something about cancer. That was why he was in a hurry to dispose of his money, as I recall. I hadn't heard that he'd died, but I suppose he must have by now. I hope some needy unit of the University did get his money."

He turned to Susan and said, in a heavy attempt at humor, "We haven't received a huge bequest lately that you haven't mentioned, have we, Susan?"

"Not recently," she said.

"Well, let's hope Mullen's money went to a good cause," Ridgeway said, looking as though he were about to change the subject.

"He didn't die of cancer," I said. "His house burned down with him inside."

"How awful!" Shelley Gardner exclaimed. "When?"

"The second of August. The reason I remember is, it's the same day Geoff Oates died."

"Killed himself, don't you mean?" Bengtsson asked me.

Susan said, "It was Geoff Oates who went out and got Mr. Mullen from his taxi and took him up to the HGRP, the afternoon he visited the department."

"What a strange coincidence," Lyle Gardner said, softly.

"What makes it even stranger," I said, "is that I think I saw Oates with Mullen on the Fourth of July."

"That's impossible!" Gardner exclaimed.

"You *think* you saw him," Ridgeway said. "What exactly is that supposed to mean?"

"It means I saw a man at Mullen's house that looked a lot like the Geoff Oates I saw in a photograph after he died. Mullen said he'd come to take him to dinner."

"But he didn't say it was Oates," Gardner asked.

"I don't remember. I wonder if perhaps Oates was picking up Mullen to take him to dinner with one of you."

"The first and only time I saw the old fellow, outside of my office, was the night we had dinner at Hightower's, and that must have been about a year ago. I haven't seen or heard from him since. I doubt that you know what you're talking about, Miss O'Neill," he added, his voice hard and flat. "Geoff Oates would have had no business with Mr. Mullen."

"You don't believe for a moment that Geoffrey Oates's death was a suicide, do you, Miss O'Neill?" Professor Bengtsson blurted out suddenly. "You think it was murder."

"I only know what the police have told me," I replied. "They think it was a suicide."

"But you don't believe it, do you?" Shelley Gardner said. "Sparky's right, you're here because you think it was murder—and maybe you think this Mullen creature's death was murder, too." She shuddered, but it wasn't a very real one. "And you want to find out if one of the distinguished men here knows something about it—as if anybody here could commit murder, with the possible exception of Troy, of course, who doesn't have a degree in anything! Lyle, would you get me a beer, please?"

Gardner ignored her. "I hope Shelley's wrong, Miss O'Neill," he said to me. "I hope you didn't come out here to spy on us, because you think poor Geoff's death was anything other than the terrible thing it was—a suicide."

"I came out here because Susan invited me," I told him and looked around at a lot of disbelieving faces.

Susan and I stayed for another half hour. When I went over to thank Brice Ridgeway for the party, he took my hand, held it firmly in his for a little longer than necessary, and stared hard into my eyes. Then he nodded and let me go.

As I said good-bye to Shelley Gardner, she smiled and winked at me.

"You must have a wonderful baby-sitter," I said, "to be able to just forget about your children and enjoy yourself like this."

The life drained out of her face. She started to say something, but thought better of it. I turned to Troy and told him good night, too. He gave me a sleepy wave, looking me up and down again with his heavy-lidded eyes.

As we were driving away, I told Susan what I'd seen upstairs.

"Too bad," she said. "Lyle Gardner's a jerk who probably neglects her and his kids, but child-men like Troy Ridgeway are no way to fix anything." After a little while, she asked, "You don't think they believed you were only there as my friend—or 'friend', do you?"

I laughed. "No. There were too many liars and cheats on the lake tonight to believe anything we said. Neither Ridgeway nor Gardner wanted me to know they knew Mullen. If it hadn't been for that graduate student and Bengtsson, we might never have found out."

As she sped off the service road and onto the freeway, Susan muttered, "I suppose I ought to have checked my brakes first, to see if they were tampered with while we were enjoying the breeze from the lake."

"Brake tampering only works on mountain roads," I assured her. "We don't have any of those around here."

Nineteen

Tuesday evening, two days after Ridgeway's beach party, Susan and I met at the gym for a game of racquetball. A guy I sometimes play with was there, looking for a match, so the three of us played a game of cutthroat, the server against the other two. You work up quite a sweat that way. Afterward, while we were showering and changing into our street clothes, I asked Susan if she'd detected any fallout from Ridgeway's beach party.

She said it had been pretty much business as usual, except for one little thing. "Your effort to save the Gardners' marriage the other night doesn't seem to have worked, Peggy. Gardner moved out of his house last night. He's living in the little apartment he keeps a few blocks from campus. The word is that they're going to see a marriage counselor before deciding whether to get a divorce."

"Damn," I said, "I hate telling lies in vain! Each one you tell," I added piously, "no matter how small, diminishes you a little. Anything else?"

"Professor Bengtsson's found an unusual number of reasons to drop into my office," she replied. "He tries to pump me about you, wants to know how long we've known each other, with a kind of arch emphasis on *known*, I think. Maybe it's just friendly curiosity, but who can tell?"

Her words reminded me of what Paula had said about the glances she and Lawrence got sometimes, walking down the street.

144

"How about Ridgeway?"

"He's been his usual preoccupied self. I rode up to the third floor with him on the elevator yesterday, and he just smiled distantly and nodded when I thanked him again for the party, as if he's already forgotten about it. I thought things were going to go badly as soon as that nerd Bill Turner blew your cover on the raft. 'She found Geoff Oates's body, she's a campus cop,' " Susan said, trying to imitate Turner's rather high-pitched voice. "Did he really ask you out once?"

"Nine or ten times, actually."

"And then Bengtsson telling everybody how he caught us looking at the budget books!" She giggled. "Jesus! I thought that would be the end of the party for us."

"But it looks like we got away with it," I said.

"Maybe. You know, Peggy, I've been thinking. What if Oates just befriended Mullen after he visited the department—you know? Maybe he felt sorry for him. I mean, Oates was all alone here, he didn't have any family or close friends, and Mullen lived alone, too, didn't he? So maybe Mullen just took it into his head one day to call Oates up and invite him out on the Fourth of July—or they met by chance on the street and agreed to have dinner together. There could be all sorts of innocent reasons that they were together—if they really were. After all, you never really saw Oates alive—just dead with his face all distorted. You can't be sure he was the person you saw with Mullen, just on the basis of a snapshot."

Even Susan! I sighed and said she might be right, but I wanted to know for sure.

I talked to Paula that night when she came in from her patrol, asked her if she'd received any response to her ad about hate mail.

"It's incredible," she replied. "We've received over twenty-five letters from people saying they've received the same kind of crap we got. Lawrence just sits there and stares at it, open-mouthed. He can't believe it either. We're actually looking forward to getting mail now." She laughed, and she'd got her old laugh back, too. "Of course, we've received a couple of pieces of really pornographic hate mail, too, but it's not the same as what our old hate mailer was sending—Mullen, I suppose. I think this is somebody else, a free-lancer."

"So what's next on your agenda? Law school starts in a week, doesn't it?" This was Paula's last week as a campus cop.

"Right. We're going to have a party! We're going to invite everybody who's answered our ad to a potluck dinner at our house. Who knows, Peggy, maybe it'll help us all to see, really *see,* that we haven't been alone with this. We might get a sense of what the others have gone through, how they've dealt with it, and how they plan to deal with it in the future, if anything like this happens again. And maybe, if we pool everything we know, we might be able to figure out who he really is—Mullen, or somebody else."

I asked her if the other people had said they'd stopped getting hate mail, too.

"Yes, nobody's received any for about three weeks, since right after Mullen died. But a lot of them have said that the mail has sometimes stopped before, although never this long. They got their hopes up before that it's going to stop for good—and then it starts again."

"It's not going to start again," I said.

"I know that. But somebody else could have Mullen's address list now and might be getting ready to pick up where he left off. Our loathsome friend Dewey, for example. We need to be prepared for that—for anything. I think a party'll be a great morale booster."

"Has it occurred to you that one of the people who responded to your ad might be the hate mailer himself, if it's not Mullen—or one of his mourners, like Dewey?"

"So what? Dewey, at least, already knows our address."

"But now he might know you're giving a party."

"Maybe he'll come," she said grimly. "I'd like to meet him. How did your friend Lillian describe him? Like something a cat with neither standards nor shame might drag in? He shouldn't be too hard to spot."

I had no place to go with my search for Harold Mullen's money. I was pretty sure it must be somewhere in the Human Genetics Research Project, but I couldn't think of any way of proving it. Besides, if it was there, it was almost certainly helping to support honest research in psychology—an oxymoron, in my opinion—regardless of what Mullen might have wanted it used for.

I also thought there had to be a connection between Mullen and Geoffrey Oates that had somehow led to their deaths, but if the homicide police couldn't prove that either of their deaths had been murder, I had no illusions that I could. But I could at least talk to Oates's office mate, Bill Turner, to see what I could get out of him.

Buck thought Bill had been withholding something. Since he lived in the Psychology Building, I waited until around 1:00 A.M. and then went inside. I took the back stairs to the fourth floor, since the place was potentially alive with people I didn't want to meet.

I knocked on Turner's office door, and as I waited for him to open up, I noticed that Geoffrey Oates's nameplate had been removed from the wall even though nobody had replaced him. After what I considered an appropriate interval, I used my key to open the door, flicked on the light and stepped in.

Turner wasn't there. Either he'd ventured out of the building for something—I wondered if pizza delivery was on strike—or he was working in one of the labs. I decided to look for him. After all, I was a campus cop with a right—even a duty—to patrol anywhere I chose.

There are no labs on the fourth floor, only offices, so I took the stairs to the third floor and walked down the halls, looking into labs. In one, I found a young man huddled over a word processor. I made a noise to get his attention. I'd seen him at the beach party at Ridgeway's, but he didn't seem to recognize me in my uniform. I asked him if he'd seen Bill Turner and he said he'd gone out with some friends.

"Bowling, can you believe it?" he said. "There's a place that's open all night."

I could easily believe it.

I continued down the hall, heading for the stairs. The door was open and the lights were on in the research library where I'd first met Carly Bachman the night Oates was murdered. I stopped and looked in.

Carly was sitting on a chrome and leather sofa in the lounge area at one end of the library, reading. She looked up as I came in, but her mind was clearly still on what she was reading, so it took her a moment to process me. Then she smiled and said hello. The small coffee table in front of her was cluttered with notebooks, computer printouts, crumpled paper, and pencils. The rest of the room was made up of rows of shelves crammed with books and journals.

I congratulated her on getting the job at Berkeley and asked her why she was still poring over books in the library right before graduation. She said she had to check some data before she submitted the final copy of her dissertation to her adviser.

On the wall above her head was a framed black and white photograph of a girl, slightly blurry, like an enlargement made from a much smaller print. The girl had dark, short hair that curled at the ends, was parted in the middle, and held at her temples by white barrettes. Even though it wasn't a very clear photograph, you could see that her eyes were crescents of happiness and her small mouth was smiling. A little plaque under the picture read Grace Sterns. The library had been named for her. I also remembered seeing her name in the budget book I'd gone through with Susan.

"Do you know who she was?" I said.

Carly glanced over her shoulder, then shook her head. "No, it's been there six, seven months, I suppose. Her parents must have donated the money for the library in her name, after she died. You'd think they would've had a better picture of her, though."

"Couldn't have been her parents," I said. "That sailor suit she's wearing is from my mother's generation."

"Her kids, then?" She shrugged and grinned at me. "You really stirred things up the other night at Ridgeway's. After you left, I saw Ridgeway, Gardner, and Sparky Bengtsson with their heads together. Bengtsson's mouth was moving a mile a minute, his ratty little ponytail bobbing with excitement, and the other two were listening as if he'd finally come up with an idea worth hearing."

"I have that effect on the psychology faculty," I told her. "I never get invited to their parties twice. Do you know why I upset them?"

"Since the Scripter story was leaked to the media, they're nervous about any kind of adverse publicity. You're really not satisfied that Geoff Oates's death was a suicide?"

"No."

"And you were at Ridgeway's spying on them—on us?"

"Yes." I try not to lie to people I like.

"That took chutzpah! Why?"

I told her how I'd become interested in Mullen and how that had led me to Oates and then to the Human Genetics Research Project.

"And you think Mullen left his money to the HGRP because he thought we were conducting racist research?" She laughed. "Well, we're not. Not anymore, anyway," she added.

I pricked up my ears. "You mean you stopped after the media found out you were getting money from Scripter?"

"I don't mean that at all! Peggy, get the notion out of your head that anybody here's doing racist research! Even when we were getting Scripter money, we weren't doing anything like that."

"Then what did you mean by 'not anymore'?"

"Only that the HGRP started out with what we'd call a 'racist agenda' today. This library was called the Roy

Heslop Library until about seven months ago, when Heslop was mysteriously replaced by Grace Sterns. Heslop was a doctor who left a sum of money to the University in the 1920s for eugenics research."

"Eugenics!"

Carly laughed at my surprise. "You heard me. Sit down and I'll tell you about it." I sat down next to her on the sofa and she continued. "I got interested in this Heslop character when I first came here five years ago, so I looked him up in the files. He was a very strange bird—an early advocate of eugenics, back when not as many people had a problem with that idea as they do now. Even Margaret Sanger was a eugenicist in those days, you know.

"Like a lot of the other eugenicists, Heslop thought we should try to improve the human race by passing laws similar to those for cattle and dog breeding. He even wrote letters to the newspapers advocating a state eugenics board to approve all marriages and state-controlled sterilization boards empowered to determine who was unfit and should be sterilized."

"Did he get anywhere?"

"He certainly did! At one point, according to a favorable article on him that appeared at the time of his death, Heslop's activities had put our state in the front rank of those that administered eugenic sterilization. But he failed in his larger plan, which was to get a state eugenics marriage law passed, which would have allowed the state to approve or disapprove of marriages on the basis of theories of 'racial improvement'."

"Who gets to decide what 'racial improvement' is?" I asked.

"Exactly. I'll let anybody design any kind of ideal dog or horse they want—it's none of my business—but who gets to decide the human ideal?"

"It's like trying to pass laws against pornography," I said. "*I* know what it is, but I'm not convinced *you* do, and I wouldn't trust even my closest friend to have the power to suppress books. I wouldn't even trust myself with that power."

"Unfortunately not everybody has your healthy skepticism, Peggy. Roy Heslop believed that things like criminality—and even bad temper—were genetic traits that could be weeded out through eugenics. In one of his articles, he claimed that the eugenics marriage board would assess people's personalities and not allow two people with 'fiery' temperaments to marry. A 'fiery' person would have to marry a 'tranquil' person, for example."

"Party time and nap time would be almost indistinguishable," I said. "And the University accepted his money?"

"Sure. We've even got his books on the shelves and his collected newspaper articles in a file drawer over there," Carly said, pointing across the room. "I'm probably the only person who has looked at any of his works since the end of World War II, but it's all still there."

"Did he spell out what he wanted his money used for?"

"He wanted it used to advance the cause of race betterment through eugenics, but the way it ended up being formulated—to make it palatable to the University—was something like 'for the study and promulgation of genetics as it applies to man.' Which is pretty much what the HGRP is doing today."

"Much nicer," I said. "How come you know so much about this Heslop character?"

She grinned and took a swallow of her coffee, which had a film of cream substitute floating on the top that made me shudder.

"I'm the devil's advocate in the Human Genetics Research Project, as you may have noticed at Ridgeway's the other night. You see, my colleagues are trying to determine why people behave the way they do. They believe—or pretend to believe, at least, since it pays so well—that they can ultimately work out the connection between heredity, environment, and character. Brice Ridgeway thinks he's discovered that the root cause of such things as temper, ambition, criminality—even good and evil—is genetic: you're born with it."

"And you say he's wrong."

"No, I say he can't be sure because all the tests he uses are flawed. You see, they study large numbers of people, using questionnaires about their family background, education, religious beliefs, etc. And they bring these people in and take measurements of all kinds—that's what all the strange equipment is in some of the labs and that's what all those grad students are doing here late at night, poring over the results as the computers spew them out. It all looks very objective, and I'm convinced that it *is* about as objective as it's possible for anybody to get who isn't God. But that's just my point. My research shows that, in the last analysis, that's not really very objective. My orientation is sociological, you see, not psychological. I can look at exactly the same results as Ridgeway or Gardner and come to quite different conclusions."

"That means your research is aimed at showing that the conclusions your colleagues are coming to are worthless?"

"No, some of their research is very good. All I'm trying to show is that they have to be more careful in what they say about behavior because their results—as well as mine—are *contingent,* and always will be."

"Contingent on what?"

"Lots of things, some of which we probably aren't even aware of yet. One obvious example is intelligence testing. There's never been a measure of intelligence that isn't skewed by the value system of the people who make and administer the test. The bottom line in all such tests is that the 'smarter' people will always be those who know the things *you* think are important in *your* culture in *your* particular time—people, in other words, who grew up in your kind of neighborhood, in your kind of family.

"Some of my colleagues," Carly went on, getting up and stalking up and down in front of me, "have developed skills tests. In the past, such tests have been used to exclude women from flying jet fighters, for example. That's turned out to be a bunch of hooey, of course. In the abstract, at least, women ought to be *better* equipped to fly a modern jet fighter than men. After all, flying jets these days is just punching buttons, isn't it? And women have been doing that kind of work at least since the invention of the typewriter.

"*But,* I hear you object," she said, pausing to glare down at me, arms akimbo, "there are other tests that show that women are less *aggressive* than men, right? So their greater button-pushing skills are negated when it comes to flying jet fighters in combat, aren't they?"

Meekly, I told her I'd heard all my life that women were inherently less aggressive than men, but I didn't believe it.

"Of course you don't, you're not a man. That conclusion is based on testing actual women, of course—which means, testing women who have lived for a longer or shorter period of time in a society that rewards them for not being aggressive! I mean, who wants an aggressive *typist,* for God's sake?"

"And people like Ridgeway and Gardner let you get away with questioning their results?"

She laughed. "Of course. They can point to me as proof that they're trying to be as objective as possible in their work. As I said, I'm the resident devil's advocate. And besides, I'm just one small, tedious voice in a sea of men's voices that utter results that look good in supermarket tabloids: 'Identical twins separated at birth both play nose harp'—that sort of thing."

I told her I was impressed that she'd managed to survive the Psychology Department as an apparently healthy human being.

"I wouldn't have survived," she replied, "if I hadn't been smarter than just about anybody else in the department and willing to work harder. And," she added ruefully, "it helps that I'm big and tall. It's harder for a man to dismiss you—or try to cuddle you—if you can look him in the eye."

"I noticed that Ridgeway did try to cuddle you at the party," I said with a smile.

She smiled, too, remembering. "I can handle it, because I know he's unaware of what he's doing—just like the blind spot in his research."

"Lyle Gardner doesn't seem to enjoy Ridgeway's arrogance," I said.

"They've got a pretty tense relationship, although I'm not sure Ridgeway notices it. But the rest of us do. Gardner's got a real father-son complex in connection with Ridgeway, made worse by the fact that he's ten years older than Ridgeway, originally brought Ridgeway here, and expected to be appointed head of the HGRP."

"What kind of a future do you think Geoff Oates had in the department?" I asked her.

"I didn't know him very well," she began, but broke off abruptly and stared at something behind me. I looked to see what it was.

Professor Bengtsson, soft, pear-shaped, was standing in the doorway. "Here again, are you, Officer O'Neill?" Light glimmered on his glasses.

I told him I was on my break.

He looked at his watch. "A long break, I think. But there's so little crime on campus that I don't suppose it matters—just the occasional suicide, such as that of the unfortunate Geoffrey Oates. What's she asking you about, Miss Bachman?"

"Mostly, I've been telling her about the kind of research I'm engaged in," Carly replied evenly. "I was also telling her about old Dr. Heslop."

"Oh, yes, Heslop—an interesting man. We used to have his portrait right above your heads, didn't we? I wonder where it is now." He shook his head, his ponytail bobbed. "Times change and, no doubt, he became an embarrassment to the project."

Bengtsson smiled at Carly and gave me a long, thoughtful stare, then he disappeared down the hall as quietly as he'd materialized.

Carly watched him go, shaking her head, then got up and said, "I know where Heslop's picture is, it's stuck behind the files over here. You want to see what a real leader in medical science, circa 1920, looked like?" She went over and dragged a huge oil portrait out from behind a file cabinet, leaned it up against the wall, and blew the dust off.

Heslop had been a fine-looking man in his time, I supposed. Heavy jowls, full lips, tight collar strangling a fat neck, and a belly like one of the early twentieth-century presidents—Taft or Teddy Roosevelt, when ponderous meant power. He probably didn't have a hard muscle in his body.

"I'm sure that when he saw the racial ideal of man, he saw himself," Carly said. "He wouldn't last five minutes in a workout program at the Y today."

Twenty

It was about five minutes to roll call the next night when Lt. Bixler's bulk filled the squad room door. "O'Neill," he said, when he spotted me, "my office. Now." He turned and stomped back down the hall.

That was succinct.

Jesse Porter looked at me out of the corners of his eyes and said, "What've you done now, Peggy?"

"I spray painted a naked picture of him on the rear wall of the building. I can't imagine how he recognized himself, since it was from the back."

I went over and poured another cup of coffee and headed for Bixler's office. This was a great improvement over the first time I'd been called on the carpet by the Rooster, which is what we call him. Then I'd been a rookie—nervous, self-conscious and defensive. But times change and people change, too—except the Bixlers of the world, of course. I was getting fairly skilled at balancing doing what it takes not to be fired with my desire not to grovel at his large, flat feet.

He was at his desk when I walked into his office, reading, or pretending to read, a sheaf of notes in front of him. His lips were moving. His lips move when he looks at pictures. I pulled a chair up to the side of his desk and sat down. I've found that if I stand in front of him, I either have to stand at attention, or shift from leg to leg uncomfortably. Neither option holds much appeal.

While waiting for him to finish his reading, I studied the man. He's a source of endless fascination—but then, so is death, which is also best experienced in the abstract.

Melvin Bixler's about fifty, with a head that would look good on a banquet table, an apple holding the mouth open. His hair is iron gray and teased into exotic configurations in an attempt to hide the baldness on top. The ruse apparently fools him. His eyes are round, mean, and close-set in a face like a bladder. The resemblance to the eugenicist Roy Heslop was striking.

I used to think Bixler was a sexist and a racist, but I misjudged him: He hates everybody and takes back on those under him what he feels he has to give to those over him. He's not a nice man.

He looked up from his reading matter and asked, mildly enough, "What're you doing in your spare time, O'Neill?"

"What do you mean?"

"Or maybe I should call you Patty Mullen," he said with heavy sarcasm.

Oops! I hadn't expected that. I'd been Patty Mullen to only two people in my life, Stanford Driggs, one of the directors of the University Club and his receptionist.

Bixler's grin at my surprise was a smear of triumph. "You have something you want to say on that subject?"

He'd got me. Suddenly I wanted to throw shrinking powder on myself and disappear into a mouse hole, a fantasy I'd had as a kid and, later, in the parochial school I'd attended, when I'd done something that had attracted the attention of Sister Mary Angelica Hitler.

"I did that on my own time," I said.

Bixler leaned back in his chair and slowly rolled a letter opener between his hands, perhaps trying to hypnotize me the way he'd seen somebody do it on television. "Did what on your own time?" he asked sweetly.

"Passed myself off as Patty Mullen to try to get some information from Stanford Driggs of the University Club."

He fell forward, his fat elbows hitting the desk with a

dull thud. "Lied to a University official is what you mean, isn't it?"

"I don't think Driggs is a University official," I said. "I was told that the University Club is a private institution with no connection to the University."

Bixler didn't know that, wasn't sure I wasn't pulling his leg. So he blustered, of course. "That don't matter, O'Neill. Whatever the situation, Driggs still works on behalf of the University and he's got a lot of pull. You hear me? You know what I'm saying?"

"Yes." I struggled to keep my eyes locked on his. If you don't move and stare them in the eye, I've heard they won't strike. I wanted to keep my job, at least until I decided what I was really meant to do with my life.

"I called your friend Hansen," he said, "to see if you're helping him with something."

Bixler knows I've helped Buck in the past, and that makes him a little nervous, even though Buck has no authority over the campus cops.

"I'm not helping Lt. Hansen with anything," I said.

"I know that now, O'Neill. He told me that. You know why you're not helping him with anything? Because there's no homicides at the University, there's nothing here to interest him! So what the hell are you doing?" He scratched his head with the letter opener, put what he may have thought was a quizzical look on his face. "Help me understand, O'Neill. Try."

This massive, stupid face is reality, I thought, fighting an urge to get up and run out of there. How can I explain to it what I'm trying to do? And what good would it do if I tried?

"A neighbor of mine told me he left his money to the University," I said. "I want to know what for."

"That's it? That's all?"

"That's it. That's all."

Bixler exploded. He rose to his full majesty—he's five eight in his lifts—shoved his chair back so it hit the wall with a bang, and glared down at me. "Using an alias, O'Neill, you invade the offices of an important and busy man—a director of the University Club who has devoted his life to raising money for the University! You tell him you think the University may have accepted money for some kind of racist research from some old guy named Mullen, and you're hoping he'll help you find out where it is! Is that correct so far?"

I nodded.

"And furthermore," Bixler continued, as if I hadn't responded, his eyes darting to the notes on his desk, "you use a secretary friend of yours in the Psychology Department to get into that department's confidential files. Then you use that same woman to help you infiltrate an official departmental gathering at the home of one of the University's most powerful and prominent professors, where you insinuate that they are doing racist research and that one of them might have murdered a graduate student—and maybe the old man, too. Is this also correct?"

He leaned over his desk at me, panting deeply, as if he were a lion who'd just brought down a gazelle and had to catch his breath before eating it.

"It's true," I replied, since I could hardly have summed it up better myself. To be sure, I wasn't the one who said I thought Oates had been murdered—Shelley Gardner had accused me of thinking that—but I didn't see any reason to get picky with Bixler after such a masterful performance. I did think I had to come to Susan's defense, though. "It's true, except that Susan Carlisle, the secretary, was an unwitting accomplice."

"A what?"

"An unwitting accomplice," I repeated. I've learned that cliches soothe men like Bixler. "She had no idea I was trying to find out what the old man did with his money. She thought I was just curious about it because I'd known him. I used her, Lieutenant. I used her shamelessly." I considered hanging my head, decided that would be slathering it on too thick, even for Bixler.

"You did?" He glanced uncertainly down at the notes on his desk, gained courage from them. "Then why'd she take you out to Ridgeway's with her? She told one of the professors she *wasn't* going to the party and the next thing is, she went—and you went with her."

My recent life was apparently an open book to a lot of people, but at the moment I had other things to think about than the implications of that.

"When Susan told me about the party," I said, "I told her I thought it sounded like it might be fun. Little did she realize I was using her as a means to satisfy my curiosity."

"You're just a natural-born liar, O'Neill, aren't you?"

I didn't contradict Bixler, but I like to think my skills in that area are as much the result of environment as of heredity. Maybe I'd ask Professor Ridgeway about it, if I ever saw him again.

"You think this student—this Oates—was murdered," Bixler probed, curious in spite of himself. "Everybody else, including your friend Hansen, thinks he committed suicide. What makes you think you know better?"

"I don't *know* better, but I think it's more than a little strange that he and Mullen died violent deaths within twenty-four hours of each other, that Mullen was interested in the research project Oates was a part of, and that they'd met."

"But you have no proof?"

"No, of course not."

Bixler kept his beady eyes on me for a long moment. I wondered if it really was just curiosity on his part, or if he was going to report what I said to Driggs or Ridgeway, or somebody else.

"Of course not," he repeated. "Because if you had proof, you'd be a good cop and tell your friend Hansen and let him handle it, wouldn't you?"

"Absolutely."

"This old man you think is a racist—Mullen—he died in a fire that was ruled accidental. And the student, Oates, killed himself. The only murder conspiracy is in your run-away imagination, O'Neill. On account of that imagination, you've annoyed and outraged some very important and very influential people connected with this University. You're going to stop it."

"Who's annoyed and outraged?" I asked, deciding to try to get a little specific information out of Bixler. "Besides Stanford Driggs, I mean?"

"I'm asking the questions, O'Neill."

"Right. Sorry."

"Not as sorry as you're going to be if you do anything to piss them off again. You're a representative of the University police at all times and everything you do reflects on us. Remember that. You've been warned—officially warned. If we get another complaint, O'Neill, you're in deep doo-doo. You understand that?"

"I do," I said. "Deep doo-doo."

He narrowed his eyes, hoping that would help him detect any evidence that I might be making fun of him. Satisfied that I wasn't, he droned on. "My advice to you is this: Steer clear of the Psych Department. You don't need to walk through that building every night, and you don't need to take your breaks in there, either, pumping students for information that's none of your business. There are plenty of other buildings on this campus to patrol. Get it, O'Neill?"

"Got it."

"Good."

He picked up the notes he'd been consulting and shook them, perhaps hoping that something really devastating would fall out. I didn't wait for it, I got up and headed for the door.

The most interesting thing about the interview with Bixler, I thought as I walked my beat that night, was learning that Stanford Driggs had been a part of the complaint against me. I wondered how he'd found out I'd got onto the Human Genetics Research Project. I hadn't mentioned to anybody at Ridgeway's that I'd talked to him. Ridgeway had mentioned that it was Driggs who'd told him about Mullen and his money and brought them together in the first place.

I wondered who had contacted whom. Had Driggs warned somebody in the Human Genetics Research Project about me before the beach party, or had somebody in the project called Driggs about me after the party, to find out if I'd been there? Bixler had also known about my going through the Psych Department's budget records and about Susan changing her mind about going to the beach party, so Professor Bengtsson must have been a part of the complaint against me, too.

It seemed to me that I'd stirred up some heat and smoke in ashes that were supposed to be cold.

Around 1:00 A.M., I spotted a car in a deserted parking lot down by the river. Lovers use the lot sometimes late at night and rapists have been known to prey on them. I approached cautiously, remembering what I'd found not long before in a car like this. A shadow in the front seat looked like a single torso with two heads. I went over and flashed my light in the window on the passenger's side. The torso separated into two normal-sized people, a young man and a woman, their startled faces trying to see me beyond the flashlight beam. I reversed it so they could see my uniform and shield and the woman rolled down her window.

"What do you want?" She was buttoning up her blouse.

Politely but firmly, I told her to get out of the car, I wanted to talk to her away from it.

"Can't you talk to me here?"

"We were just about to leave anyway," the man hollered, leaning around her.

"Come out," I said to her, and to him, "you stay there."

The door opened and she got out, straightening her jeans and tucking in her blouse. I kept my eye on the man as she walked toward me.

"I've got a pistol," I told her, "and I know how to use it. That man can't hurt either of us. Are you with him voluntarily?"

She laughed, suddenly understanding, a warm, erotic laugh. "You bet! It's okay, officer."

I could see that it was.

I wrote down the license number, gave him a warning citation and stood in their dust until their taillights disappeared over the hill.

A hand fell on my shoulder, hard. I swung around. It was Troy Ridgeway, a sleepy grin on his young-old face.

"A little slow, officer," he drawled. "I could've killed you, and you wouldn't have known what hit you."

Struggling to breathe normally, I asked him what that was supposed to prove.

"That you oughtta make sure your ass is covered before you charge," he said. "Didn't they teach you that in cop school?"

"They taught us we're pretty much slow-moving targets to the crazies, Troy. That comes with the job. What do you want?"

He threw out his long arms to show he wasn't carrying a weapon. "Nothing! I just came by to see what campus cops do, walking around all alone in the middle of the night. Like I told you, I'm thinking of becoming one."

The only way he could have found me down here by the river was if he'd followed me. That wouldn't have been hard to do on the Old Campus.

I started walking up the road back to the campus. He fell in step beside me.

"I liked the way you put a scare into those heterosexual kids making out back there," he said.

"What do you want to be a campus cop for?" I asked him. "I thought you owned some kind of sports bar, shaped like a baseball, out on the strip. Shouldn't you be there this time of night, glad-handing the customers, counting the receipts?"

"That's none of your business," he said, his lazy voice suddenly becoming harsh. "You're making a lot of things your business that aren't, aren't you?"

I stopped, turned to look at him. "Is that why you're

here? To tell me to mind my own business? I guess I really must have upset your dad the other night, huh?"

"You kidding?" His face came alive, briefly. "Who do you think you are—you think a campus cop could upset a man like my dad? Give me a break!"

"I upset somebody in the Psych Department enough to have him lodge a complaint against me," I said.

"My dad wouldn't bother. You're insignificant," he said. "Believe it: My dad doesn't even know you're alive. But I do."

He assumed a batter's stance and took a wicked swing at an imaginary baseball. It couldn't have been a curveball, though, since he shielded his eyes with one hand and watched it sail over a distant center-field fence. Then he turned to me and said with a grin, "Hey, a woman who walks around campus in the middle of the night can't afford a lot of enemies, can she? So let's be friends."

"I'll just be more careful," I said, and headed into the Old Campus, leaving him standing there.

The next morning, I called Ginny Raines and asked her if she'd do a background check on Troy Ridgeway for me. Ginny's got a good working arrangement with her detective counterparts on the city police—they often ask her help in locating students wanted for various crimes.

"Who's Troy Ridgeway?"

"A former minor league baseball player who lives with his parents. He owns a sports bar out on the strip—A Whole New Ball Game. Last night he scared the piss out of me. He looks like trouble and I wonder if he's got a record. I'd also like to know how he was able to afford a bar on what he made playing ball in the minor leagues."

There was a long pause, broken only by the sound of Ginny chewing thoughtfully on something that had the crunch of something lo-cal and tasteless.

"Bixler warned you to stay away from the Psychology Department and everything connected with it," she said.

"I am," I said. "That's why I'm asking you to do this for me."

"Why?"

"You mean, the ultimate *why*, with a capital *W*?"

"Yeah—that's the *why* I had in mind."

"I think the Psych Department owes a little old lady a new roof and porch."

"That's one of those Zen answers, right? I didn't know you were into that now, Peggy. I'll see what I can find out for you."

"Thanks, Ginny. Dinner's at my place next time. We'll watch *The Band Wagon* with Fred Astaire and Cyd Charisse, and do take-out from one of those gourmet delivery services. How does barbecued ribs, Texas toast, french fries and coleslaw sound?"

"Skip the coleslaw, it doesn't travel well."

Twenty-One

Ginny called me back the next afternoon as I was watching the molecules that would constitute my lunch writhing in the microwave.

"Troy Ridgeway had to go to the nursery," she said.

"And sit in the corner?"

"Not that kind of nursery. I mean the kind where you buy trees and shrubs. There's a family in town that owns a small one. If you're strapped for cash and your credit's not all that good, or the reason you need money doesn't look appealing to your bank's loan officer, you might consider going to the nursery, if you're stupid enough."

"And the interest rates are high," I said, catching on, "and the penalty for nonpayment severe."

"You got it. And Troy doesn't own A Whole New Ball Game anymore, either. The place is boarded up—has been for several months. My source tells me it's just an empty shell of a baseball, sitting out there surrounded by thriving nightclubs run by smarter businessmen than Troy."

"In a word, he went bankrupt."

"Right. He declared bankruptcy—except that the nurserymen don't take ten cents on the dollar."

"Was he able to pay them off?"

"The last time you saw him, did he have kneecaps?"

"Yes."

"Then he paid 'em off."

"How much did he owe?"

"A quarter of a million bucks. Maybe a little more."

I whistled. "Thanks, Ginny."

Professors of psychology make plenty of money, I knew that. But I wondered if they made enough to keep up beautiful and expensive places on Forest Lake, one of the most exclusive lakes we have around here, and give their kids allowances big enough to cover debts to loan sharks.

That night I decided to avoid the river—no sense making myself an easy target for the Troy Ridgeways of the world. Besides, there was a chill in the air, as summer began leaning into fall. Instead, I sat in one of the deserted lounges in the student union and drank a cup of coffee and tried to work out a chronology.

Harold Mullen had retired two years ago. He'd sold his property to his lawyer, Dell Baker. A little over a year later, he discovered he had cancer and thought he had only a short time to live.

He talked to Baker about what to do with his money, and Baker had put him in touch with the University Club. Someone there—probably Stanford Driggs—created a living trust for Mullen that named the Club as trustee when he died.

Sometime in the late fall of last year, Mullen had visited the Human Genetics Research Project. That's when he first met Geoff Oates. Sometime later, Brice Ridgeway had taken him to the University president's for dinner, yet at the beach party on Sunday, Ridgeway had trouble remembering Mullen—or pretended to. And nobody else would admit to knowing Mullen, either, or remembered his visit to the HGRP, until the graduate student blurted it out.

A disturbing thought struck me: Someone in the HGRP had heard about my visit to Stanford Driggs. Who, I wondered, and when? If it was before the beach party on Sunday, then some member of the faculty had known from the beginning why I was there. It's an odd feeling, realizing somebody might have been watching me while I thought I was watching them unobserved.

I was supposed to die this winter, Mullen had told me with a gleeful chuckle. *The doctor gave up on me, but I fooled him.*

The Fourth of July rolled around, he was still alive— and going out to dinner with Geoffrey Oates. A month later, both he and Oates were dead.

Where did Oates fit in? His office mate, Bill Turner, told Buck he thought Oates had been depressed the last few weeks before his death, but he couldn't, or wouldn't, tell Buck why. The last time I'd tried to talk to him, Bill had been out bowling. Since then I'd been warned to stay away from the Psych Building.

Bill might not want to talk to me there, either, assuming he wanted to talk to me at all. Up in his office/home he was as safe from me as if he were surrounded by a moat with a fire-breathing monster swimming around in it. I supposed I could disguise myself as a pizza delivery person, but that seemed a little extreme. Pizza did, however, seem to be the way to lure Bill down from his aerie, assuming he was lurable.

As soon as I got up the next morning, I called his office and got an answering machine that began, "Geoff Oates and Bill Turner can't come to the phone right now." I didn't want to leave a message, so I just hung up.

When I called again that evening around six, Bill answered on the first ring.

"What's up?" he asked cautiously, when I told him who I was.

"I had a sudden desire to take you out for pizza, Bill. Genio's." Genio's makes the best pizza in town.

He laughed nervously. "You've been banned from the Psych Building, huh?"

"Not quite. But I've been told I'm not supposed to bother you people anymore, asking questions about Geoffrey Oates and stuff like that. So I thought I'd bother you over dinner instead."

There was a long pause. "Why me?"

"You were Oates's office mate. You knew him better than anybody else in the Psych Department."

"Jesus!" Something seemed to dawn on Bill. "You really do think Geoff was murdered, don't you? And you're working undercover with the city police on it, right?"

"Wrong. The homicide cops have dismissed his death as a suicide. They aren't interested in him at all. And I don't think anything yet. Maybe his death really was suicide. But I want to know the connection between Oates and Harold Mullen, the old man we talked about at Ridgeway's."

"I don't know anything about that. Honest, I really don't. And I told the cops everything I know about Geoff."

"Let's have dinner and talk about it," I said.

Another pause, long enough to make me question my Mata Hari appeal. "Professor Gardner kind of told us—without really telling us, you know?—that we shouldn't talk to you. The HGRP doesn't need negative publicity—not after the Scripter Fund flap. I could get in trouble if it gets back to anybody that I talked to you."

"We could wear false noses and mustaches," I said.

He laughed, not sure if I was serious, but after a little more hesitation, he agreed to meet me at Genio's that night at eight.

It was raining by the time I got there, a cold late August downpour announcing that summer was almost over. I parked and ran inside. Bill Turner was in a booth way in back of the restaurant. He stuck his head out into the aisle and waved. Either the rain had plastered his unruly hair to his head, or else he hadn't combed it recently. He looked the way he'd looked when I woke him up the morning of Geoff Oates's death. But he had shaved, which was something—a special treat for me, maybe.

Genio's is the way pizza restaurants used to be, according to people I know who are old enough to remember the good old days; candles in Chianti bottles, red-and-white checked tablecloths, and the pizzas are hand-tossed and made in brick ovens in the kitchen wall. There's now a selection of yuppie pizzas littered with the kinds of ingredients Buck Hansen might use—eggplant and duck liver, cilantro and mesquite-smoked chicken—but the waiters and waitresses always ask you if you're sure you really want that and treat you rudely if you insist you do.

We ordered a house salad each and a large pizza, half pepperoni, half Italian sausage, with green olives over the whole thing. Bill ordered a carafe of Chianti for himself, and I ordered a lime sparkling water. Bill was visibly nervous and he kept checking the aisle, even though Genio's is a long way from the University.

"You told the homicide cops you thought Geoff Oates had been depressed over his future in psychology for several months before he died," I said. "Nobody else would admit they noticed anything like that. You were Oates's office mate and you saw a lot of him, so you must have had some reason for saying what you did."

He watched me as I talked, and I could see that he was trying to make up his mind about something. When I'd finished, he said, "You're really not working with the city cops?"

"I told you, they think his death was suicide."

"So it's just you who thinks it was murder?"

"And you."

"Not me!" He threw up his hands, almost tipped over his wineglass. "I don't think anything."

"If it was murder, do you want Geoff's killer to get away with it—maybe kill again?"

He changed the subject, trying to get off the hook. "This old man, Mullen. He burned up in his house, right?"

"Right. He was a racist who sent out hate mail to people."

"So it could've been one of his victims who burned him up, couldn't it, if it wasn't an accident?"

"Sure, if one of them had managed to find out where he lived. But he was pretty careful. He'd done it for years without getting caught. And then, a month after I saw him with Geoff Oates, he burned to death—right after Oates died."

"You really did see Geoff with him?"

"I'm pretty sure I did."

"Pretty sure. What if it's all in your mind, Peggy?"

"Then I'll have gone to a lot of trouble for nothing," I said, "and you'll have got a free pizza out of it."

"And a lot of trouble, too, if any of the HGRP finds out I've talked to you."

"Well, you've already gone against orders just for being here with me."

He laughed. "And if I don't tell you everything I know, you'd probably tell them we were together tonight."

Bill was stalling, trying to work up the courage to tell me something. "Oh, I would," I assured him with a smile. "I'd call Brice Ridgeway—anonymously, of course—and tell him I'd seen you and a redheaded campus cop with your heads together in a pizza parlor."

He suddenly turned serious. "Geoff and I spent a lot of time in that office together, but he wasn't an easy guy to get to know. Very hard-working, very earnest. And he'd set his mind on getting a Ph.D. in psychology and getting a position in a college or university somewhere."

Bill paused, gulped a swallow of wine, stirred his salad with a fork, and then shoved it away abruptly.

"He ran Professor Gardner's errands for him last year," he went on, staring up at me. "This year, too, until he—died. All Gardner's students have to do some of that, of course—me, too—but Gardner's known for picking out one grad student to be his regular gofer, and these last two years it was Geoff. It's not a good omen, becoming Gardner's gofer, because it means he doesn't think your research is as important as some of his other students', so your time isn't as valuable.

"Anyway, one morning in June, he called Geoff into his office and told him to drive out to his house and get some papers he'd forgotten. Gardner lives about half an hour from here—that's why he keeps an apartment in town, in case he stays at the U late and is too tired to drive home. Geoff drove out there. He'd been there before, of course, at little gatherings Gardner had occasionally, so he knew the way.

"Gardner had told him where he'd find the papers—by the swimming pool in the backyard. He told Geoff to just walk around the side of the house, open the gate, and go through to the pool. He said his wife wouldn't be home— she had taken the kids to day care and then had a tennis lesson.

"So that's what Geoff did. He went through the gate and around the house to the pool and, lo and behold—Shelley Gardner wasn't off somewhere at a tennis lesson. She was lying on an air mattress beside the pool and lying on top of her was—can you guess, Peggy?"

"Easy," I said. "Troy Ridgeway."

Bill looked at me in surprise. "Troy? No, but you're close. His dad."

The pizza arrived then, a great, reeking wheel of tomato, cheese, olives, mushrooms, and meat that the waiter slid onto the table between us. Bill and I both turned our attention to it—sometimes I do have my priorities straight. Ten minutes later, when we'd been reduced to nibbling indifferently on crusts, Bill continued his story.

"To a passing stranger," he said, "or in a movie, it would have been a comic scene, but Geoff wasn't a passing stranger and he wasn't watching a movie. He was watching his life pass in front of his eyes."

"He told you all this?"

"Yeah, in our office—speaking very softly, too. We were both working there one night a few weeks after it happened, and he asked me if he could talk to me. I knew something had been bothering him, so I said sure. He was pretty slow to get to the point—he wasn't even sure he wanted to—but finally he did. He said he wanted my opinion about something. He knew I wouldn't spread it around, and I haven't. I was even sorry he told me! You're the first person I've repeated it to. If it gets back to Ridgeway that I know the story, my career's as dead as Geoff."

"I believe you."

"Geoff tried to backpedal out of there as fast as he could, but he didn't get far. Brice Ridgeway, as everybody knows, is a very direct man. He came after Geoff, his face white with anger. He caught up with him, dragged him back to the pool, and threw him in. When Geoff climbed out, he made him stand there, right in front of Mrs. Gardner, and he told him a few things—'home truths', he called them."

Bill poured the rest of the wine into his glass and took a swallow. "You'd have thought it was Geoff who'd been caught in a shameful act and was standing there naked. Ridgeway swore that, if Geoff told Gardner, he'd destroy him, he'd make sure Geoff never got a job anywhere, in any field, in any college or university in the world. Geoff believed him, and so do I."

"What happened then?"

"A few days later, after thinking it over, Geoff went to Ridgeway and said he wanted to leave the University and enroll in a program somewhere else. Ridgeway told him no, said he'd have to stay here and finish up. Geoff asked him what kind of future he had in the department and Ridgeway laughed and gave him a hearty slap on the back, just as if they were old buddies.

"He said he'd already put the little incident at the Gardner's pool out of his mind and he was surprised that Geoff was still concerned about it. He said it wasn't entirely Geoff's fault, and he added that it had probably taught Geoff a good lesson about knocking first before coming in. As long as Geoff kept quiet about what he'd seen, he'd be okay."

"Did Geoff believe him?"

Bill sagged back in the booth, suddenly looking tired. "I don't know," he said. "I sure as hell wouldn't have. If I'd been Geoff, I'd have switched to some other field—a field as far from psychology as I could get. Men like Ridgeway have long reaches. But Geoff wanted to believe him. He wanted that Ph.D. in psychology and that academic job so badly! That's why he told me the story, I think. He was hoping I'd tell him what he wanted to hear."

"But you didn't."

"No, I told him what I thought, but I don't know if I convinced him. He'd put a lot of time and effort into his work, and he was trying to fool himself into thinking Ridgeway meant what he said and that he'd be okay."

"Do you remember the exact date he came to you?"

Bill shook his head. "Not the exact date, but it was late June, a couple of weeks after the graduation picnic at Ridgeway's. That was June 10."

"You should have told the police this," I said.

"I thought about it," Bill said. "But it seemed to be such a clear case of suicide. And if I told the police, and it got back to Professor Ridgeway, I'd be where Geoff was when he killed himself—was killed, I mean."

"And it didn't occur to you that Brice Ridgeway might have murdered Geoff?"

"For maybe a second. But then I decided that was nuts. Why would he? He knew Geoff wasn't going to tell Gardner. Geoff told me it wouldn't help him any, anyway, it would just hurt Mrs. Gardner and maybe get back to Professor Ridgeway's wife, too. He said he didn't have any hard feelings against either of them.

"And besides, Peggy," Bill added angrily, "you can be damned sure Ridgeway wouldn't kill anybody to keep his affair with Shelley Gardner a secret. That sort of stuff goes on all the time in the academic world. Ridgeway's wife probably knows that as well as anybody. She probably knows her husband's unfaithful to her, even if she doesn't know the names of the women."

I agreed with him there, remembering how Mrs. Ridgeway had sat over in the shadows on the patio, knitting and looking about with her incurious eyes that probably didn't miss anything—including me, in the shadows opposite her, looking about with my incurious eyes that tried not to miss anything, either.

"So I figured Geoff couldn't think of anything he could do to save his career," Bill went on, "no matter what he did. He couldn't hurt Ridgeway, he could only hurt Mrs. Gardner for nothing. So he just said, 'To hell with it,' and hurt himself instead."

"Is that how it often happens?" I asked him since, after all, he was the student of psychology.

"Yes," he said earnestly.

Geoff Oates sounded like a nice guy who'd ended up in the wrong place at the wrong time. It was generous of him not to want to tell Lyle Gardner about his wife because he didn't want to get her into trouble, even though she was half the reason his career was threatened.

But I didn't think it added up. Oates thought he got on Brice Ridgeway's hit list because he stumbled on him having sex with a colleague's wife. Would he commit suicide just because he thought his career was down the drain? Suicide's a drastic step.

I told Bill I'd heard that Gardner and his wife had split up.

"Yeah, they have," he said. "Nobody seems to know why. I mean, if Geoff had told him about Ridgeway, you'd think they would've split up a long time ago."

Maybe he did tell him, I thought, and maybe Gardner was able to put Ridgeway *père* behind him, but choked on Ridgeway *fils*. I sat there staring into space until Bill said, "Hey, you've gone away and left me sitting here with pizza crumbs and an empty wine carafe. I hope you're not going to stick me with the check, too."

I looked up into Bill's face, too young for his age, which is often the way it is with people who've stayed too long in school. "Sorry," I told him with a smile. "I was off in a world of my own."

"Maybe I could join you there sometime."

"You can come in as far as espresso and dessert."

He shrugged, said, "I suppose that's better than nothing."

I wondered if Mata Hari had ever got so much information so cheaply. Of course, in the end they shot her.

Twenty-Two

As I walked my patrol that night, the cold rain thudding on my raincoat and dripping from the hood, I thought about what Bill Turner had told me. I'd try to find some other solution before I'd consider suicide—not that I would ever consider it. Once, a long time ago, when my life had looked unremittingly awful, I'd considered *considering* suicide, but my curiosity about whether things were going to get worse or better kept me from going any farther than that. Of course, having no interest in an afterlife helps considerably: As I understand it, there are no unanswered questions in Heaven, so what do you do there for excitement?

I wondered if Oates had decided to try something else before killing himself or running away—assuming he'd ever thought of doing either.

What if he'd heard something—from Gardner, from Ridgeway, from Bengtsson or somebody else in the project—that made him think Mullen was giving his money to the project for racist research? And what if he thought he might gain something from finding out if it were true or not—a little judicious blackmail, or perhaps a lever he could use to keep his future in psychology alive?

I wondered if Geoff Oates had really been as forgiving as Bill Turner thought he was, and hadn't gone to Lyle Gardner and told him what he'd seen by the Gardners' pool. What would Gardner have done, in that case?

Maybe I should ask Shelley Gardner about it. Of course,

I could get fired doing that, if Shelley told her husband. But would she, now that they'd separated?

I thought it was worth a gamble.

Wet, cold, and tired, I finished my patrol, filled out my report, and drove home. I made coffee and showered and then, instead of going to bed, waited until eight-thirty and called Susan in the Psych Department. She'd just come in.

I asked her if she was alone and when she said she was, asked her when Lyle Gardner usually came in. I wanted to know where he was while I was out talking to his wife.

She answered in a low voice, as if there were spies everywhere. "Around nine, if he didn't stay here late the night before. If he did, he might not get here until later. Of course, it could be different, now that he's not living at home. He's got a little apartment near campus, you know."

I asked her to call me when he came in, and I went to bed.

An hour and a half later, she called back and whispered, "The coast is clear."

The rain had tapered off by the time I found the Gardners' home. It was in an expensive housing development—no two homes exactly alike, but all clearly members of the same family—that had been farmland until fairly recently. It was about half an hour's drive from the University.

I thought of doing what Geoff Oates had done, go around the side to the pool, but it was raining and I didn't think I'd see anything as dramatic as what he'd seen. I rang the doorbell instead, and after about half a minute, Shelley Gardner opened the door. She was wearing a rose-colored, knee-length silk nightshirt, and her bare feet were buried in the fluffy white carpeting on the floor.

She didn't look particularly surprised to see me, although she did raise one eyebrow. She looked me up and down and said, "Don't you know what the job market's like out there?"

"I thought maybe you wouldn't tell on me."

Her laugh crackled out into the wet morning. "You

mean, otherwise you'll tell Lyle about me and Troy? Haven't you heard the news yet—Lyle's moved out?"

"It sounds to me like things have worked out just the way you wanted them to. Or are you all broken up over it?"

"No, I'm not all broken up over it." She stood away from the door. "Come on in. I haven't the faintest idea what you want, but we might as well be comfortable while you tell me."

I asked her if she was alone and apt to stay that way for a while.

"Yes and yes," she replied. "But I do have to go out in a little while."

She led me into a sunken living room, with sliding glass doors opening onto the infamous swimming pool, desolate in the rain, and beyond it, a view of rain-shrouded farmland.

The furniture and carpeting in the house were all in soft, muted colors, perhaps to better set off the paintings on the walls—bland representations of children with large, soulful eyes who were playing with toys that dwarfed them. They were all signed Shelley and belonged to the Clown School of Painting.

I asked her about them and she told me she'd been an artist before she married Gardner, but now her kids didn't give her time to concentrate on her work. She'd sold a few through a gallery before becoming a mother.

I looked around, saw no evidence she had kids, asked her where they were.

"School just started," she said. I raised my eyebrows questioningly. Sometimes, that's all you have to do to put people with guilty consciences on the defensive. "Kids chop the days up," she rushed quickly on. "You need large blocks of time, if you're really going to get into a painting."

"Whereas affairs can be fitted nicely into time's little nooks and crannies," I said, keeping my voice neutral.

She gave me an uncertain smile, then nodded.

She offered me coffee or a drink. I chose coffee, and she disappeared into the kitchen. After a while, I heard her speaking in a low voice. Since I couldn't hear another voice filling the pauses, I assumed she was talking on the phone.

She returned a few minutes later with a cup of instant coffee. Better than nothing for somebody who'd had less than two hours sleep. For herself she had a tall glass of what looked like tomato juice over ice. Yum.

"I wasted a lie, out at Ridgeway's," I told her. "When I came back to the patio from the house, your husband asked me if I'd seen you. If I'd told him what I'd seen, he might have left you sooner and you'd have had a couple of extra days of freedom."

"Yeah, well, thanks anyway," she said, smiling uncertainly again. "But I'm not sure Lyle and I are breaking up for good, you know. Maybe we'll try counseling. It's just that Lyle's been in psychology so long, he doesn't think counseling works. He's too cynical, I guess."

"But you'd give it a try?"

"Sure," she said, without a great deal of enthusiasm. "On account of the kids, right?" I thought she meant she was thinking of their well-being, but she went on, "I mean, isn't it easier if you don't have to be always shunting them from one parent to the other, having to learn the names of the stepparents and stepbrothers and sisters, and trying to remember whose turn it is to have them for which holiday?"

Here was a woman truly committed to family values. "I wouldn't know," I replied. "But you'd have to give up Troy Ridgeway if you and your husband tried to work it out or at least be more careful. Or was Troy just an attempt to give your husband a wake-up call?"

"That's right," Shelley said eagerly, "that's all Troy's good for, believe me. Troy and I dated a few times, before Lyle and I got married. It was when Troy came home after the baseball season had ended and he was hanging out at his dad's place. That's how Lyle and I met, in fact—I was at Ridgeway's with Troy, and Lyle was there. Lyle swept me off my feet," she added. She made it sound like he'd done that literally, perhaps with a broom.

She cocked her head and looked at me curiously. "What do you want, Peggy? Out at Ridgeway's, you said you were trying to find out what some old man did with his money. You must think somebody in the Psych Department, or the HGRP, has it. Is that right?"

"I don't know," I said. "I don't think the old man—Mullen—would have knowingly given his money to something I might think was appropriate, but I could be wrong. I just want to be sure. You've been around the Psych Department a long time. Is it possible that somebody could take money under the table to do racist research?"

She stared at me over her glass. "I suppose so, if they thought they could get away with it and if there was enough money in it. Some guy in behavioral psych got caught fudging the results of a tranquilizer for a big pharmaceutical company a year or so ago. There was a lot of money under the table there, I heard—and he got away with only a slap on the wrist because the University didn't want to offend the drug company. But I've never heard anything about racist research in the Psych Department—not that I would, necessarily," she added, staring down into her glass.

"What about the Scripter Fund?"

"You heard what Brice told you at the lake," she said. "Scripter gave that money to the project with no strings attached." Shelley shook her head. "You know, Peggy, you're way off track—you must be. Nobody in his right mind would do racist research."

"What about research that was just slightly slanted that way?"

She shook her head. "I don't think so. For it to mean anything, whoever did research like that would have to put his name on it and publish it, wouldn't he? And if he did that—and the research was no good—he'd be ruined. It

would have to be for a lot of money and done by somebody who didn't have anything to lose."

"Is there anybody in the HGRP who fits that description?" I asked her, knowing there was.

"Sure," she said brightly. "Sparky Bengtsson. He might
be dumb enough to do something like that, if he had a
chance. I mean, he doesn't have any money or any status,
and you just know he wants both. From what Lyle says,
he's just drifted from one project to another, mostly just
looking for ways to cause trouble, since the University
made him stop torturing animals. He reports anything he
thinks is against regulations, no matter how small— a regular little whistle-blower. Lyle thinks it was Sparky who
put the newspapers onto the Scripter money, just to cause
trouble.

"But I seriously doubt Sparky's clever enough to con
money out of anybody, even an old man. A lot of people
in the Psych Department might want to con old men out of
their money, you know."

"Who?"

Shelley took a swallow of her tomato juice, etc., and
glanced quickly at her watch at the same time.

"Not my husband, I can tell you that," she said, as if
reading my mind. "For one thing, he wouldn't have the
guts to do anything criminal, and for another he wants
power, not the kind of money he could cheat out of an old
man."

"Do you know how much money we're talking about
here?"

"No. Do you?"

"At least a million, I think."

"But he still wouldn't do it," she said, a little too
quickly. "He's not like that."

"What about Ridgeway? He's got all the power he
needs. Does that translate into all the money he needs,
too?"

"You saw how he lives. Does he look like he needs to
steal from an old man?"

She obviously didn't know about the money Troy owed the nurserymen. I wondered if Brice Ridgeway had the kind of money needed to pay them off.

"Ridgeway stole from your husband," I said.

Her eyes opened in surprise and then her face slowly turned red. "Would you care to explain that remark?"

"I heard a story a few days ago," I said. "It was about a poor fool who stumbled upon a man violating the tenth commandment with a woman violating the seventh."

She took her drink over to the glass doors and stared out at the swimming pool and the farmland beyond it waiting in the rain to be transformed into homes for people like the Gardners. "That didn't tell me anything," she said. "Confirmation was a long time ago."

"You, Brice Ridgeway, and Geoff Oates is what I mean. But I missed one part of it, Shelley: Did Oates get the papers he came out here for that morning?"

She turned to me suddenly, her face white now. "Who told you?"

"It doesn't matter. Did he?"

She stood there stiffly a minute longer, then made a visible effort to relax. "Yes. Brice stood there, buck naked, and waited until poor Geoff pulled himself out of the pool. Geoff started to slink away but Brice called him back, wanted to know why he was there. When he was through threatening Geoff, he made him pick up those goddamned papers, and leave. All I'd been able to do was roll over on my stomach. It didn't matter to Brice that we were both naked, but it mattered to me! I really gave Brice a piece of my mind."

"Did you ever see Oates again?"

"No. Lyle had a party and invited the HGRP people a few weeks after that. I wasn't looking forward to meeting Geoff face to face again, here or anywhere. But he stayed away, made some excuse."

I told Shelley I'd heard that Oates was afraid Ridgeway was going to ruin his career because of what he'd seen.

A thoughtful look appeared in her eyes. "Would he do

anything that cruel? I wonder. I mean, it wasn't Geoff's fault, it was Lyle's for sending him out here—and mine, I guess," she added as an afterthought.

A horrible thought seemed to strike her. "Was that why the poor kid killed himself? No, I don't believe it. Why wouldn't he tell my husband first, to try to hurt me and Brice?"

"How do you know he didn't?"

"I'm sure he didn't," she said, uncertainly. "Lyle would have told me. He sure as hell confronted me fast enough when he found out Troy and I were lovers!"

Lyle Gardner might have had something else in mind, I thought. Maybe Geoff Oates did tell him, but Gardner didn't confront his wife with it because he didn't want Ridgeway to know he knew. He might have had some plan for getting revenge on Ridgeway—a plan that involved both Oates and Harold Mullen.

"Your husband keeps a little apartment near the University," I said. "Do you think he could be cheating on you, too?"

Shelley laughed scornfully. "Lyle? No. Believe me, he's too busy for affairs—and they're too messy for a man like him. Besides, he feels guilty that he can't spend more time with his daughters—not with me, you understand, with his daughters. All Lyle really wants in life is his own big research project. That's what drives him."

"Do you think he's ever going to get one?"

She shrugged. "It could happen, if his research is good enough." She stared out the glass doors again, beyond the pool to the farmland waiting in the rain for the developers.

"I suppose Ridgeway would have to give him a strong recommendation, wouldn't he?"

"That would help," she replied. She looked at her watch. "Your time's up. You have to go now."

"Who's your date with?" I asked her. "Troy—or his father?"

Red spots appeared on her cheeks. "Neither—not that it's any of your goddamn business."

I followed her to the front door. Something on the wall of a room off the entryway attracted my attention, above a cluttered, modernistic desk. It was a wooden paddle, with Greek letters on it, the same kind I'd seen in the office of Mullen's lawyer, Dell Baker, and in Brice Ridgeway's study.

"Is this your husband's study?" I asked Shelley.

"Yes. Whenever Lyle was home, this is where he was."

"Is that the same fraternity Brice Ridgeway belonged to?" I asked her, pointing to the paddle.

She nodded. "In order to get in, the boys have to make them themselves—go to a lumberyard, pick a suitable piece of wood, cut it according to a plan provided by the frat house, sand it, stain it, and burn the fraternity's Greek letters and the date into it. Then, on initiation night, they pull down their pants and hand the paddle to each member of the fraternity and let them swat them on the bare ass with it." She shook her head. "They call it a bonding ritual, you know? I'm surprised Lyle didn't take it with him when he moved out. It's of great sentimental value to him."

"I suppose your husband still keeps in touch with his old fraternity buddies."

"Some of them."

"Dell Baker's probably a good friend of his."

"Who? I don't know most of their names."

"Did Ridgeway paddle your husband or vice versa?"

She smiled sadly. "Brice is the younger. In fact, it was because they belonged to the same fraternity that Lyle supported Brice's candidacy for a position in the department."

"And now it's Brice Ridgeway who's wielding the paddle," I said. "That must ache on more than just your husband's butt."

She looked at me with large eyes, as if she'd never quite thought of it that way before. I thanked her for her time and started out the door.

"What are you really after, Peggy?" she asked.

I turned around and said, "A sick old man—sick in

more ways than one—left his money to the University. He also left his sister living in something close to poverty. I'd like to be sure the University's doing something useful with that money. That's all I'm after."

"It could be like pulling on a piece of yarn in a sweater, though, couldn't it? You could lose the whole sweater."

"It happens that way sometimes."

I thought of parking around the corner from the Gardners' house and waiting to see who came calling or—if Shelley went out as she'd said she was going to do—following her to see where she went. But what difference would it make?

I was sure that Shelley Gardner's love life had been important once—it might even have cost two men their lives, although I didn't see how yet. But it wasn't important now—at least, not to me. And probably not to her either.

Twenty-Three

That night I took a roundabout way to the University so that I'd pass the property on Twenty-ninth that Harold Mullen had sold to Dell Baker. It was a few minutes after ten and the street was nearly empty. The lights were on in some of the offices in the law building, and I could see shadowy figures moving around inside—law clerks, probably, forced to neglect their lives, wives, and kids in hopes of someday making partner—a little like psych majors at the U. Paula said she wasn't planning to work for a big law firm. She wanted to start as a public defender, then go into private practice after a few years.

I straddled my bike in the nearly empty parking lot and looked over at the property next door. Somebody had bought it the year before Dell Baker bought Mullen's but for a quarter of a million dollars more. It was an old, one-story strip mall, featuring a cleaners, a laundromat, a bakery, and a little cafe.

I thought Baker must have bought his property from Mullen for a very good price.

As I was about to continue on to the U, the cafe door opened and Dell Baker came out, strolling my way. I waited until he'd almost reached the car I was standing next to, a cream Mercedes, and then called his name.

He glanced up, keys in hand. He tried to look puzzled, but I saw the spark of recognition in his eyes.

"Peggy O'Neill," I said. "I talked to you a couple of weeks ago about a client of yours, Harold Mullen."

"Right, right! You wanted to know what old Harold did with his money, didn't you?" He grinned, with watchful little eyes. "How'd you make out at the University Club?"

"The way you said I would. I got nothing."

"So what're you doing now to keep busy?"

"Not a whole lot. I was surprised to learn that you owned all this," I said, gesturing at the law building.

"Were you?" What little pleasure he'd felt in my company up to then faded. "How'd you find that out—and why? Am I supposed to have been involved in Harold's hate-mail project, too?"

"Well, I wanted to know how much money I'm looking for, so I went to the courthouse and asked about this property. It's amazing how much you can learn about other people, if you know where to look, isn't it? What was here before the law building besides Mullen's little store?"

"A couple of small businesses. My law office was here, too, which was why I was interested in buying the property."

"And then you put up this building?"

"Not alone—I couldn't have afforded that. With some friends looking for income property," he said. He unlocked his car door and started to open it.

"Friends," I repeated. "Old fraternity buddies like Brice Ridgeway? Lyle Gardner?"

He turned and stared at me. "What?" Then he laughed, a noise without humor, and shook his head. "No. My partners are some of the other lawyers in the building who needed more space."

"It's a thriving business," I said, "the law."

"We live in litigious times, Miss O'Neill." He started to get into his car.

"Harold must have trusted you greatly, to sell you his property."

He paused and glanced up at me. "What's that supposed to mean?"

"Since you were his lawyer," I told him, "there must have been a possible conflict of interest."

"Harold did trust me," Baker said, his voice quivering with righteous indignation. "He trusted me more than he should have, Miss O'Neill. At my insistence, he hired another lawyer to represent him in the sale of his property to me. He didn't think it was necessary—just an added expense for him, he said—but I made him do it—to avoid a possible conflict of interest."

I wondered if the other lawyer—assuming there really had been one—was one of those who'd gone in with Baker on the law building.

"That property over there," I said, "sold for almost a quarter of a million more than you paid Mullen for his."

Baker's face turned blotchy with anger. "I don't know why I'm standing here talking to you, I really don't, listening to your sleazy insinuations. I know nothing about that property over there—and may I remind you that you don't either? You're a campus cop, not a real estate agent, not a private eye. I paid Harold Mullen fair market value for his property. If somebody sold the property next door for more money—good. Business is business, Miss O'Neill. But I didn't cheat Harold. As I told you at our last meeting, I liked Harold."

"I'm sorry if I came off sounding as though I thought you did," I said. "Harold Mullen interests me, and I guess I just don't know where to stop."

"I don't think you do, either."

He started to get into his car.

"You ever hear of a friend of Mullen's named Geoffrey Oates?"

It may have been my imagination, it may have been the light, but I thought he hesitated a second.

"No," he said, from inside his car, "that name doesn't ring a bell."

The door slammed and the engine purred into life.

I went over, rapped on the window. His face a mask of

suppressed rage, Baker pressed a button and the window came down partway.

"How'd you know I was a campus cop?" I asked him.

"You told me, in my office. How else would I know?"

"That's what I'm wondering," I said.

If looks could kill. The window went up again and his car accelerated out of the lot with a screech of rubber. I pedaled after it, watching Baker's taillights grow smaller and finally disappear around a corner. When I'd talked to him in his office, I'd tried to avoid mentioning what I did for a living. Of course, it might have slipped out, but I didn't think so—which meant somebody had been talking to Dell Baker about me, or he'd contacted them. Which of his frat buddies? Ridgeway or Gardner? Or both?

Twenty-Four

Paula had invited me to the party she and Lawrence were giving on Sunday night for the victims of the hate mailer.

"After all," she said, "you've suffered with us and spent a lot of time and energy trying to find out who the creep is."

I hadn't suffered, but I said I'd be happy to come.

It was probably the strangest party I've ever attended, and I've attended a few real doozies in my time. Milling around in Paula and Lawrence's newly remodeled living and dining rooms, carrying plastic cups of beer or wine and plates of food, were couples and families of every racial mix, the only constant being that one member of each was white— "Nordic," they called themselves, laughing disparagingly.

"According to some of the hate mail I received," a tall, fair woman explained to me, "when I married Tony, I married a mongrel." She looked her husband up and down, squinting critically.

"Italians are mongrels?" I asked.

"You bet," her husband said, not without a certain pride. "If you knew your history, you'd know that Rome was created by Nordics who swooped down on the unsuspecting inferior people living in Italy at the time—sort of the way they do today in cruise ships. They killed or enslaved the indigenous people and then created the Colosseum, the Forum, Caesar, and the Roman legions."

"The Forum was Greek," somebody pointed out.

"It doesn't matter," Tony replied with an expressive

hand gesture, "since ancient Greek civilization was Nordic, too. Anyway, everything went well for a while, but then these Nordics—great, good-hearted people that they are when they're not killing, raping, burning, and pillaging—decided to give the surviving inferiors equal status in their society—integration, you see—and the next thing you know, those pesky inferiors were intermarrying with the Nordics and—BAM—that's the end of the great Roman civilization. The Wop you see standing before you at this very moment," he added modestly, "is the result of the Nordic race's fatal attraction to inferior peoples once they've stomped on them. Now, instead of building temples and throwing slaves to the lions for laughs, we croon to the moon about *amore*."

"I wanted a gladiator and I got a pasta chef," his wife wailed.

"Ours is a similarly tragic story," a woman with long, dark hair and an olive complexion said. "I'm a mongrel, of course, and my husband lusted after me in his placid Nordic way—they just can't leave us mongrels alone. I can understand *that*," she went on, "but what I can't understand is how a hot-blooded Spaniard like me ended up marrying a pure-blooded Nordic named Brad. I *must* be degenerate!"

"I'd resent that, if I weren't so Nordic," Brad said placidly.

"Why do we Nordics lust after the dark-skinned peoples to the south of us?" somebody declaimed, her face a mask of mock anguish.

"If you'd ever spent time in Oslo," a black man said who'd just joined the group, "you wouldn't have to ask."

"It was the Devil's work," somebody else put in. "The Devil enjoys thinking of interracial sex almost as much as racists do. It's a remarkable coincidence."

"I'm Jewish," a short, balding man said. "You'd think that would make me special, considering that Christ was supposed to be Jewish, too. But it turns out Christ was Nordic after all."

"He was?" I asked.

"Yeah, he was a member of one of the ten lost tribes of Israel who left the Holy Land. My people stayed behind and became the degenerate Jews of today. Christ and his people became—guess what?"

"Nordics!" about ten people chanted in unison, and we all laughed.

"What I thought was strange," the Spanish woman said, "was how often this hate mailer compared human beings to creatures lower on the evolutionary scale. He kept asking things like, 'Does the mud fish mate with the trout?' and 'Do monkeys marry gibbons?' It's strange that he'd want humans to model themselves on fish and monkeys. I mean, if we're going to copy the lifestyle of other creatures in one way, why not in other ways? Why don't we eat our young, or go around naked, or shit on the streets?"

"You said a no-no!" a Korean child told her, giving her a stern look.

The child's blond mother said, "It got so darned tiresome after a while, all that poisonous ignorance—but we had to read it, day in, day out—just in case the creep changed his tactics and started to make real threats. You never know when somebody like that's going to flip out and get himself an automatic weapon or start making bombs."

"Sometimes it would stop for a while," the black man said, "but we still waited for it every day. Even now, we're waiting for it to start up again. We probably always will."

"We didn't start getting hate mail until my mother died," a middle-aged woman said. "When we got home from her funeral, our mailbox was crammed full of it. My mother was of Swedish descent and my dad's Russian. The letters told me that my mother had betrayed her race and I was going to hell, even though it was no fault of my own. The best thing I could do was to testify publicly about the evils of miscegenation, to spare others my terrible fate."

There was a long silence after that one, broken finally

when Paula came by, offering servings of her famous Szechuan chicken salad.

A Chinese woman tried some. "It's very good," she said politely. "What is it?"

"Is something burning?" somebody asked.

I smelled it, too. It was coming from outside, through the partially open sliding glass doors to the deck.

I ran outside and looked over the railing. Smoke was seeping out from under the door of the apartment that Lawrence was refinishing, and I could see light flickering inside through a window. I started for the stairs, but Lawrence ran past me and plunged down, with Paula right behind him. A car started up down the street, the grinding noise of an old engine slow to catch.

When I got to the bottom, Lawrence was running to the street. I ran after him, and we stood there and watched as an old car turned the corner at the end of the block, its tires squealing, a large, old, green car. Dewey.

We ran back to the house. Most of the guests were standing on the lawn, a few people still coming downstairs. Paula had a garden hose in her hands, water gushing from it. She kicked open the door to the apartment and plunged into the smoke.

"Paula!" I shouted, and went in after her. The smoke was too thick for me to see her at first. I followed the hose across the floor and found her kneeling, spraying water onto the fire that was eating its way across the floor and up the wall. The stench of gasoline was strong and the smoke and heat almost unbearable.

I grabbed her and tried to pull her back, but she jerked away, her face a mask of rage and determination. Lawrence came in then, put his arm around her, and shouted, "Water isn't doing any good, Paula. We've got a bucket brigade started, with sand. Get out of the way now!"

I led her out of there, both of us almost doubled over with coughing, past a line of people—men and women, who were just dark shapes in the smoke, passing buckets of sand, from one of Lawrence's masonry projects, across the room and onto the fire.

The fire was out by the time the fire trucks arrived.

None of the guests left. An hour later, we all traipsed back upstairs. Neighbors who had come out to watch were still milling around. Halfway up the stairs to the deck, Paula turned to them. Her clothes and face were charcoal-smeared and she looked as though she could do a good imitation of Al Jolson singing "Mammy." Instead, she croaked, "We're having a party. There's lots of food left and plenty of stuff to drink. You're all welcome to join us."

A number of neighbors, somewhat hesitantly, followed her upstairs.

Twenty-Five

Most of the next week passed uneventfully, except that Paula was no longer a campus cop. Although law school didn't start until the day after Labor Day, she had vacation time to use up, so she'd quit a week early. Lawrence took that week off, too, so they could work on the house together, especially the fire-damaged apartment downstairs. They needed to rent the apartment, since Paula wouldn't be bringing home any income for a while.

Lawrence had switched to the first watch, to be there when Paula came home from school, so instead of seeing both of them in the squad room when I came to work at night, I'd only be seeing Lawrence when I came off duty in the morning.

On Thursday I got a call from my Aunt Tess, who lives in a little town north of here. She informed me that she was coming down to the big city for Labor Day and that I was going to take her to dinner, since she wasn't about to eat lasagna again at my place, thank you very much.

"Fine, be that way," I said, as she hung up. I decided to invite Lillian Przynski, whom I hadn't seen in a while, to join us, so on Friday I drove to her place.

Lillian said she'd be delighted, as she fussed around her kitchen looking for the tea and muttering about her absent-mindedness. As I carried the tray into the living room, I thought of the time I'd had tea with her brother in his cheerless house on the last day of his life.

I told her about the fire.

"It's that friend of Bud's, I suppose, who'd behind it," she said, picking up her arthritic little poodle and placing him in her lap, "Dewey."

I said I thought so, too. I asked her if she'd seen him since the day he came up and talked to her when she was out walking Rufus.

"No, and I'm glad I haven't! Such an unfortunate man. It can't be easy being Dewey—not that I'm making excuses for him, you understand," she added quickly.

"But look at you and your brother," I said. "You had the same upbringing, and yet you turned out completely differently."

"I know, I know." Lillian shook her head. "Life's such a mystery, isn't it? I sometimes think the remarkable thing is not how much evil there is in the world, but that there's any good in it at all—especially when my arthritis acts up! Life's so short and it always ends so badly. We all know it, and yet some people still take the time to think of others besides themselves. Not many, I suppose, but it's a miracle any do at all. Why do they, I wonder?" she asked, raising her head as far up as it would go and shooting me a hard glance from her pale eyes. "I wish I had a phone, so you could have told me you were coming, Peggy. I would have saved one of my oatmeal scones for you. They're very good, if I do say so myself."

"That must be why there aren't any left," I said.

"Yes, that's why," she agreed with a smile. "Oh, and by the way, I sent your landlady a little note thanking her for taking the time to send me that book of Bud's." She nodded at the old book lying on the little end table next to her.

I picked it up, put it in my lap, and opened it.

"It's strange, isn't it," Lillian went on. "It's all that's left of him, that and a few snapshots I have in a photo album from when we were children."

It was the book of names Mullen had brought to the picnic on the Fourth of July. When he'd seen Geoffrey Oates across the street looking for him, he'd rushed across to meet him, and left the book behind. Mrs. Hammer had taken it, meaning to return it to Mullen, but forgotten about it. She'd asked me for Lillian's address so she could mail it to her.

It was part of my first memory of Harold Mullen, when he was telling us what our names meant. Mine meant "champion," or "military hero." I should tell Bixler about that, I thought, maybe he'd appreciate me more.

Mullen had suggested that Lawrence and I would make a nice couple because Lawrence's name meant "laurel-crowned," which is kind of the same thing as "champion." He must have thought that together we'd produce a super race. The major drawback was that Lawrence was in love with Paula, and I wasn't in love with anybody. I suppose a eugenics marriage board would have set our priorities straight for us.

Mullen hadn't shown any interest in Paula's name, I recalled, so I looked it up now. It was the feminine form of Paul and came from the Latin for "small." And, of course, it was the name of a zealous missionary, too. I tried to find some significance in that, but couldn't. Paula was neither small nor inclined to spread anyone's gospel, she just wanted the freedom to live her own life, love, and be loved by Lawrence. Not an impossible dream in a sane world.

I flipped to the *L*s and looked up 'Lillian'. "Your name means 'Lily'," I told her.

"Well, of course it does—what's that?"

A slip of red paper fell out of the book and landed on the floor at my feet. I picked it up.

It was a bookmark with printing on it in black Gothic letters: The Nordic Advocate. Books and periodicals. Catalogues available on request. The address was about half a mile from Lillian's house. The owner's name was Duane Sween.

"I don't suppose this is yours," I said, showing the bookmark to Lillian.

She put on her glasses to read it, her bent head trembling slightly. Then she peered sharply up at me.

"It sounds like the kind of book store Bud would have patronized, doesn't it?" she said.

I finished my tea in a gulp, arranged a time to pick Lillian up on Monday, kissed her on the forehead, and headed for the door.

"Do be careful," she said. "They're probably not very nice people."

It was in an old neighborhood shopping center that progress, in the form of malls, had sucked the life out of. On one corner a mom-and-pop grocery store with a tattered awning advertised specials on milk and cigarettes. Next to it was a hardware store, with used lawn mowers and new wheelbarrows on display on the sidewalk out in front. Down the block, a submarine-sandwich shop, part of a chain that had failed, was boarded up and graffiti-sprayed, and the marquee over the theater across the street was blank.

Next to the theater was a sign over a door that said Books. I crossed the street. The display window was empty except for a faded American flag and some kind of dispirited plant that was somehow able to live under airless, sunless conditions. The backs of bookcases blocked the view into the store. A sign in the window said Open, Come In. I pushed open the door, heard a bell jangle somewhere in the back, and stepped in.

A single, naked bulb burned above a desk in one corner with an old cash register on it. On the wall behind it, a banner exhorted me to obey God's laws and come in and browse. Tall bookshelves filled the room and lined the walls, illuminated by cheap track lighting on the ceiling. An exhausted-looking American flag, as if crucified, hung on nails on the fourth wall, below a sign that said The Nordic Advocate.

I heard a toilet flush in the back somewhere.

A sign on one of the bookshelves caught my eye: Why

are you called a Caucasian? I went over and pulled one of the books off the shelf and thumbed through it, reading a passage at random: "When two people of different races mate, the resultant DNA is defective, and disharmony in the organism will be the result." I was so startled by this news that I almost failed to hear the man come out of a door in the back. I glanced up.

"Hello," he said. "Is there anything I can help you find?"

I asked him if he was Duane Sween.

His eyes narrowed slightly. "Yes. Why?"

"I just wondered. I found a bookmark from your store in a friend's book. I thought I'd like to check you out."

He nodded and went to his desk and sat down. "Like I say, if I can help you, let me know." I could feel his eyes on me as I wandered around the store.

He was about thirty-five, with brown hair and a short, military-style haircut. He was lanky and a little taller than I, but his height was distributed mostly above his waist. He would have been good-looking, in a boy-next-door way, except for a lack of animation in his face. At some time in his life, I thought, he'd learned that there was no point in feeling anything or at least in letting feelings show. His eyes were light blue and deep-set, and he was wearing a western-style shirt and blue jeans.

I love books, but I'm sometimes appalled when I see what dreadful things they can contain between their covers. The books I saw in Duane Sween's book store were among the worst I'd ever seen—and I'd once been in a so-called adult book store. At least porn shops don't have intellectual pretensions, they just show the goods. In this store, the books and pamphlets made crude attempts to justify scientifically the most hideous forms of racism.

When I'd seen enough, I asked Sween how late he was open that night.

"Until five," he said.

It was a little after four. I wanted to show this place to Paula and Lawrence, since I was sure that it was the source of the material that had almost ruined their lives and those of others.

"I'll be back," I told him.

He just nodded, watched me leave.

I drove over to Paula and Lawrence's house, about a fifteen-minute drive, climbed up to the deck past the boarded-up windows on the downstairs apartment, and rapped on the sliding glass doors. The lingering smell of wet, charred wood reminded me of the ruins of Harold Mullen's house across the street from me.

Paula came out into the dining room and opened up.

"Hi, Peggy," she said, a look of great distraction on her face. "I'm trying to finish a poem and if I don't do it before school starts, I'll probably never do it. Come back some other time, okay?" Without waiting for my answer, she padded barefoot back to her study. My, I thought, the muse must really be riding her hard today. She'd never told me to go away before. Ignoring the exasperated glance she gave me over her shoulder, I followed her back to her study, wondering how the world was going to take a lawyer-poet, or poet-lawyer.

A long, white table with a bright red architect's lamp clamped to it takes up most of one wall of Paula's study. A computer sits on one corner of the table along with a dictionary, a thesaurus, pens and pencils, and a photograph of her and Lawrence. That afternoon, fat law books that looked almost criminally boring were piled on one side of the table.

The opposite wall is one long bookcase, a jumble of slim volumes by modern poets I've never heard of, and her martial arts books and magazines.

Pictures of her family—she's got two brothers and a younger sister—hang on the walls, along with a framed copy of her first published poem, in a journal called *intruders*. A futon was rolled up in one corner of the room. I doubted she was still sleeping on it. She probably kept it there as a reminder—to herself, to Lawrence—of the recent past.

I glanced at my watch. If I was going to show her the book store I'd discovered, we were going to have to hurry. "A spring of love gushed from my heart, and I blessed them unaware," I recited.

She looked up from the sheet of paper she was bent over. "What's that supposed to be?"

"Coleridge," I told her. " 'Rime of the Ancient Mariner,' the poem he was writing when his neighbor came to borrow a cup of potato chips to sprinkle on the tuna casserole. He lost the thread and was never able to find it again. But—as you can hear—I can still recite a couple of snatches of it, which means it must be pretty famous, even if it's incomplete. Then there's Schubert's *Unfinished Symphony,* which is still played. Would it be, do you think, if he'd finished it?"

Paula looked at me closely. "Peggy, I think you're hysterical. Why are you here?"

"Not hysterical, but a little giddy, perhaps. Poems are made by fools like you, but only I could find the place where Harold Mullen got all the material he mailed out."

She stood up. "Where?"

"It's a book store, in the same way adult book stores are. I thought you and Lawrence might like to come and see it."

"How'd you find it?"

I told her.

"Lawrence is at the lumberyard, getting glass for the windows downstairs, but he ought to be back in half an hour or so."

"That would be too late for today," I said. "We can wait until tomorrow."

"No. I want to go there now."

I avoided the freeway on account of the rush-hour traffic, but still got to the book store with a few minutes to spare.

"The Nordic Advocate," Paula said grimly, when we'd gone inside. "I like that."

Duane Sween came out from his back room and stopped in his tracks. Paula was almost certainly the first black who'd ever stepped into his store.

"Hi," she said, and gave him her best smile. "I'm from another planet, just here on a visit."

"I'm closing now," he said.

"According to the sign, we've got ten minutes," she replied. "Try to close early, we'll sue you for false advertising and racial discrimination. Besides," she added, "I want to find out why I am a Caucasian." She started over to that shelf of books.

"This is Duane Sween, Paula," I said. "Duane, Paula's received a lot of literature from your store through the mail."

"I don't know what you're talking about. I only send my literature out to people who want it."

"What makes you think I wouldn't want it?" Paula asked.

His expressionless eyes blinked, but getting caught in a small inconsistency didn't seem to bother him much. "I do a mail-order business," he said. "If you ordered something, and your check cleared, you got it."

"Is that how Harold Mullen did business with you?" I asked.

"Mullen?" His eyes narrowed again. "I don't know anybody named Mullen. What are you after?"

"He was a customer," I said. "He had your bookmark."

Sween shrugged. "Lots of people have my bookmark. I don't know the name of everybody who comes in here to buy something."

"No, I'm sure they just become a blur after a while," Paula called over to him. She was going slowly around the store, looking at titles, pausing every now and then to pluck a book off a shelf and open it.

"Here's something I'll bet you didn't know, Peggy," she said. "The mulberry spots on the lower spine of the Japanese and other dark races is a sign of Negro descent. We sure do get around."

"Why haven't I ever heard about that mulberry spot?" I demanded.

"It's part of a Jewish conspiracy to mix the races," she replied airily. "Through their control of the media, they're keeping it a secret. See, it says so right here: 'Few people realize that the Jews are at the forefront of the movement designed to mix the races.' "

"Those rascals! How come?"

"They want to pollute the blood of the Nordics. They're jealous of their purity."

"Won't Edith Silberman be shocked, when I tell her I'm on to her," I said.

"Okay, that's it," Sween said. He went over and opened his door. "I'm closing. You two bitches get out of here, now, or I'm calling the police."

Just then I heard footsteps coming slowly up the stairs from the basement. The door opened and a man carrying a carton of books emerged. He stopped just inside the room. I'd seen him before, coming down the steps from Harold Mullen's house the afternoon before the fire.

He didn't see Paula, standing behind him at the bookshelf next to the basement door in the dim light. He glanced at me, glanced at Sween, and then back at me. He didn't seem to recognize me, but he knew something was wrong.

"Paula," I called softly. "Guess what? Dewey's here."

Twenty-Six

She turned. Dewey looked over his shoulder, saw her, let out a scream, and dropped the carton of books. He bolted toward the back of the store, tripped over the box, picked himself up, and kept going. Paula caught up with him. He let out a squeak and tried to kick her, his arms flailing.

As I've mentioned, Paula's a student of exotic ways of killing, incapacitating, or simply bemusing you into helplessness, all according to the needs of the occasion. What she did to Dewey was too fast for me to see in any detail, but he sat down suddenly. She was still holding the book she'd been reading, her breathing slow and even.

"Dewey, is it really you?" she asked affectionately.

"Duane, do something!" he yelled. "This is the Negress who killed Harold Mullen and burned up his house!"

"Negress—oh my God! Dewey, *where* have you spent the past quarter of a century? As if I couldn't guess!"

Duane Sween crossed the room to his desk, but not to pick up the phone to call the police. He pulled open a drawer, reached inside. I got there in time to slam the drawer shut on his hand with my hip. I waved my shield in his face.

"I'm a cop," I said.

His expressionless eyes looked at the shield, came back to me. "So what do you want? We aren't doing anything against the law here. Haven't you ever heard of the First Amendment?" I relaxed the pressure on the drawer enough so he could bring his hand out empty.

Dewey tried to burn down a house—her house," I said, nodding at Paula. "That's carrying freedom of speech a little too far."

"That's a lie, you can't prove nothin'," Dewey hollered from the floor.

I pushed Sween away from the desk, reached inside and pulled out a loaded .38 revolver.

"I've got a permit for it," he said.

"Show me."

I backed away from the desk, and he pulled open another drawer, got out a piece of paper, and thrust it at me. Sadly enough, it was a valid permit.

"Trying to burn down her house was a hate crime," I told him. "You run a racist bookstore, and the arsonist works for you. We've got hundreds of pieces of the garbage you sell here, mailed to her and to the people who were in her home when the fire started. To a jury, it's going to look like you and Dewey were in on the arson together."

"That's a bunch of crap," he said. "I ain't responsible for what Dewey does in his free time, I'm just a bookseller." A sly look appeared on his face. "I read something in the paper about a fire—last Sunday, wasn't it—at the home of some mixed-race couple who were having a party, or something like that. Was that you?" he asked Paula. He was almost grinning. "I can't really say I'm sorry. But Dewey was here with me that night, from about eight o'clock on. We were doing inventory, weren't we, Dewey?"   •

"That's right, Duane," Dewey said gratefully.

"We saw Dewey's car, speeding away from the scene of the crime," I told him, stretching the truth a bit. "I think we've got enough evidence to take you in for questioning. You can call your lawyer from downtown."

Sween looked suddenly worried. "I'm telling you the truth—Dewey was here with me. I don't have the money to hire a lawyer!"

"That's too bad," I said. "But maybe we can work

something out. My friend here and I want to spend a little time with Dewey. What do you think?"

Sween thought about it, his eyes moving from Dewey to Paula and back to me, still holding his gun. Then he shrugged. "Why should I mind?"

"We'd like to be alone with him," I said. "We've been wanting to talk to him for a long time. Why don't you just go on home to whatever's waiting for you there. We'll let ourselves out when we're through here, and if we don't take Dewey off to jail, what's left of him will lock up. Does he have a key?"

Sween nodded.

"For God's sake, Duane!" Dewey cried from the floor. "I told you, the Negress killed Harold! The two of 'em are in it together. What do you think they're going to do to me and the book store when you're gone?"

"Do we look like killers and arsonists to you, Duane?" I ran my fingers through my hair which, even in low afternoon light coming through dirty windows can look quite incendiary, and flashed a pyrotechnical grin.

Sween gave both Dewey and me a disgusted look. "You don't have anything on me you can make stick," he told me, "but you can cause me trouble I don't need. However, I'm warning you: if my store's wrecked when I come in tomorrow, I call the cops, no matter what. You understand?"

I nodded.

"When you and your friend are through with him, make sure the gun's back where you found it and the door's locked behind you." He walked out his front door, pulling it shut.

"Talk about loyalty!" Paula said, turning to Dewey.

He tried to scramble to his feet, keeping his back against the wall, his eyes never leaving Paula. She kicked his feet out from under him and he sat down again.

"Dewey what?" I asked him.

"Fesler."

"Fesler!" Paula exclaimed. "It just gets better and better,

doesn't it? Can't you just see his parents taking their first look at the little tyke and saying, 'Dewey Fesler.' And the thunder rolled," she intoned.

"Let's see some identification." I held out my hand and he passed me his wallet, so old it looked like somebody had chewed it up and then spit it out. There were a few dollar bills in it and a driver's license. I noticed that he lived just a few blocks away from the store.

"Why do you think Paula killed your friend Harold and then burned his house down?" I asked him. "What makes you think we didn't burn the house down around him while he was still alive and screaming?"

Dewey was trembling all over. His thick head of hair, combed straight back and held rigidly in place by grease of some kind, began at least an inch beyond his high, sloping forehead, like a wig that was sliding off the back of his head. His face was pitted with acne scars and dotted with blackheads like cracked peppercorns, and his nose and ears seemed to have been molded from some soft material that hadn't held its shape. He actually looked worse than Lillian Przynski had indicated with her description. Of course, it could have been the light.

"Harold told me you'd been in his house that morning and you'd accused him of all kinds of things. He told me you were a friend of ... of hers," he said, glancing at Paula and quickly looking back at me, the lesser of two evils. "Then she came to his house that night and burned it down. Maybe she didn't mean to kill Harold—maybe it was kind of an accident. . . ." His voice took on a hopeful tone.

"No," Paula said, shaking her head ruefully, "it was no accident, Dewey. When Peggy told me about Mullen, I lost it. I waited till it was dark and then I drove over to his house with a can of kerosene and sprinkled it all over him the way I'm going to do you—"

"I swear to you, I didn't think Harold should've been sending out that stuff, I told him he'd get in trouble someday on account of it."

"I thought you said he didn't do it." Paula said.

His eyes leapt around the room, looking for answers. "All right—so he did it. But he wasn't breaking no law. You shouldn't of murdered him—he sincerely believed in what he was doing. He thought it was important, to make people understand."

"I'm sure you're right," Paula said, very softly. "And you thought it was important, too, and you mailed out his garbage for him."

"Only since he got sick, honest! I felt sorry for him, he was so old and weak! And besides, he paid me. I don't have much money."

I reached down and slid my hand into his shirt pocket and pulled out a crumpled pack of cigarettes and matches. I tossed the cigarettes across the room and struck one of the matches and watched it burst into flame as if fascinated by the sight. "Confidentially, I love a good fire," I said. "Except for the smell when there's something nasty in it." I continued to stare at the match until the flame started to burn my fingers, and then I shook it out.

"What do you want from me?" Dewey said, his voice climbing several octaves. "Sending out that stuff wasn't my idea. It was Harold's, it was his mission. Anyways, you can't kill people for what they believe! Haven't you ever read the Constitution?"

"I flunked civics,' Paula told him, and took the matches out of my hand. "I think it's genetic."

"Tell us about Harold's basement," I said. "Describe it to us."

"You mean, like where he worked down there?"

"Yes."

Dewey looked at me as though he thought I was crazy. "It was just a room he'd fixed up—he called it his study. It was cluttered with lots of books and stuff he brought home when he sold his store. There was paper everywhere, too, and his old typewriter—and a machine he used to copy stuff for his mailings. He sort of lived in that room, just went upstairs to eat and sleep. He had a radio and a

TV down there, and he liked to listen to tapes on his tape recorder, too."

"He listened to tapes?" I asked. "Music?" For some reason, I couldn't imagine Harold Mullen listening to music down there in his lair.

"Not music, far's I know. Tapes I brought him from here—you know, speeches by people who thought the same way he did about things. And he recorded stuff off the radio, too—things he liked and didn't like."

That fit better with my image of the man.

"Harold left his money to the University," I said.

"I know that."

"What for?"

"You don't know?"

"I asked you, Dewey."

"Something scientific," he said, stumbling over the word, "that was gonna show that whites shouldn't mix their blood with ..." he shot a look at Paula "... with other people's blood."

"Who was doing this research?" I asked him, holding my breath and waiting.

"I don't know," he replied.

I lit the match I was holding in my hand and stooped down and stared through the flame into Dewey's eyes, which bulged like fat, dark marbles through the folds of skin around them. "Yes, you do," I said.

"I don't," he said, his voice rising. "Honest to God, I don't! All he told me was that the University—he didn't say who at the University—just the University was gonna get his money when he died. He told me he gave them a little—for starters, you know—but they'd have to wait until he was dead for the rest."

"When was this?" I asked.

"A year ago, maybe? A little more? I don't know. It was around the time he was bragging about how he'd had dinner with the president of the University—he thought that was a big deal. Anyway, he said he couldn't give them all his money at once because he didn't know how much the cancer was going to cost him—radiation treatment, the hospital, medicine, and such. He didn't have health insurance, so it could of been ruinous. So he hung onto most of his money and then—he doesn't die, the cancer goes away!"

Dewey was getting into the story now. "He thinks it's God's will that he's going to live—maybe he's even going to live for a long time. So the next thing I know is, he starts telling me about how he's going to buy a chair at the University. You know what I mean by a chair?"

"We know what you mean," I said. "An endowed chair. When did he start talking about that?"

"It wasn't very long before he . . . died," he said, shooting Paula a frightened glance. "He said somebody he'd talked to at the University told him about these chairs. He was gonna pay over a million bucks—everything he's got except what he needed to live on, and Harold didn't need much, you know, except when he had the cancer, for this—what kind of chair?"

"Endowed chair."

"Yeah, right. The doc told him to be careful, the cancer might come back any day, and the University wouldn't give him his money back if he needed it, but Harold just laughed. He didn't believe the cancer was going to come back, he thought he was cured."

Dewey's eyes went to the front door longingly, like an old cat at the pound staring through the wire of the cage.

"Then what?"

He shrugged. "I don't know. I guess then he goes to the University and tells them he wants this chair now, he don't wanna wait. Something like that. The University tells him it's gonna take time to arrange all the details, you can't just get one of these chairs overnight. Harold didn't understand that, he wanted it right away."

Dewey paused to reflect. "I think the cancer changed Harold, or maybe the treatment did. He was on some kind of medicine that really screwed up his head for a while. That's when I started coming in and helped him. He could act real strange sometimes, get real mad if things didn't go the way he wanted 'em to—fly off the handle. Although it got a lot better towards . . . towards. . . ."

"The fiery end," Paula said.

His eyes darted to her, back to me. "Harold told me he wanted to see that chair while he was still able to enjoy it. I told him he should be patient. 'Harold,' I said, 'you know how these big institutions operate. These things take time.' "

Dewey stopped talking again.

"What else?"

"Nothing else. You—." He shot a nervous look at Paula. "He died."

"Think, Dewey," I said. "He must have given you some idea of who he was talking to at the University or which department he was dealing with."

Dewey stared at me. All of a sudden, a great idea struck him square in the face and his eyes flew open. "Hey," he said, "wait a minute. Why're you asking me all these questions?"

"We're curious," I answered. "We like to know all about the people we burn alive. About their hopes, their dreams—"

"You didn't kill Harold, did you?" he said, almost whispering, as if it were our secret.

"Don't be so sure." Dewey was rapidly losing faith in Paula and me as arsonists and murderers. He tried to scramble to his feet. I pushed him back down.

"You didn't kill him, though," he said, still whispering. "I got it wrong." His face lit up with something not unlike intelligence. "Yeah, that's right," he went on. "I should've realized broads like you couldn't kill nobody, not even a sick old man, and then burn his house down."

He sneered and then the sneer turned into a grimace of pain. He hollered and rolled over, pulling his foot up to where he could reach the match Paula had stuck in his shoe and then lit.

"I've never given anybody a hotfoot before," she said,

awed at its effect. "Anything else you want from Dewey, Peggy?"

I asked him where Mullen had heard about endowed chairs—according to Dewey, he'd started talking about endowing a chair shortly before he died.

"He didn't say," Dewey muttered.

"There's no chair at the University named after Harold Mullen," I told him.

"So? That don't mean—." He stopped abruptly.

"That don't mean what?"

"That don't mean nothin'," he said, struggling to his feet but keeping his back to the wall, his eyes moving between Paula and me.

"You thought of something, Dewey," I said. "Tell me, or we're going to take you to jail."

"You gotta be kidding," he said, sneering. "What for?"

"Arson." It was a pathetic effort. For some reason, he'd lost interest in us.

He shrugged, as if going to jail for arson were an everyday occurrence in his life. "Go ahead. Like Duane said, I was here the night of the fire."

"Going to jail's going to cost you money."

He shrugged again. "No, it ain't. Public defenders are free. Besides, ain't there something called false arrest?"

I glanced over at Paula. She shrugged. "This is an area where Dewey seems to have some knowledge, Peggy. Maybe he went to law school, too."

I was sure he was keeping something back, but the threat of arrest wasn't going to make him talk. And he was right, we didn't have any evidence against him that was stronger than Duane Sween's testimony that they'd been together in the store.

Paula saw my shoulders sag. Dewey did, too, and grinned his yellow grin.

"C'mon, Peggy," Paula said, "let's get out of this place."

I oughtta get a lawyer and sue you both," he said.

"Yeah, you oughtta," Paula said.

We started out and than I remembered something. I turned and went back to Dewey, and got a certain pleasure in seeing him flinch back against the wall again. I said, "The night of the fire at Harold's, Dewey, why'd you go back to Mullen's place?"

His eyes flickered and tried to meet mine, slid away. "To help him," he said. "He asked me to come back when I got off work, to help him with something."

"With what?"

"You know, getting stuff ready to mail out." His eyes moved around the room.

"That late at night? What was the big rush? You'd already mailed out two big bags for him that day."

"I told you—Harold was a little strange, on account of the medicine he was taking, I guess."

I stared at him a long time. I didn't believe him. "If you'd gone into Harold's house as you were supposed to, instead of following Paula, you would've burned up in that fire, too, Dewey. Maybe you have Paula to thank for your continued miserable existence."

He stared at Paula in amazement.

We left him in the store, among the books and pamphlets scattered around him, and walked out into the bright evening, the clean, early fall air.

"It was nice," Paula said, "finally getting to see the source of the evil—and getting to meet Dewey, too. Thanks, Peggy."

"You're welcome. But only you and Dewey got anything out of it. I'm no farther along than I was."

"What did Dewey get out of it?"

"Until now, it never occurred to him that somebody might have cheated Mullen out of his money."

"Why should it?" Paula asked. "He thought I'd killed Mullen." She suddenly burst out laughing. "Anyway, it was kind of fun, wasn't it, terrorizing the little rodent?"

"The hotfoot was unconscionable," I said, giving her a hard look.

She nodded, giggling. I'd never heard her giggle before.

"If Lawrence had done it, I wouldn't have approved at all."

"Too bad Lawrence couldn't have been with us," I said.

"Oh, I don't know. Sometimes it's more fun when it's just us girls."

Twenty-Seven

I called Edith Silberman when I got home and I asked her what endowed chairs cost.

"It depends," she said. "In the humanities, you might get one for as little as a million bucks. In the sciences, one and a half million would probably be the least you'd expect to pay."

"Why so much?"

"Well, the endowment has to pay for more than just the professor's salary, which would have to be quite large, since endowed chairs go only to stars. The fringe benefits—health insurance and retirement—have to come out of it too. In the sciences, you'd also expect to pay for a lab for the guy, plus give him an equipment allowance and a personal secretary. It all adds up."

"How about in psychology?" I asked her.

"The psychologists think they're scientists and they've fooled a lot of the rest of the world into thinking they are, too, so you wouldn't expect to fund an endowed chair for less than a million and a half. What's all this about, Peggy? You're still trying to find out what that dead old bigot did with his money?"

"That's right."

"You think he left it for an endowed chair?"

"I think he thought he did."

Aunt Tess arrived on Sunday and we spent it at a shopping mall, worshiping. Tess, when she finally does drive down to the big city from her little town, turns into a compulsive shopper with a specialty in hats, the odder the better. She managed to force on me a green suede cap that made me look like an overgrown Girl Scout.

"It goes perfectly with your eyes and hair," she said. "No man'll be able to resist you—although that's not the problem, is it? If I were you, I would have followed that delightful young man—Gary, was it?—to Belize. It would be quite an adventure, and you could always come back here if things didn't work out, you know."

Mutter, mutter. The cap would go into the back of the closet with a lot of other accessories Aunt Tess has bought me over the years, as soon as she'd returned home.

The next day, Labor Day, we drove to Lillian Przynski's. She was waiting for us on the porch, a tiny figure in a beige cloth coat and a matching beret with a little pom-pom on the top. After I'd put her in the backseat and introduced her to Tess, she said, "My, you look very nice in that outfit, Peggy. I've never seen you looking so spiffy."

"I'm not surprised," growled Tess.

"And that cap is nice, too," Lillian went on. "Were you ever a Girl Scout?"

As we were finishing our after-dinner coffee, she said, "Is it all right to talk business, Peggy?"

"Sure."

"I had the strangest conversation yesterday with Dell Baker, Bud's lawyer," she said.

"Who's Dell Baker and who's Bud?" Aunt Tess asked.

When I'd told her, Lillian continued, "Baker came over yesterday evening. He wanted to know if I knew where Dewey lived."

"On a Sunday?" I asked.

Lillian nodded. "He said Dewey had called him on Saturday and left a message on his answering machine. He had something important to tell Baker about Bud's money, but he didn't leave a phone number where Baker could call him back."

Lillian shot me a shrewd glance. "I thought Mr. Baker's story sounded fishy. Maybe I didn't hide my disbelief too well because he explained—talking just a little too fast, if you ask me—that a good lawyer likes to tie up loose ends quickly. You get into less trouble that way, he said, with that loud laugh of his. Well, you know, Peggy, he'd seemed a little eely the first time he came to see me, asking all kinds of questions about Bud, and this time he looked nervous to boot. And what information would Dewey have about Bud's money that would be so important that Baker would drive all the way over to my place on a Sunday to get it? So I told him I had no idea where Dewey lived. He stared at me a long time, as if trying to see into my heart of hearts, and then sighed and gave me his card and asked me to contact him if I heard from Dewey. I'm sure you know where that card is now, Peggy."

"Are you poking that sharp little nose of yours in where it doesn't belong again, Peggy?" Tess demanded.

I admitted it.

Tuesday afternoon, as soon as I'd got Tess on the road home, I drove across town, to the address I'd taken from Dewey Fesler's driver's license at the book store. Paula and I seemed to have stirred things up a little: It was probably not a coincidence that, the day after we'd talked to him, Dewey tried to contact Dell Baker, and Baker immediately went looking for Dewey.

Dewey lived in an old apartment house next to the railroad tracks, a four-story square of dingy brick about half a mile from The Nordic Advocate. I parked and went up to the door, found Dewey's name next to the number 6, and went in. The place smelled of disinfectant and stale cigarette smoke.

Apartment 6 was in the basement. I followed the threadbare carpeting downstairs and along a dimly lit hall, the sound of country music getting louder as I went. It was coming from the apartment next to Dewey's. I knocked on Dewey's door and waited. Nothing. I tried again, with the same result.

The hall was empty, so I stooped down and peeked through the keyhole, but it was too dark to see anything inside. I rattled the door. It was locked, but the door had shrunk away from the frame over the years and I could see the old lock's tongue.

I walked back down the hall to the laundry room, went inside, and flicked on the light. At the end of the room was a workbench with tools on it. I chose a screwdriver that looked like it would do, took it back, and pried open Dewey's lock. It took about two seconds. I went in and flipped on the light.

It was a single room with one curtainless window, the blind pulled down, an old overstuffed chair in one corner, a rickety lamp next to it, and a newspaper on the bare floor in front of it. There was a bed against one wall, neatly made and covered with a gray chenille spread worn thin in places.

A table against a wall held a radio and a number of cassette tapes, but no tape player. The cassettes were mostly of country singers I'd never heard of. I wondered what it sounded like when both Dewey and his neighbor had their country music playing at the same time. Badly worn paperback novels were scattered on the table, too—soft porn, hard porn and westerns, but no racist stuff. He probably got all he needed at the book store.

I went over to a closet and looked inside: A few un-ironed shirts on hangers, a couple of pairs of pants, a dresser that contained a few pairs of socks and underwear, and nothing else.

I walked back out into the room, stood and listened to the steady thump and whine of the music next door. I felt like Snow White, visiting one of the dwarfs who'd decided to strike out on his own and ended up in this dismal dump.

I closed the door behind me and walked back down the hall. A man was coming my way, wearing an undershirt over his enormous belly, his trousers open all the way, revealing boxer shorts.

"You looking for a room? We got vacancies."

"I'm looking for Dewey Fesler," I said.

"Dewey?" He took a second, considerably more interested, look at me. "What'd'ya want with him?"

"Are you the caretaker?"

"I own this place."

"I owe Dewey some money," I said. "He did some work for me—painted a fence."

"Yeah, well, that's about Dewey's speed, I guess. He went to his mother's for Labor Day."

"His mother?" The knowledge that Dewey might have a mother was startling—disturbing, too, for some reason. "Do you know where she lives?"

"No idea." He gave me a skeptical grin. "You're so anxious to give Dewey money that you wanna take it to him at his mother's?"

"Did he say when he'd be back?"

"A week, maybe. He wasn't sure."

I drove back to the book store, parked on the side street, and went into the alley, looking for Dewey's car. It wasn't there, it wasn't in front of the store, either. I pushed open the door and stepped in, hearing the bell jangle in back.

Duane Sween came out from the back of the store and stopped in his tracks when he saw me.

"I'm looking for Dewey," I told him.

"Oh yeah? What d'you think I am, his social secretary? I figured he was in jail—thanks to you and your Negroid friend."

"I heard he was visiting his mother."

"If you say so."

"He works here, doesn't he?"

"You could call it that."

Sween was grinning at some private joke, and talking too loudly. He'd also closed the door to the back room behind him when he'd come in. He hadn't done that the first time I'd been in the place.

"Thanks," I said. "I'll try again some other time."

"You do that."

* * *

Since Lillian Przynski lived only a few minutes from the book store, I drove to her house. She offered me tea, I helped her make it, and then told her that I couldn't find Dewey—he'd gone home to visit his mother.

She gave me a shrewd look. "And you don't think so, is that it?"

I shrugged. "I don't know. But when he's looking for Baker and Baker's looking for him, it seems a little odd that he'd leave town for a week."

I described the scene in the racist book store on Friday, when Paula and I had terrorized Dewey. Lillian listened and smiled sadly at the parts I thought were funny, but she didn't laugh.

"I can understand how you feel about him, Peggy," she said, "and especially your friend Paula. Maybe he really has gone home to visit his mother. There's good in everbody, I think—even Dewey."

"Paula and I didn't have time to look for that," I replied.

"Or the inclination, either. I know." Sometimes it was hard to know when Lillian was shaking her head sadly, and when her head was just shaking because that's what it did.

As I was about to get up to go, she said, "I've been thinking a lot about the past, Peggy, since you first showed up on my doorstep and told me the awful things you thought Bud had done. A few days ago, I got out my picture album from when we were kids and went through it. I could remember some of the things I was doing when the pictures were taken more than sixty years ago as if they'd happened yesterday—the adults' voices, telling us to be still, the laughter and the crying of the children."

Her big eyes grew brighter when she looked at me.

"I'd like to show you a few pictures of Bud when he was a child. He wasn't bad then, you know. He was just different."

She pulled herself up out of her cushioned rocker and went to a side table.

"Scoot my chair over by you, will you, Peggy?" she

said when she returned with an old photo album. She sat down next to me, opened the album, and put it in my lap.

We sat there like two old ladies sharing memories. The pictures of Harold Mullen as a child bore only the slightest resemblance to the old man I'd seen, briefly, on two occasions. He looked shy and always seemed to be standing apart, his head cast down or his eyes averted, or both. As a child, Lillian had the same mischievous smile she had now, and the same big, open eyes.

We almost missed it. As she was about to turn a page, Lillian paused and said, "Oh, look. Here's that girlfriend of Bud's I told you about—you remember, the little girl he carried a torch for from the time he was just a little boy." She'd told me the story, I remembered, the first time we'd sat here together.

It was a small picture, of a girl of about fourteen with a round face, cute smile, and curly hair.

"I think she was the first and last date Bud had in his life," Lillian said. "Now what was her name?"

"Grace Sterns," I said.

She looked up at me, startled, and said, "Why yes! How'd you know?"

I told her about the account in Grace Sterns's name in the Psych Department and the research library that was named after her. "That's what your brother did with his money—with some of it, at least," I said.

"Oh, but Peggy, Grace wouldn't have wanted him to do anything racist with his money. You remember, I told you she married a Jew!"

"I guess that must have been the point," I said.

Twenty-Eight

When I got home, I called Susan at the Psych Department. It was a few minutes after four-thirty, quitting time, but she answered anyway. I told her I'd found out where Harold Mullen's money was.

"Good heavens!" she said in mock horror. "Now what're you going to do for a hobby?"

"Ha, ha! It's the Grace Sterns account."

"Grace Sterns! You mean that sweet little girl in the photograph in the library was a frothing-at-the-mouth racist?"

"No, but it's a long story. Can you find out how much is in that account?"

"I'll call you back in a few minutes."

Ten minutes later, she called and said, "The University Club deposits about $20,000 in that account a year. If we're the only unit in the University getting Mullen's money, and our twenty thou is the interest on the principal, that means Mullen left the University about $150,000."

"That's *all*? Mullen must have been worth at least a million dollars when he died, Susan—probably more."

"You know, Peggy, Mullen's money doesn't all have to be coming to us. It could be going into accounts all over the University."

"I don't think so," I said. "He was talking about an endowed chair. That takes a lot of money, all in one place."

"Well, we've got three endowed chairs in the Psych Department. We've had them for years and years, so none of them is funded by Mullen's money. Give it up now, Peggy. At least you've found a piece of Mullen's money. The rest of it could be in any of a hundred places within the U."

I thanked her, made a racquetball date for the next day, and hung up.

I was sure I'd found all of Harold Mullen's money that the University had. I wasn't at all sure I'd found all the money Harold thought the University was going to get.

Should I call Buck and tell him about the Grace Sterns account? Would that be enough to convince him to get a court order to allow him access to the University Club's files to look for Mullen's money?

Probably not. As Susan had said, I still had no proof that Mullen's money—in the capable hands of Stanford Driggs and the University Club—wasn't exactly where Mullen wanted it to be and doing what he wanted it to do. After all, this wasn't part of a homicide investigation. I was still the only person, besides their killer, who thought Harold Mullen's and Geoffrey Oates's deaths were murder.

I still wanted to try to find out what Dewey Fesler had to tell Dell Baker that was so important. So, a little after six that night, I drove back to Dewey's place and knocked on his door. This time, the basement was mercifully silent. When there was no answer, I bent down and peered through the keyhole. The room was dark.

As I straightened up, the door next to Dewey's opened and a woman stepped out, bringing with her the stench of stale tobacco. It almost knocked me over. She was wearing a country-western outfit—short white leather skirt and matching boots; fringe was everywhere. It was hard to tell how old she was, anywhere from forty-five to seventy.

"I'm over here," she said. "I thought it was gonna be a guy."

I started to say what anybody would say in that situation—"Huh?"—but caught myself in time. "Why'd you think that?" I asked.

She shrugged. "Dewey kept saying a guy'd be coming with the envelope."

"I'm Lucille, his secretary," I said, stepping into a story without a script. "Right at five, when he knows I gotta run to pick up the little one at day care, he asked me to come over here—oh, he asked me politely enough, of course, but what am I supposed to do, say no? You have any idea what the job market's like out there?"

"Yeah, ain't it the truth?" she said, shaking her head sympathetically.

"Just out of curiosity," I asked her, "what are you supposed to do with this precious envelope once you get it?"

"Keep it 'til Dewey calls, then open it and read it to him over the phone. Sounded a little nuts to me, but what the hell, ten bucks is ten bucks."

"Well, thanks," I said, and turned and headed back down the hall.

"Hey, wait. Where's the envelope?"

"What envelope?" I asked and got out of there.

I guessed that the man she'd been expecting was Dell Baker, but I couldn't imagine what information he was supposed to be bringing Dewey in such a complicated way. It seemed obvious, though, that Dewey didn't trust Baker enough to get whatever it was from him directly.

I drove slowly past the book store. A Closed sign was visible in the display window. I thought there was a good chance Dewey was temporarily living in the store now. From the way Duane Sween had acted yesterday, I suspected Dewey might even have been in the back room or the basement when I was there asking about him.

I parked in front of the store and walked around the block looking for Dewey's car. It was a chilly night, and I wished I'd worn a jacket or sweater. On the street behind the book store, many of the old houses had been turned into apartments. Music leaked from windows, closed now in the early fall, and television light flickered behind drawn blinds.

Halfway down the block, a man who'd been walking

ahead of me crossed the street briskly and got into a car. As I approached, the headlights blinked on and the car pulled away from the curb. As it passed beneath the streetlight at the end of the block, I thought it looked like Dewey's huge clunker, except the driver looked too big to be Dewey.

I broke into a half-run, to try to get a glimpse of who it was, but I was too late. I stood half out in the street and watched it disappear around a corner. Old gas-guzzlers had made a career of pulling away from me lately. At least the driver of this one wasn't Dewey Fesler, I was sure of that. I continued around the block, past the boarded up movie theater and back to the book store. I rattled the door disconsolately, but it was locked. I knocked and listened. It sounded like something inside was holding its breath, but it was only me, outside, holding mine in order to try to hear. I started to leave and then heard what sounded like footsteps inside.

I knocked again, louder, and listened, but there was only silence.

I walked around the block again and turned down the alley in back of the book store. Dim yellow light glowed faintly through the blind in front of a barred first-floor window that I knew was the back room of the store. At ground level, just to the right of the back door, was a narrow window with a grill in front of it. I went over, knelt down, and tried to see through the gap.

It was a basement storage room, cluttered with boxes, shelves, and books, illuminated by a naked light bulb hanging from the ceiling by its cord. Dewey Fesler lay sprawled faceup on a floor that was littered with books and paper. His arms and legs were splayed out, his heavy lids only partially covered his eyes, and the handle of a knife protruded from his blood-soaked chest.

I scrambled to my feet, turned, and started to run out of there. The back door swung open in my face, knocking me backward, and Brice Ridgeway stepped out. He had a pistol in his big hand.

"I'm very good with these," he whispered. "Come inside." His voice was shaking slightly, but the pistol wasn't. Keeping his eyes on mine and the revolver steady on my chest, he backed away from the door, a foot at a time. Still dazed from the blow from the door, I followed him into the narrow passageway. Ridgeway flattened himself against the wall and indicated with his head for me to go past him.

As I did, I grabbed for the hand holding the gun and tried to twist sideways, but he must have been expecting that. He pushed away from the wall behind him and slammed me against the opposite wall with his heavy body, knocking the breath out of me and pinning me there. Out of the corner of my eye I saw the pistol rise and come down, and I tried to duck away. I heard Ridgeway's grunt of effort, and something like a bottle exploded in my head.

Twenty-Nine

I tried to raise my head, but the pain made me lower it again onto a rough surface of some kind. I opened my eyes and focused on a pair of large running shoes. They looked expensive. I remembered Brice Ridgeway.

I raised my head again, more slowly this time, and tried to straighten out my body. A sharp, burning jab in my side made me cry out and squeeze my eyes shut. When I opened them, the running shoes weren't there. I carefully turned my head, to see where they'd gone. Brice Ridgeway was lowering himself onto a wooden chair a few feet away. He put the revolver on a wooden table next to him.

I moved my eyes to Ridgeway's right. A shapeless form that I knew was Dewey's body was where I'd seen it from the basement window, in the pool of light from the naked bulb above him. Inconsequentially, I heard Lillian Przynski's voice saying, "It can't be easy being Dewey." It wasn't easy being Peggy O'Neill just then, either.

I glanced back at Ridgeway. He was watching me incuriously, his face pale. In spite of the pain, I slowly inched my way into a sitting position, my back against the lowest step of a flight of old wooden stairs. It took forever. Something was horribly wrong with my shoulder and side, and I couldn't move my right arm.

"You threw me down the stairs, didn't you, you bastard?" I croaked.

Ridgeway didn't reply, just went on staring at me.

"Look behind you," I tried again. "There's a corpse on the floor."

Apparently undergraduate humor left him cold. He looked at his watch.

"What are you waiting for?" I tried to keep the panic out of my voice. I wanted to hear him speak.

"Baker." He cleared his throat nervously, tried again. "Dell Baker."

"He drove off in Dewey's car. Why?"

His eyes moved away from me. "Miss O'Neill, I don't want to talk about it."

"You've killed three people and you don't want to talk about it to your next victim?" I whispered hoarsely. "At least tell me what it's all about! It'll make the time go faster for both of us, won't it?"

"You know what it's all about," he said dully. "It's about Harold Mullen's money. Dell and I stole it. That's what you wanted to know, that's what brought you here to-night. Are you satisfied now?"

"How?"

He reached into his jacket pocket and pulled out his pipe, took his time lighting it, puffs of smoke like blue clouds floating around his distinguished head, but I noticed that his hands were trembling slightly.

"Mullen wanted to do something useful with his money," he said, just as I was about to ask him again. His voice was flat, drained of all emotion. "I'm sure you know what he meant by *useful*. He went to Dell—to Baker, his lawyer. Mullen had read about the Scripter Fund business in the newspaper. He wanted to know more about the type of research we were conducting. Dell contacted me—we go back a long ways, I guess you found that out, too, didn't you?"—and arranged for us to meet. I cultivated the old man, had him shown around our labs, and introduced him to the other members of the faculty. I even took him to dinner at the president's, as I told you. He said some pretty awful things, but money was involved, so

Hightower pretended not to hear. There isn't much a university president won't ignore when there's money involved."

Hearing his own voice seemed to relax Ridgeway, the way it does so many professors.

"After that night, Miss O'Neill, I had Mullen eating out of my hand. Quite frankly, he worshiped me. I was the scientist who was going to bring his ideas out of places like this"—he waved his pipe around the book store's basement— "and make them respectable."

"And you took advantage of that worship and his lack of knowledge of how the University works."

"Of course I did—why not? Think what he might have done with his money, if Dell and I hadn't taken it. We were doing the world a favor."

Ridgeway sucked on his pipe, took it out of his mouth, and looked at it critically. Then he brought out his box of wooden matches and relit it, concentrating on what he was doing. His hands were steady now.

He glanced at his watch again and then continued speaking. "Dell and Mullen went to the University Club and arranged for Mullen's money to go to the Human Genetics Research Project after his death. In the meantime, we talked him into giving the project some of his money while he was still alive. The afternoon Mullen came to the Psych Department to see our labs, I asked Geoff Oates to show him the Roy Heslop Library. You know about Heslop?"

"Yes."

"Heslop's just a curiosity now, of course, but we still have some of his eugenics nonsense in the files and a few of his books on the shelves. He was virulently opposed to the mixing of the races. Mullen was delighted. Those old books convinced him we were seriously interested in 'racial betterment through science.' The upshot was, Mullen wanted a library, too. I would have talked him out of that—he was a little unstable, and I didn't want his name associated with the project, at least not while he was alive—but then it turned out he didn't want anything in his own name, he wanted it in the name of an old flame of his."

"Grace Sterns," I said.

He nodded, not particularly surprised or impressed that I'd got that far. "To hear him talk about it—and I did, Miss O'Neill, ad nauseum—it was the love story of the century, but poor Grace died before they could marry. She shared his beliefs about race and racial purity."

Ridgeway made a face. "Dell Baker and Stanford Driggs set up an account for Mullen in the University Club and I had old Heslop's name and portrait taken down and hers put up in its place. It took a couple of hundred dollars and ten minutes of your friend Susan's time," he added dryly.

"Harold Mullen thought that, when he died, the trust would get the balance of his money—and it did, too, except that Dell and I had taken most of what he thought he had by then. Mullen wasn't in very good shape by then, you know, and he was also taking some powerful medication. Dell had power of attorney—he'd got that when Mullen first became ill—and we took him for just about everything he had."

Ridgeway paused to relight his pipe again. Between puffs, he said, "It looked like everything was going to go just the way Dell said it would."

"Except that Mullen's cancer went into remission," I put in.

A faint hint of annoyance crept into Ridgeway's voice. "The old fool was supposed to die last winter! Dell and I didn't want to murder anybody! I talked to Mullen's doctor myself—a cancer surgeon I know slightly at the University hospital—and he assured me Mullen couldn't live six months. I ought to sue the son of a bitch for malpractice!" That was the only humorous thing I ever heard from Brice Ridgway—assuming, of course, he didn't mean it.

"That was a blow," he went on with feeling. "You can't imagine how horrid it was to me, to see Mullen start to blossom again. But still, everything would have been fine. Mullen suspected nothing and couldn't live forever."

"And then along came Geoffrey Oates," I said. "He thought you were going to ruin him, and he figured out there was something fishy going on between you and Mullen."

"Goddamn it," Ridgeway exploded, "I assured Oates I didn't hold what happened at Gardner's against him! What did he think I was, some kind of monster? But he didn't believe me. All right, I did lose my temper and throw him in the pool. But I apologized, didn't I?"

"No, I don't think you did. And you are some kind of monster," I added.

He waved that away. "Mullen sometimes called me at my office, although I discouraged it—but obviously I couldn't forbid it. Once, Oates took the call and spoke to Mullen for a few minutes—he'd shown Mullen around the project, and Mullen remembered his name—and Mullen invited Oates to dinner. I don't know if Oates already suspected something, or if he really wanted to go to dinner with the old man. In any case, they agreed to have dinner on the Fourth of July, and that's when Oates learned enough to figure out what Dell and I were doing."

"He tried to blackmail you?"

"You could call it that, I suppose. He wanted two things, a letter from me recommending him to another university—a letter so strong that I couldn't very well hurt him at some later time without making a fool of myself— and he wanted me to put Mullen's money into an endowed chair!"

I laughed and then wished I hadn't. "Why didn't you?" I asked, when the pain had subsided a little.

"I would have written the letter, gladly," Ridgeway said, "although it would have been an embarrassment for me professionally, since Oates wasn't a very promising student. But there was no way I could get an endowed chair for Mullen. There wasn't enough of his money left for that."

"Couldn't you have done what Troy did," I asked, "and gone to the 'nurseryman'?"

"You found out about that, too?" He shrugged. "I couldn't go to them. Can you imagine what their interest rates are? Those people would have owned me! And besides, Dell wouldn't go along with that and Mullen wouldn't have, either. He wanted that goddamned chair Oates told him about, and he wanted it immediately! So there was no other way than to kill him."

"Tell me, Professor Ridgeway," I said. "Do you think you were born bad—if you'll excuse a value-weighted, old-fashioned word like that—or did you become bad through environmental factors?"

He gazed thoughtfully at me, as if I were a student in a seminar. "What I've done, Miss O'Neill," he said finally, "was completely rational and from the purest motives: I did it to save my son, Troy. A father has a right—even a duty—to save his son's life. I didn't know it would involve murder when I took the first step—but I would have done it, even if I had known. After all, Mullen's was a worthless life."

"But not Geoffrey Oates's," I said. "And he died along with Harold Mullen, then Dewey Fesler, and now me—not on account of some high moral purpose but because Geoff Oates—running an errand for Lyle Gardner—stumbled on you making love to Gardner's wife. And instead of realizing the fault was yours, you took your shame out on Oates. The reason for all the blood on your hands, Professor Ridgeway, is because you're a morally sick man who's worked too long in a corrupt system that's given you too much power."

He stared down at me as I crouched on the floor, and tried to say something. Then he closed his mouth and looked away.

"Did you share her?" I asked him. "You and Troy?"

His eyes came back to me. "Who?"

"Shelley Gardner."

"What do you mean?"

"Troy's having an affair with her now—didn't you know?"

"He is?" A grin of paternal pride split his distinguished face. "I'll be damned!"

Thirty

There was a sudden noise upstairs, the sound of the back door opening and shutting and then heavy footsteps crossing the floor and starting down the basement stairs. They stopped halfway down. I looked up, moving my head slowly. Dell Baker was standing there, two large red cans of gasoline in his hands, staring down at me.

"Hi," I said.

"What the?—" Then he saw Ridgeway and came the rest of the way down the stairs, stepping over me, keeping his eyes on me. "What's she doing here?" When Ridgeway told him, he said, "Why's she still alive?"

"I didn't want to use the gun."

"So get the knife out of Fesler, Brice. Okay?"

"I'll bet you two guys were real mischief-makers in the frat house," I said.

"Cutups," Baker said, matter-of-factly, "we were real cutups. But sometimes Brice needed a little encouragement. He still does."

"He's been telling me the story I've been trying to figure out for the past month, but we hadn't got to Dewey over there yet."

"Dewey Fesler," Baker said, giving the object under discussion a contemptuous glance. "He got it into his head for some reason that a black friend of yours burned down Harold's house. When it dawned on him that she hadn't, he decided it must have been Brice who did."

"Why'd he think that?"

"He got hold of a tape Harold had made of a conversation between Harold and Brice," Baker said. He was kneeling by his gas cans. unscrewing the caps. "You see, old Harold worshiped the ground Brice walked on, and he was so delighted to discover that Brice shared his views on all kinds of issues that he taped their conversations! Hell, maybe he was even wired when Brice took him to the president's for dinner. You think so, Brice?"

Ridgeway shrugged. He seemed to have grown smaller since Baker had arrived.

"I don't think Harold taped their conversations because he didn't trust Brice," Baker went on. "I think he just wanted to have the tapes to play sometimes. His was a lonely existence."

He walked to the back of the basement and began sloshing gasoline from one of the cans on the shelves and floor. He paused to pour some on Dewey, too.

I remembered how Baker had referred to Mullen as a corn chip on our first meeting. I suppose lawyers take classes on how to avoid becoming sentimental about the innocent people they have to destroy for profit. I hoped Paula wouldn't be a lawyer like that—and realized suddenly I wasn't gong to live to see Paula's progress through law school, or be there when she graduated.

"How did Dewey get hold of one of the tapes?" I asked.

"We don't have the time, Miss O'Neill," Baker said, walking toward me with the second can of gasoline. I thought he was going to pour it on me, but he went around me to the area behind the basement stairs and began pouring gasoline there. The room was filled with the nauseating reek of the fumes, adding a headache to my other pains.

"You can die as you lived," he went on, coming back and standing in front of me, "with lots of unanswered questions. Brice, give me your matches, and either kill her or we burn her alive."

Ridgeway was standing now, too. He hesitated, looking from the corpse on the floor to me. There was confusion on his face, as if he were trying to understand how life had brought him to this moment and this place.

"Now, Brice!" Baker's voice had the shrill finality of a paddle on a bare ass.

Ridgeway handed Baker his matches and went over to Dewey. Baker crumpled a piece of newspaper and set it on fire with one of the matches.

I slid my legs under me, almost screamed at the pain as I glanced over my shoulder to locate the stair railing I'd have to try to reach to pull myself up. I knew I didn't stand any chance at all, but I had to act as if I did.

The floor above us creaked. Ridgeway swung around, staring up, the knife in his hand, and then he turned and looked at Baker, panic in his eyes. Baker tossed the burning paper at the gasoline and lunged for the stairs, grabbing the pistol off the table as he went. He jumped over me. Ridgeway followed, the bloody knife in his hand, as the room burst into flame.

I screamed, twisted my body and strained to reach the railing to try to pull myself up. Pain unlike anything I'd ever felt before tore through my shoulder and side. I couldn't lift myself to reach the railing, and my arm was useless anyway. Behind me the shelves were blazing and sheets of fire were running up the books and boxes stacked against the walls. Over the roar of the blaze, I heard a shot above me and then another, and then I heard a shout that sounded like Paula's voice.

Using only my legs, I lifted my body onto the lowest step. The smoke and heat were becoming unbearable, but the pain was worse. Thin streams of fire began running across the floor to the gasoline-drenched clutter under the stairs beneath me, and I kicked desperately at the next step with one foot, just for something to do, and then I started to lose consciousness.

Then Lawrence was beside me, his beautiful face close to mine, as in a dream. The pain of being lifted was too much and I lost consciousness.

Some Last Things

I was bandaged up pretty tightly the next morning and still in pain, but I refused codeine and demanded coffee instead, to kill the taste of the hospital breakfast. A couple of ribs and my left wrist were broken, and they'd put stitches in various sections of my head, too, where Ridgeway had cracked it with his pistol and where I'd hit it when he'd dragged or thrown me down the basement stairs. A surgeon said I also had second-grade splenic lacerations, and she wanted to remove my spleen, but I told her no. She went away mad, as surgeons will.

Lawrence came in. "Sorry I had to be so rough when I picked you up," he said, looking around for a place to put the flowers—mums in fall colors. "I was afraid I'd killed you."

"It was either you or the fire. Where's Paula?" I remembered the gunshot I'd heard.

"In class. She'll be over tonight." He came over and kissed me on the forehead. "I hope you realize it's because she's studying law that you're alive."

"That's not the first explanation that would've occurred to me, Lawrence, but what do I know?"

"If she wasn't in law school," he explained patiently, "she'd still be working the second watch, right?"

"So?"

"She'd have been patrolling the campus while you were burning up."

"Possibly true," I admitted, "but that doesn't make it immediately clear to me how the two of you came riding into the book store at the last moment and rescued me."

"Well, if Paula wasn't in law school, I'd still be working the second watch, too. So I wouldn't be able to drive to the University to pick her up at night and bring her home. I do that because I don't want her out on the streets after dark alone—not now, when she doesn't have her uniform, pistol, and portable radio anymore."

"Nice mums, Lawrence," I said, weakly. "Are they from your yard?"

"Yeah. So anyway, I picked her up in front of the law library last night, and as we were driving home she asked me if I'd be interested in driving by the book store where all the hate mail had come from and where you'd found Dewey. It's just a little out of the way and I hadn't seen it yet.

"I thought about it for a moment or two," he went on, in a futile effort to build suspense, "whether I wanted to see the store or go right home, I mean. But I knew that, when we got home, Paula would just eat the tuna-noodle casserole I'd fixed that was waiting in the oven, then disappear into her study, and that's the last I'd see of her until bedtime. So I said, 'Sure, why not?'—not because I really cared one way or the other, you see, but because I like being with her. So we drove past the book store, and guess what we saw out front?"

"Golly," I said, "let me think. My little Rabbit?"

"Right, and we wondered what you were up to. So we drove around the block and saw an old car pulling into the alley behind the book store. It looked like the car you and I'd seen speeding away from our house the night of the fire. So we thought it would be a good idea to see what was up. I mean, we couldn't just drive home after that, could we, and go about our business?"

"I don't know," I said. "That tuna-noodle casserole sounds pretty tempting to me."

A nurse came in and took my temperature, blood pressure, and heart rate. "My heart rate's probably going to be elevated," I warned her. "I'm under the spell of a master storyteller."

"Seems normal to me," she said and departed.

"Paula peered through a crack in the blind over the basement window," Lawrence went on. "I thought she was going to have a heart attack. We tried the back door and it was unlocked—maybe Baker and Ridgeway figured they needed to get out fast—and went in."

Lawrence got up and strolled to the door. "The rest is history," he said.

"Come back here, you idiot!"

"Why?"

"Then what happened?" I said more quietly. Hollering had been a mistake.

"Oh, well, if you really want to know." He came back to my bed. If I didn't know Lawrence so well, I would have sworn he was trying not to laugh at me. "They came rushing upstairs, Baker first, waving a pistol," he said. "He pointed it at me, I guess because he thought I was the dangerous one, but as he pulled the trigger, Paula kicked him in the nuts, which can really throw a guy's aim off. His second shot went even wilder because he was trying to avoid what Paula was going to do to him next. Ridgeway rushed at me, and I hit him and then left him to Paula because I heard you scream downstairs and smelled gasoline. And that's it. We managed to drag Ridgeway and Baker outside, too, before the book store went up, like a rocket on the Fourth of July."

I reached up carefully with my good arm and put it around his neck. "Lawrence the Laurel-Crowned," I said. "Thanks."

I was home two nights later, propped up on the couch in my living room, still in a little pain. Paula and Lawrence were there, of course, as well as Mrs. Hammer and Lillian Przynski. Susan Carlisle was there with Kate, her partner, since Susan had played an important role in the story. Ginny Raines had also managed to insinuate herself into the group, just as she'd done on the Fourth of July, probably because she knew there'd be dessert. We were all eating popcorn and listening to Buck Hansen finish the story Dell Baker decided he and Ridgeway didn't have time to finish for me. I was drinking coffee and Lillian tea, and the others had bottles of beer in front of them.

"A few days before he was killed," Buck said, "Mullen gave Dewey Fesler his tape player to be fixed. Fesler had done simple electronic repair work for Mullen when Mullen had his store. Fesler took it home and fixed it, but forgot to bring it back the day of the fire. Mullen told him he needed it by the next morning because he wanted to tape something important—most likely a conversation he expected to have with Brice Ridgeway about the endowed chair."

"Dewey must have been returning the tape recorder when he spotted me leaving Mullen's house," Paula said.

Buck nodded. "If Fesler had arrived a little sooner, Baker would have killed him, too, and the tape Mullen left in the machine would have burned up with both of them."

"So it was Dell Baker who killed Mullen?" I asked.

"Right."

Susan asked Buck why Baker had burned down Mullen's house.

"To try to make it look like an accident and also to destroy the evidence of Mullen's hate-mail activities. Ridgeway didn't want anybody looking too closely into Mullen's life in case it ever came out that he'd left his money to the University. People might wonder if a university should take money from somebody like that."

"And also, some nosey-parker might start asking questions," Ginny said, speaking around a mouthful of popcorn and looking at me.

"But surely it must have been a very big risk for a man like Ridgeway to get involved with somebody as unstable as Bud," Lillian Przynski said.

"Ridgeway didn't know about your brother's hate-mail

activities when he first became involved with him," Buck told her. "When Mullen finally told him—he thought Ridgeway would be impressed—Ridgeway was horrified, but it was too late for him to back out, even if he'd wanted to. He and Baker had already taken a lot of Mullen's money, and Ridgeway had used most of his share of it to pay off his son's debt."

"I suppose Ridgeway killed Oates," I said.

Buck nodded. "That little parking lot's right next to the river bluffs. Ridgeway waited in the trees until he saw Oates come out of the Psych Building, then followed him to his car. Ridgeway left the way he'd come, via the riverbank."

Recalling the animals' heads hanging from the walls of Ridgeway's house, I supposed that stalking and killing unsuspecting creatures came easy to him.

"And as Mullen's trusted lawyer, Baker wouldn't have any trouble getting into Mullen's house and killing him," I said.

"Right." Buck chewed a handful of popcorn, chased it with a swallow of beer, then looked thoughtfully at the flavored salt on his fingers. It's my secret recipe. "So Mullen and Oates were dead and Dewey had the tape. It's a conversation between Mullen and Ridgeway that contains just about everything but Ridgeway's last name. It's 'Brice this' and 'Brice that' and 'What do you think about this, Brice?' in Mullen's high, reedy voice. And Ridgeway expands with enthusiasm on every racist notion Mullen proposes, in his deep, professorial voice. It would play well at a Ku Klux Klan rally, and if it had got out, Ridgeway would have been ruined. With Dewey's testimony to back it up, it would also have led to an investigation into Mullen's finances, and that would have ruined Baker, too."

"What did Baker need money for?" Susan asked.

"He didn't need it. But he saw it there, ripe for the taking, and knew his old fraternity buddy Brice needed money desperately. Together they decided it would be almost a righteous act to steal it."

"It must have been a little like that question we used to

pose when we were children," Mrs. Hammer put in. "If by pressing a button that killed a man somewhere in China you'd get a million dollars, would you do it? A lot of people would because they wouldn't have to know the consequences of their actions."

"Harold Mullen wasn't as innocent as the man in China," Buck said, "but Geoff Oates was. And Peggy, too."

"I'm not innocent," I said. "I'm responsible for Dewey Fesler's death."

"Oh, Peggy!" Lillian and Mrs. Hammer said simultaneously.

"Don't be grandiose," Ginny growled.

"I was the one who made Dewey realize Paula hadn't killed his friend Harold," I said, "and that Harold's money wasn't where it was supposed to be. That must have been when he remembered the tape and played it."

"I hope you're not going to lose sleep over it," Paula said.

Buck drained his glass, poured some more beer. "According to Ridgeway, Fesler knew Baker was Mullen's lawyer, so he called him to find out who Brice was—almost certainly ruining Baker's Labor Day holiday. Baker played dumb and asked Fesler what Brice's last name was. Fesler didn't know, he just knew he was the professor at the University who'd promised to use Mullen's money to buy an endowed chair. So, of course, the two aging frat boys had to go into action again. Fesler didn't entirely trust Baker, so he made a complex arrangement with Baker to deliver the name to a neighbor of his, and moved into the book store's basement. The owner says he didn't know anything about it, by the way—claims he didn't know anything about what Dewey was up to, or Mullen, either.

"It's too bad Dewey didn't stay in his apartment," Buck went on. "He would have had a better chance to survive, since Baker didn't know where he lived, but Ridgeway remembered the name of the book store Mullen had told him about—apparently Mullen had recommended it highly to Ridgeway—and that's where they found Dewey and his tape. And that's the end of that."

I asked Buck if there was any way Lillian could get Mullen's money.

"Oh, Peggy," Lillian protested, "don't worry about me! I have enough for my needs."

"She probably won't get what the University has," Buck answered. "The contract Mullen signed with the University Club is legal and the money's being used for a legitimate purpose—the Grace Sterns Library."

"But Lillian can sue Baker and Ridgeway, can't she," Paula asked, already becoming litigious, "to recover what's left of what they stole from her brother?"

"You'll have to talk to a lawyer about that," Buck replied.

"They shouldn't get away with it, Lillian," I said.

"But they aren't getting away with anything," she said. "Thanks to all of you, they're going to go to prison for a good long while. And it'll do them good."

After a while, Susan and Kate served the cake they'd brought. After only one forkful, Buck asked for the recipe.

As we were eating it, Mrs. Hammer remarked: "You know, Peggy, none of this would have happened if you weren't such a lousy liar."

"Me?" Nobody'd ever said anything that insulting to me before.

"You," she said. "Remember how I invited you to the Fourth-of-July block party and you said you had other plans with your friends here?"

"So?" I turned a little pink because I do have a tiny residue of shame in me.

"Well, I could see you were just making that up so you wouldn't have to mingle with your neighbors. So I called Paula and invited her and Lawrence—just to thwart you."

"My God!" Paula exclaimed, her eyes growing huge. "It *is* all your fault, Peggy! If you'd been a better liar—or a better neighbor—Lawrence and I wouldn't have come to

Mullen's attention in the first place, and we wouldn't have received any hate mail."

"And if we hadn't received that mail," Lawrence said, "you'd never have gotten interested in what Mullen did with his money."

"Dewey wouldn't have thought I burned down Mullen's house or tried to burn down ours," Paula went on. Fortunately they were sitting close together, their arms around each other, so I didn't have to swivel my head from one to the other to follow their routine. "And the distinguished careers of Dell Baker and Brice Ridgeway would still be thriving."

"I guess there's a moral there somewhere," Lawrence said.

"Let's hope not," Paula said. "Peggy might go looking for it."

Ginny asked if there were seconds on the cake.

Meet Peggy O'Neill
A Campus Cop With a Ph.D. in Murder

"A 'Must Read' for fans of Sue Grafton"
Alfred Hitchcock Mystery Magazine

Exciting Mysteries by M.D. Lake

AMENDS FOR MURDER 75865-2/$4.50 US/$5.50 Can
When a distinguished professor is found murdered, campus
security officer Peggy O'Neill's investigation uncovers a mur-
derous mix of faculty orgies, poetry readings, and some very
devoted female teaching assistants.

COLD COMFORT 76032-0/$4.50 US/$5.50 Can
After he was jilted by Swedish sexpot Ann-Marie Ekdahl,
computer whiz Mike Parrish's death was ruled a suicide by
police. But campus cop Peggy O'Neill isn't so sure and launches
her own investigation.

POISONED IVY 76573-X/$3.99 US/$4.99 Can

A GIFT FOR MURDER 76855-0/$4.50 US/$5.50 Can

And Coming Soon
MURDER BY MAIL 76856-9/$4.99 US/$5.99 Can